Divorcing A Dead Man

Book Two of The Thomas Hall Series

Beth Sorensen

Contents

To my parents, Harry & Betty Bryant

Thanks for never saying no when I asked for a new book as a child.

I love you both!

Chapter One

THE MOMENT I OPENED my eyes, my head began to pound, and I was aware something had gone terribly wrong. The air smelled of stale cigarettes and as I strained my neck to look around, I realized I was in a motel room but had no idea how I got there. My first thought was that I needed to get out of this place, but when I tried to sit up, I could not and found I was pinned down in a spread-eagle position, flat on my back. My wrists and ankles were bound to the bed. The filthy bedsheets made my stomach turn and that's when I realized I was wearing nothing but a black lace bra and matching boy shorts.

I looked at the nightstand and saw a phone. Even if I could reach it and make a call, I had no clue where I was or how I had gotten there. I closed my eyes and tried to remember anything that would have brought me to this place, but my head throbbed so hard I could not think clearly.

Out of nowhere, I recalled who was responsible for this and that he was probably still in the room.

"Hello?" No answer. No footsteps. Nothing. Only silence.

I noticed the sun shining through an opening in the drapes. And then I saw him. A single beam of sunlight spotlighted my estranged husband, Tony, lying face-up on the floor. His eyes were open, his body motionless, and it did not appear he was breathing. Clutched in his right hand was a scalpel and as I looked up, I noticed more surgical knives on the dresser. They were laid out haphazardly next to a cooler of partially melted ice.

I decided not to wait around to see if Tony was dead. I stretched my left arm as far as I could, managed to reach the phone cord, and pulled until the phone and receiver were next to my hand. I awkwardly dialed 911 and pushed the receiver toward my ear.

"County 911. What's your emergency?" a voice asked.

"I've been kidnapped," I said. "I need to talk to Detective Hayes immediately."

The operator lowered her heavily-accented voice and spoke softly. "What's your name, dear?"

"My name is Cassandra Martin. I was in Lucky Shots when I was taken. Brian was at the bar when it happened."

The operator gasped. "Oh, thank God, you're alive. The whole county is looking for you. Where in the world are you?"

"I'm not sure. I think I'm in a motel room somewhere."

"Hold on. I'll trace the call while I put you through to Detective Hayes. Officers will be on their way as soon as I have your location nailed down."

There was a moment of silence and clicking while the emergency operator patched me through to Brian's cell.

"Hello?"

I knew he would recognize my voice. "Brian, don't let anyone know it's me. Is Edward with you?"

"Y-yes." He spoke slowly and deliberately.

"Your operator is tracing this call. Please come get me, but don't tell Edward. I don't want him to see me like this."

"O-okay."

I could hear Edward's voice on the other end asking if it was news about me. When I heard the first word leave his mouth, tears began to run down my cheeks. I heard Brian tell Edward there might be a lead and told him to stay put in case someone called the house. Then I heard the door close behind him.

"Are you all right?" Brian asked. "We were all beginning to think ..." He let his voice drift off and failed to complete the sentence even though we both knew how it should end. Everyone had begun to believe I might be dead.

"I know. I'm half-naked and tied to a disgusting bed in a filthy motel room. I don't know exactly where I am or how I got here, but my head feels like it's about to explode."

"Okay, the emergency operator just texted me your location. You're in Bay Grove at the Ocean Breezes Motel. I'll be there in ten minutes."

"Brian, you're gonna need some help. I think Tony's dead."

I laid there, waiting to hear the sound of sirens and trying to remain calm, wondering how my life had gone from bliss to total insanity. Somewhere along the way, I had lost control of everything. And after a moment, I remembered exactly how it all began to unravel. It was the same way most major events in my life began, with a phone call. Actually, this time, it was a series of phone calls.

Chapter Two

I HAD SPENT MUCH of the last six weeks happy, and while life for me was almost always good, it was leaning towards perfection. I was still laughing at a joke Henry told me when I answered the phone.

"Hi Cassandra, it's Kelly." I knew it was my fiancé's assistant as soon as I picked up the phone. Her voice was unmistakable. It was a little after four-thirty in the afternoon.

"Hey, what's going on?"

"I thought you might want to know that Edward is on his way to Thomas Hall to surprise you." Most people would be angry that Kelly would call and blow that kind of little surprise, but I was thankful. There was rarely a surprise in my life that turned out well, and while I would never insult anyone by showing my frustration, I hated the unexpected. This was a fact that eluded my fiancé, but not his assistant.

"Thanks for the heads up. What time should I expect him?"

"In about an hour."

I hung up the phone and looked across my desk at Henry, my soon-to-be brother-in-law. His build, eyes, hair, and smile were nearly a carbon copy of his late father, Senior.

"Let me guess, you're about to bail on getting Chinese food with me because my big brother is on his way home." His smile was confirmation enough that it was fine for me to do so, but I still felt a little guilty. The thought must have shown in my expression because he was quick to continue. "Oh no, no guilty face, Sis. The two of you don't get to spend enough time together as it is. We can grab dinner any night after work. Go on home and get ready. I'll call up to the main house, have them send dinner over for the two of you, and tell Mom I'll be joining her for dinner tonight."

"She'll like that," I said, both happy and grateful. "Thanks." I stood up, walked to the other side of my desk, kissed Henry on top of his head, and grabbed my coat. Henry was on the phone before I was out the door.

As I made my way down the path and watched the dried grape leaves blow across the fields lit by the dim light of the sinking sun, I thought about the place I had called home for the last six weeks. The place I planned on calling home forever. Thomas Hall was the Baker Family compound as well as a small winery. Within the gates, a long, main drive circled around onto itself. Where the loop formed sat the main house and at the opposite end was the production warehouse, where the business offices and the wine production areas of Thomas Hall Winery sat. Along the loop between the main house and the production building were Henry's house and the home Edward and I shared. Phoebe, my soon-to-be sister-in-law, also had a house on the loop, but it had recently been reduced to a pile of rubble in a fiery explosion. The construction crews were working as swiftly as possible to clear the debris in hopes of framing the new house before the first frost of winter slowed production. Edward's late father, Senior, and his mother, Vivian, built the houses several years earlier with their children and their families in mind.

Senior left me controlling interest of the winery in order to keep me close to Edward, although I knew nothing about running a winery. When the Bakers first met me, I was winding down from a case of wanderlust that led me on a year-long trek around the world. Senior, along with Edward, feared that one day I would leave Thomas Hall and never look back. However, the reality remained when I arrived at the Northern Neck winery for what was to be a weekend event, I never left. And had no desire to. Ever.

"Sweetie, are you here? I'm home." I heard Edward say as he closed the door. I had only been home long enough to shower and change, but in that brief amount of time, the sun had set and most of the house was dark. The only light on was in the kitchen, where I had just taken a casserole out of the oven. My heart leapt with joy whenever I heard his voice, and that night was no different. I placed the food on the stovetop, turned off the oven, and hurried into the living room to meet my fiancé.

"You're home," I said, turning on a light as I entered the room. "And on a Tuesday night. What's the occasion?" He met me halfway across the room and wrapped his arms low on my waist. I let out a sigh of complete contentment.

"The occasion is that in a month we'll be on our honeymoon." He leaned in and pressed his warm lips against mine. Pulling back a bit, I gave Edward a look that usually made him confess the truth and this time was no different. "My last appointment of the day canceled, so I decided not to stay in D.C. tonight. I hope that's okay."

I smiled as he released his embrace to take off his coat and scarf. It had been unusually cold for the last few weeks and everyone was wearing winter coats even though it was only November. Winter had arrived early in the Northern Neck of Virginia, too early for my taste. But coastal Virginia had crazy, unpredictable, sometimes non-existent, seasons, and that year autumn only lasted a couple of weeks.

"Of course it's okay. You mean someone actually canceled on the great Chesapeake Biotech CEO, Edward Baker?" I asked in a silly, joking tone. "That's unheard of."

"It happens every now and then," he said, half laughing at my playful mocking of his position. He laughed, leaned in, and kissed me once more, running his fingers around the back of my neck and through my hair as he usually did. His chocolate brown eyes met mine as we both smiled.

"Something smells yummy. What did you make for dinner?"

"I made nothing," I said as we walked toward the kitchen. "The kitchen at the main house sent down a casserole. All I have to do is warm it up and open a bottle of—"

The ringing of my cell phone interrupted me. I walked to the coffee table, picked up the phone, looked at the number, and set it back down.

"You're not going to answer that?" Edward asked.

"I've been getting prank calls off and on all day from this number."

Edward's expression went from happy and carefree to that of concern. "How many? What kind?"

"Only a few. Just heavy breathing. I'm sure it's nothing. Probably some bored teenager dialing random numbers."

"Cassandra, we've talked about this kind of thing before. These things are never nothing when you're a Baker. You've got to tell somebody." I let out another deep sigh, and not a happy one this time. This is what I didn't love about being in love with Edward Baker. His wealth and power made the people he loved targets for mischief and mayhem. Two things I had experienced more than my fair share of over the course of my twenty-six-year lifespan. "You need to call Brian."

Brian Hayes was Willow Creek's Police Detective and had quickly become my best friend in town. He was my window into the real world, which was a far cry from the modern fairytale existence of life at Thomas Hall.

"I'll call tomorrow, I promise. I just want to enjoy my night with you." I walked back to where he stood and squeezed him with a big hug. "Let's eat."

He looked at me with a long, lingering desire and whispered in my ear. "In a little bit, but first things first."

I squealed when he picked me up and carried me to the bedroom. A sound that turned to laughter when we fell into bed, where we stayed until long after our dinner had turned cold.

I woke the following day alone, and not to my alarm clock, but to the sound of my cell phone ringing. I pulled the phone off the charger and checked the number before answering it.

"Good morning, Brian."

"Did I wake you? You sound groggy."

"It's okay. I needed to get up anyway." I looked at the clock. It was six-thirty. My alarm wasn't set to go off for another hour. I sat up and leaned against the headboard. "So what do I owe the pleasure of this early morning call?"

"I just got off the phone with Edward. Why didn't you call me yesterday about these prank calls?"

I let out a deep breath before answering his question. "Edward's making a mountain out of a molehill."

"Why don't you give me the number and let me be the judge of that."

"Fine." I rattled the number off to Brian, confident my fiancé and friend were making far too big of a deal about this. "I'm going to be in town this morning for Mass. Do you have time for some coffee afterward?"

"Sure, I've got a few little things to handle at the station but nothing pressing. Call me when Mass is over and I'll meet you. Maybe, I'll have this prank call problem wrapped up by then."

"Are you sure you have time? What with those two teens still missing?"

"The sheriff from the county where they went missing is getting ready to call off the search. He seems pretty certain the two have just eloped. He's following the whole Romeo and Juliet theory of star-crossed lovers."

"Oh God, I hope not. Romeo and Juliet both ended up dead," I said.

"Funny, I said the same thing."

A few hours later, after a quick trip to the office and Wednesday morning Mass, I parked my car on Main Street. It wasn't exactly the car you'd expect a billionaire's fiancée to be driving, but it was mine and I liked it. I bought the Volkswagen Beetle about three weeks after arriving at Thomas Hall. It was a tiny car compared to the limos that most of the family used, but it got me where I needed to go, and even though I did not like to drive, I liked the independence it granted me more.

As I stepped out of the car, I saw a dark blue Porsche with California tags speed down Main Street. Every time I saw a Porsche, my stomach turned at the thought of who I had known that owned one. My late husband's car had been canary yellow, but every time I saw a car like it, I was reminded of the man who tormented my life for too many years.

I took a deep breath and stared upward. The gray clouds sat low in the sky and the harsh wind stung my face. I was still trying to clear my head of the memory of Tony when I found Brian Hayes standing beside me. I hadn't seen him leave the station and walk down the street.

"You okay, Cassandra? You look a little rattled." I heard the clicking of cameras across the street and knew the paparazzi were catching every possible shot of Brian and me together. I hated the constant invasion of privacy that the press had imposed since the start of my involvement with Edward. Two weeks earlier, they would have been inches away, not yards, but Edward had put a stop to that, although I am not sure how. I suspected that having a police officer as part of my social circle had not hurt my cause either.

"I'm good," I said, pasting on a convincing smile. "I just hate all these cameras. Let's get some coffee."

When we walked into the coffee shop, everyone turned and looked at us. Their previously loud voices lost volume and became hushed gossiping whispers. Brian and I heard the rumor about the torrid affair we were supposedly having and laughed about it.

However, in a small town like Willow Creek, it was big news. Even if it was not true.

Brian tried to shoo me off to the closest available table, but I refused. We placed our orders, and as he reached for his wallet, I told the woman behind the counter to put the coffee on Edward's tab. She gave me a dirty look. Brian opened his mouth to comment, but I shook my head and he obeyed. When our drinks were ready, we made our way to an empty table and sat for what seemed like only a split second before Edward flew through the door.

I am certain the entire coffee shop, along with the paparazzi, who now had their camera lenses pressed up against the windows, expected him to react differently when he knelt down beside me and took my hand in his. He must have taken the helicopter because the wind from the blades had transformed his always perfect brown hair into a messy mop but in a sexy, disheveled way. "Are you okay?"

I had recently discovered the helicopter Edward used was not corporate, but one he purchased for private use and how much it cost each time it left the ground. It didn't matter to him, though. He claimed it was worth the convenience. However, I didn't like the idea of anyone spending money frivolously on me. Edward knew this and the fact he felt compelled to get to Willow Creek so quickly concerned me.

I looked back and forth at both men and saw the tension in Brian's face and the worry in Edward's eyes. "What's going on?"

Edward took the seat between us. "You haven't told her yet?"

"No, I thought it best to wait until you arrived."

My shallow breathing quickened. I braced myself for the worst thing I could imagine. That would be something happening to my Uncle Fred, my only living relative. So there was no possible way to prepare for what I was about to hear.

"Brian found your prank caller," Edward said, hesitating as though there was something he wanted to add but couldn't find the words.

"Cassandra," Brian continued for Edward. "The calls are coming from a number registered to an Antonio Scarpelli Martin."

"That's impossible. Tony's dead." As I said the words, the Porsche I had seen moments earlier raced through my head.

"I know. That's why I called Edward. I hope you don't mind."

I stood up, leaned on the table, and shook my head from side to side. As I did I could feel the muscles in my body tensing and my head beginning to pound. "No, this can't be right."

"Cassie, sit down." Edward's voice was soft and calm. It was just convincing enough for me to follow his suggestion. As I did, the cameramen, whose lenses were pressed against the window, snapped photos as fast as they could. Edward brushed the back of his hand against my cool cheek. I am certain he hoped it would produce the same calming effect his loving touch normally did. However, it did nothing to help.

I looked at Brian. "Are you sure? I mean absolutely? Maybe all this is a mistake. A different person? Perhaps a cruel joke?"

"I've tracked him down to the Creekside Motor Lodge. A man matching his description checked in yesterday under the name Tony Martin."

I froze. It was as if the world, at least my world, had come to an abrupt halt. A week ago my biggest dilemma had been whether to buy a green cocktail dress or a burgundy one. Now my life was being turned inside out. Was it really possible the man I thought was dead could still be alive? My body language must have been an indicator as to what I was thinking because Edward squeezed my hand tighter. I closed my eyes for a moment and inhaled sharply. When I opened them, both men were staring at me.

"No, this is impossible," I said desperately fighting back tears.

"Edward, why don't you drive Cassandra back to Thomas Hall?" Brian suggested. "Maybe it would be better if you two discussed this at home. Away from the press."

"Good idea." Edward looked at me. "Let me grab some coffee and then we'll go. Are you okay to sit for a minute?" I nodded and he kissed the top of my head as he stood up.

Brian stood as well and the entire coffee shop went silent. If the customers were waiting for the classic "two men fighting over the girl" scene, they were disappointed.

The two men made their way to the counter and Edward ordered while they continued to talk. More than once, Brian looked over to check on me as Edward spoke. Each time he did, his expression was slightly different and by the time Edward had his coffee in hand, Brian lips were turned downward at the corners and his brow wrinkled. However, it was obvious that Edward thanked Brian when he shook his hand before heading out the door.

Chapter Three

THE RAIN BEAT HARD against the windows within moments of our arrival home. Edward sat at the kitchen table, sour-faced, reading the prenup our family attorney had drawn up last week. I left it on the table when I was sorting through some paperwork and he discovered it while I was pouring us iced tea.

"I'm not signing this."

"Yes, you will," I said. Suddenly the glass in my hand slipped through my fingers and crashed to the floor, creating a sea of liquid across the ceramic tiles. I shook my head, exasperated by both my clumsiness and the conversation. "It's designed to protect you and your family's assets."

"They don't need protecting. We aren't going to be one of *those* couples."

"Then you shouldn't have a problem signing it." I grabbed a mop from the broom closet to clean up the mess while we talked.

"We have people who can do that for you, you know. And I'm not signing this. It feels like we expect our marriage to fail." I heard the sound of papers rustling and turned in time to watch him toss them back onto the table.

"Do I have to get your mother involved? Because I will. And I'm sorry, but I'm not calling the main house to have someone come down here during this storm to mop a floor."

"Keep Mom out of this. I know who she'll agree with and I don't like the idea of being ganged up on by the two of you." He paused for a moment and I knew him well enough to know he was looking for a compromise that would make us both happy. "I tell you what, I'll get my legal staff at corporate to look at it. Okay?"

I finished mopping, walked into the living room with the tea, and Edward followed. I set the glasses on the side table before sitting on the sofa. I looked at Edward, who sat across from me, as the events of the morning replayed in my head.

"This doesn't make any sense. I mean, I buried him, Edward. He was cremated. I watched them bury Tony's ashes in the ground. I just don't understand."

"I know. It's okay," he said. "Come and sit with me, my love."

I stood and walked to the oversized chair and sat on his lap. I closed my eyes as he stroked my hair while he held me.

"Brian said his name was Antonio Scarpelli Martin. He's not one of *the* Scarpelli's, is he?"

I opened my eyes and lifted my head before answering. "His grandfather is Poppy Scarpelli if that's what you mean."

"Whoa! You married into *that* family?"

"You didn't do your research very well. Didn't you know I was married to the grandson of Chicago's famous mob boss?"

After a chance first meeting, Edward had gone to great lengths to find me again. He had no idea that I would show up at his parent's house four short months later. Of course, neither did I. During that four-month period, he'd hired a private detective to find me and in the process, the detective had discovered numerous things about me. All of which he passed on to Edward.

"No, somehow that part of your husband's family got past me."

"Well, it wasn't as bad as it sounds. Poppy was always good to me. He still is." I thought about Tony and his family for a moment.

I knew what I had to do but I wasn't sure if I had the nerve to actually see it through. I was certain that if I thought about it for too long, I'd wimp out. So I took Edward's hand and kissed it before I stood up and picked up my cell phone from the desk. I flipped through the incoming numbers and when I found the one I was looking for, I dialed.

"Who are you calling?" Edward asked as he stood up and walked up behind me. I didn't answer but waited as the phone rang.

"Hello?" I was more than stunned. There was no doubt this was Tony's voice on the other end of the line.

My husband was still alive.

The reality struck me with the force of an unforgiving wind and I felt the oxygen being pushed from my lungs.

"Hello? Is anyone there?" He asked.

"It's time to end this Tony. Be in my office tomorrow at one." I could hear my voice shake as I spoke.

"Baby girl, where's your office?"

"If you can find me in Virginia, you can find my office." I hung up the phone and blew out a deep breath. As I turned around, I saw the anger on Edward's beet-red face.

"What in God's name did you just do? Have you lost your mind? You just invited that sorry son-of-a-bitch to Thomas Hall. I don't want him anywhere near you!"

"Honey, calm down," I said, putting my arms around him and trying to reassure both of us that I had just done the right thing. "I have my reasons."

"Would you mind sharing them?" He asked. His expression was strained. I had never seen him as stressed as he was at that moment and considering our history that was saying something.

"If Tony is here, at Thomas Hall, on my terms, then I can control the situation. I'll feel safer too."

"I'd prefer you not see him at all. But what about someplace neutral, like the police station, preferably with him behind bars?"

"No, I need to meet with him someplace where I'm in charge," I said, suddenly obsessed with controlling the meeting I needed to have with Tony. "I've got to keep this whole thing under my control."

"I understand the need to control things, I may have even invented the concept, but there has got to be a better way."

"No, I want this resolved now. If this guy really is Tony, I have to get him out of my life immediately." Even though I had heard Tony's voice, and knew in my heart it was him, I still wasn't ready to face the truth.

Every feeling that raced through me, terror, panic, disbelief, must have shown on my face. Edward looked at me and despite his mood, took me in his arms. "I know. We'll get this worked out."

"I wish I knew the *how* part. How are we going to fix this? The wedding invitations went out last week."

"Don't worry." He held me tightly and I rested myself against him. "One way or another, I'm going to make sure that man never hurts you again."

I felt as though I had just closed my eyes when I stirred from sleep to the light from the evening's full moon pouring in through the windows. The rain had stopped and the now dissipated clouds allowed the night sky to shine. I was quiet for a moment, thinking about the day's events, before turning over in bed to discover I was alone and a note rested on Edward's pillow.

> *Sweetie, Ran into town. Be back soon. Forever Yours, Edward*

The clock glowed with the numbers twelve forty-two. I could not think of anything that Edward would need to do in Willow Creek in the middle of the night and wondered what he was up to. As I picked up my cell phone to call him, I heard the front door open and then close. I sat up, laid my phone back on the nightstand, and waited for Edward to come into the bedroom. As he entered, the surprise of seeing me awake caused him to step backward momentarily.

"Did I wake you?" He asked, sounding prematurely apologetic.

"No, I woke up a few minutes ago. I was just about to call you."

"I'm surprised you're up," he said as he slipped off his jeans and black turtleneck sweater. I was not the kind of person to judge someone based on their looks, but whenever I looked at my fiancé I felt like I had won the lottery. In addition to being crazy about me, his body looked as if he had been sculpted by Michelangelo himself. He had a god-like body, handsome face, perfect hair, and a smile that warmed my heart. "You normally don't wake up in the middle of the night."

"Well, it wasn't exactly a normal day." He turned his bedside lamp on and I watched as he threw on some sweatpants and a t-shirt before he crawled into bed next to me. "Where did you go?"

"I went to see Tony."

I felt my eyes widen and my chest tighten. "You did *what*?!"

"I made him a business proposition."

"Oh no." I wondered if there was anything else that could be done to make the situation worse. I worked to stay calm, with no success.

"What?"

"Just tell me exactly what you did first."

"I offered Tony an annual stipend in exchange for a quick divorce and no contact with you – ever."

Edward's world was different from most. He had unlimited resources at his disposal and used them generously where I was concerned. He learned quickly that money didn't mean much to me, that all I wanted was him. Still, he was a firm believer that any problem could be fixed with the right amount of cash.

I groaned, rubbing my temples. "I wish you hadn't done that."

"Why? Are you mad at me?"

"No," I said softening my voice. I knew his heart had been in the right place. "I know you were just trying to fix this mess. But Honey, you've probably just opened a Pandora's Box."

"What do you mean?"

"Tony is stupid and greedy. I doubt we've seen the last of him."

"He shouldn't be greedy with what I offered." He reached over and turned out the light.

"I don't think I want to know, but how much?" I asked.

"A million –"

"You think I'm worth that much?"

"A million a year? Every penny and then some." He reached over and held me. I melted into him.

"So what did he say?"

"No deal. He's determined to meet with you, which I really hate. But I need to tell you one more thing about Tony ..." I didn't hear a thing he said. I drifted off to sleep again, safe in his arms, long before he finished his sentence.

Chapter Four

IN THE MONTH AND a half we lived together I had never asked Edward to take a day off work to stay with me. We actually argued on more than one occasion about it. He would insist on staying with me when I knew he was needed at work. Some events warranted his staying, like when his former sister-in-law, Darla, tried to kill me. Others, though, were completely ridiculous. It was beyond all logic that his staying at Thomas Hall would help me recover from a cold. However, this time I was thankful when he didn't return to Washington D.C. the following morning. He should have been back in his office at Chesapeake Biotech, a company his mother inherited several decades earlier, but he voluntarily chose to stay with me as I confronted my past.

Edward and I never got much work done when he attempted to do business from my office. It always ended the same. We would arrive at my office around eight-thirty. I would check my e-mail and maybe even return a phone call before Edward would bring me a cup of hot tea. I would join him on the sofa by the window and snuggle up against him while I sipped the warm liquid. We would talk about our lives, both together and apart, and somehow he would always get me to tell him a story from my travels. The next time I looked at the clock in my office, I would discover it was lunchtime.

That morning was different though. It was spent on the phone with Zachary O'Keefe, the Baker family's attorney. During the call, there was much discussion about my lack of residency, timelines, potential court dates, and how to dissolve the situation in the most prompt manner. I periodically found myself drifting in and out of the conversation. I knew all of this had to be handled, but I kept checking out mentally in order to avoid my current reality. Divorce was the one thing I had always sworn to myself I would never let happen and yet, it was exactly what I was about to do.

I wished I had never called Tony, but I knew there was no backing out now. I stood at a floor-to-ceiling window in my office, staring at the vines. I watched as a few of the grape leaves floated in the icy wind toward our house and wished I was back in bed, next to Edward, who was now sitting at my desk, watching my every move.

Outside in the driveway below, I saw Michael and Sarah's car pull up in front of the production building. Sarah Abbott was my best friend from college. I called her the night before and told her everything that had happened. As the couple exited the car and headed toward the door they looked like they were engaged in an intense discussion and paid no attention to the sports car pulling up next to them as they walked into the building.

It was a midnight blue Porsche.

"I should've known," I said, not even realizing I had spoken the words.

"Known what, Sweetie?" Edward asked as he walked across the room to me. He put his arms around me but the tension that filled my body was not calmed by his touch.

"I should have known that Tony was alive, I guess." I turned from the window and faced my office.

I had not done much to change it since I inherited my job from Edward's father. The large Oriental rug still covered the industrial, warehouse floor and the oversized desk was the focal point of the room. A sofa, side table, and lamp sat along a window. The only things I added were a few pictures. There was one of me with Senior that someone snapped in the fields the first day we met. While I didn't have the pleasure of knowing him but a brief time, I missed him. I was certain that if he were alive now, he would know exactly what to say about this whole mess, and probably make me laugh in the process.

The phone at my desk buzzed. "Yes, Libby-Mae?"

Libby-Mae Jett was my receptionist. I hired her at the beginning of October to work part-time for the winery. She was a senior at Willow Creek High School but only had classes until noon, so she worked at Thomas Hall from one to six. Libby-Mae was smart, quick, efficient, and polite. I had already decided if she continued to work out, I would offer her a full-time position after graduation.

"Mr. and Mrs. Abbott are here to see you."

"Send them in please," I replied. "Could you also ask Henry and Alex to come up?"

She said something that I didn't quite hear and as she did Sarah and Michael Abbott came into the room.

When I called Sarah the night before and told her I had heard from Tony, she was shocked. However, she was even more stunned when I told her about the meeting I arranged with him. She was insistent that both she and Michael be there and I agreed, under one condition. She had to tell Michael everything she knew about my relationship with Tony. Michael never knew about Tony's abusive behavior toward me and now that Tony was once again alive, I felt it was important for him to know the whole truth.

Sarah walked over to me and whispered, "Don't worry, everything will be all right."

Michael gave me a warm hug but not before taking a long look at me first. I knew the look. It was the look I received when someone found out I had stayed as long as I had in an abusive marriage. Before either of us could speak, Libby-Mae buzzed in again.

"Miss Cassandra, there is a Mr. Martin here. He says he has an appointment with you."

"I'm sorry," I said. "I didn't put it on the schedule. Could you please show him in?"

I was regretting my decision to meet with Tony more and more with each passing second. Edward knew this was going to be a challenge for me as he was one of the few people in whom I had ever confided my entire past. He held me for a moment and looked into my eyes. I closed mine, thinking about how wonderful it would be for the two of us to be somewhere, anywhere but in my office, in the middle of what I certain was about to turn into an apocalyptic event. I opened my eyes, sat, and he rested his hands on my shoulders. His touch made me feel safe, secure, and even a little brave.

The door opened and Libby-Mae bounced her way across the room with the energy only a teenager had. She was a beautiful girl and it was obvious she was of Irish descent with her fiery red hair and freckled skin. She was shapely but her proportions were well-suited to her tiny frame.

Tony followed her. I had hoped and prayed that the man I was about to see wasn't my dead husband, but he was. I let out a deep breath and spoke to Libby-Mae.

"I need you to hold any non-urgent calls for the rest of the day."

Libby-Mae looked around. I did not know if she sensed something was amiss or if some new gossip about Tony being alive had already reached her, but I could tell she was analyzing the situation. "Of course, Miss Cassandra. Is there anything else I can do to help?"

"No, but thank you." I watched as she left the room with the same energy she had entered. I was about to call out to her and ask her to close my office door, only to realize she had left it open to allow Henry and Alex, Edward's half-brother and wine master at Thomas Hall, to quietly enter the room. I had spoken to each of them individually the evening before and they were both insistent on being present at this meeting. If for no other reason, they wanted to make certain there were enough men in the room to protect me from this man.

I watched Tony as he walked across the room and sat in the chair opposite my desk. He looked pretty good for a dead guy. He was definitely not movie star good looking, and nowhere near as sexy as Edward, but he wasn't a hideous swamp creature either. He was of Italian descent and had the trademark olive skin and thick, black hair. I noticed a few silvery hairs trying to creep into the mix. The last few years had aged him, and it looked good on him. He was wearing blue jeans, a white t-shirt, and black leather jacket.

"Hey, Baby Girl. I'm back," Tony said. "Did ya miss me?"

I feared that the ongoing hysteria I had semi-successfully concealed for the last twenty-four hours would burst forth the moment I spoke. I nervously twirled a strand of my hair and stared at him.

"I'd be lying if I said yes."

He leaned back in the chair looking relaxed and in charge. "Really, Baby Girl? Really?"

Tony moved his focus from me to Michael and Sarah. "Well, at least I know somebody missed me, right?"

I wasn't prepared for what would happen next. As Michael walked toward Tony, I thought about the relationship they once had. They were college roommates, best friends, more like brothers; I didn't know of two guys who were as close. Michael reached down and roughly pulled Tony to his feet by his collar, and sent a strong right hook to Tony's face, catching his eye on contact. I sat and watched as Tony's left eye began to swell.

"You sorry bastard! I swear to God, if I had known for a second what you were doing to C.C. I would have beaten the crap out of you back then!" He dealt Tony a few more blows and dropped him to the floor. After the fourth or fifth hit, I had the sense to react.

"Michael! Enough. He's not worth it. He is *so* not worth you going to jail," I said.

Michael stopped and took a step back. Tony peeled himself off the floor and straightened his jacket, smiling smugly as he did so.

"Still in love with her, huh?"

"What?" Sarah and I said in unison.

"You two still don't know?" He snorted out a laugh. "That's rich. The night we met at that frat party, you know, the one C.C. got kicked out of 'cause she was only fifteen. That night, Michael here told me he thought he was in love with C.C. He wouldn't act on it though 'cause of her age."

I thought back to that night. It seemed like a lifetime ago, not just a decade. Sarah helped me put on makeup for the first time and convinced me to wear a v-necked sweater and dress boots with my jeans instead of a t-shirt and tennis shoes. I remember wanting to put my hair in a ponytail but she had other ideas and made me leave it down.

Sarah always attracted men wherever we went, so I was pleasantly surprised when Michael and Tony walked over and struck up a conversation with me. Michael made me laugh with all his crazy jokes and Tony kept telling me how cute I was.

It wasn't until about three hours into the party that one of the frat guys recognized me from our quantitative methods of statistics class. I remembered him because he had been struggling with the class, although I felt like it was overly basic. It wasn't long after that the head of the fraternity politely informed me that I needed to leave. The house was already under investigation for serving alcohol to underage students, and while he knew I wasn't drinking, they couldn't risk having me there. Sarah insisted on leaving as well, and the guys walked us back to the apartment my uncle arranged for Sarah and me to rent off-campus. After all, there was really no appropriate place on campus for a fifteen-year-old to live.

I thought that getting kicked out of the party was the beginning of a laundry list of reasons that Michael did not like me. Only recently, I found out differently, but in love with me, there was just no way it could be true.

Sarah looked at me. I shrugged at her and she turned her attention to Michael. All of this was news to me too.

"Oh my God!" She paused for a moment before a look of revelation appeared on her face. "Michael no! There is no way this is happening! When you told me in couple's therapy you were in love with someone else and had been for a long time I had no idea it was C.C.! Why the hell didn't you tell me?"

"How? How was I supposed to tell you it was C.C.? She didn't even know." I felt my face burning and knew it was red as a strawberry. I was certain this was a conversation I should not be hearing, but they did not seem to care about the lack of privacy and continued.

"But you told me the money you took out of our retirement account was for this woman you'd been in love with." Sarah looked me straight in the face. "Was Michael funding your little trip around the world?"

"No." I snapped defensively, before turning my attention to Michael. "What money?"

Michael spun around to face Sarah. "How else was C.C. gonna get out of that prison in China?"

It was suddenly as if all in the room were frozen statues. No one moved or spoke. I couldn't keep silent any longer. I looked at Michael, my rescuer. "How did you know I was there this summer? How did you find me?"

Michael looked at everyone in the room with a self-satisfying grin stretching across his face as he shoved his hands into the pockets of his jeans. He was thrilled to be rid of the guilt of taking the money without telling Sarah exactly why it was gone, along with the pride of having saved me from some untold horror of prison in a foreign country. Alex, who had stood in silence the entire time, asked the question everyone wanted to know.

"Cassandra, what on earth did you do to end up in a Chinese prison?"

"Nothing. It was a misunderstanding." I was afraid to but knew I needed to see Edward's reaction. Would he still want to marry me now that he knew I'd been in jail? I slowly brought my gaze to his face.

He leaned over, half-smiling, and whispered in my ear, "Who knew I was marrying such a bad girl?" I found myself constantly wondering what Edward did or didn't know about my past. And it drove me more than a little crazy.

Tony, in his ever arrogant state, sat on the edge of my desk and looked me up and down as though he could see right through me. "I don't remember you looking this hot. Are all of these guys so in love with you they're willing to share? Because if that's the case, I think I might have to start charging them for –"

Henry moved until he was inches away from Tony and cut him off. "Don't you dare talk about my sister-in-law like that!"

I watched Henry's face go red from anger. When he raised his voice it told me things were beginning to spiral out of control. I needed to reign it all back in.

"Henry, it's okay. He's just trying to stir up everyone." I silently motioned to Henry to back away from Tony and he obeyed my request. "Tony, why did you come to Virginia and what do you want from me?"

"You're a wealthy woman, Baby Girl."

"You need to stop calling me that. I am not a baby and I'm definitely not your girl." The irritation his arrogance caused began to show in the tone of my voice. I could feel Edward's warm hand on my shoulder press in a little more. While it was silently comforting, I could tell by the tension in his hands that he was resisting the desire to interfere. I knew what he was dying to tell Tony. "Cassandra is mine. All mine. Don't even think about it." But he seemed to understand Tony's type well enough to know that it would have only fueled the fire that was his massive ego.

Edward's behavior helped me maintain what little self-control I was struggling to hold on to.

"I'm not as wealthy as you think. The insurance money's gone. I used it to pay back the money you embezzled from your last employer. I ate up a good chunk of my trust fund traveling. The rest of it I gave away to charities, trusts, churches, schools, families – whoever needed it."

Edward did not know I had given away most of my money. I wasn't wealthy, but always managed to live comfortably. When others needed the money more than me, I had no problem parting with it.

Edward looked at me lovingly, longingly. I knew why. He often said the thing that drew him to me was my selflessness. As I exhaled, I thought about how he would react had we been alone. The soft, wet kisses down the side of my neck, the sudden absence of clothing, the afternoon in bed. And I longed for it all.

It was easy to tell from his body language that Tony was infuriated. He had come out of hiding for the money and it was becoming clear to me that he thought he could get more than Edward offered him the night before. However, he was beginning to understand that there wasn't any of my money left.

"But you're the boss here, at least that's what I heard. There's gotta be some big bucks in that."

"On paper, maybe. But in reality, I've used up my resources. So the cash cow, as you used to refer to me, is milked dry."

While I was in charge of the winery, the shares I inherited from Edward's father weren't worth the paper they were printed on.

Thomas Hall had never turned a profit and it had quickly become my sole mission to turn the winery around.

"So which one of these guys is the man keeping you in cash?"

"That is none of your business," I said.

"So, you're not going to tell me, huh?" He began to pace around the office as he assessed the possibilities. "The money man, let's see. It's not Michael, because Sarah would never allow that. This guy," he said pointing to Henry, "referred to you as his sister-in-law so it can't be him. Mr. Edward 'social page' Baker here has plenty of money, and he cares enough about you to try to buy me off in the middle of the night, but I don't think so. He's way too old for you. Maybe he has a son? Or the blond? What's your name?"

"I wish I was marrying Cassandra," Alex replied. "My brother is one lucky guy."

"He's related to your fiancé too? Are they all?"

"All but Edward. He is my fiancé," I said. Reluctantly telling him what he wanted to know.

"Holy shit! Got some unresolved daddy issues, Baby Girl?" Comments about the age difference between Edward and me irritated me for a multitude of reasons. One of which was the fact that in no universe had I ever thought of him as any kind of father figure.

"No, just the need for a decent husband."

"You really gonna divorce me?" Tony asked, sounding as bewildered as he looked. He plopped down in a chair and continued. "Who the hell are you and what did you do with my wife?"

"I may be your wife on paper, but you were never a husband to me, at least not in any way that counted."

"What's that supposed to mean?" He asked.

"Remember Neil? I found a letter he wrote you in your dresser a few days after the funeral. I'm guessing he was one of the reasons you faked your death." I'd never said anything about Neil's letter to anyone, not even Sarah.

Every eye in the room followed my movement as I stood and walked slowly around the office. Everyone was astonished I was a pillar of stability, everyone except Edward. He was always in control and it seemed completely natural to him that I would act the same. Tony sat open-mouthed, expecting me to fall apart while revealing this secret.

"I'm sure you remember Neil. He was your lover. You know, the one who gave you the ultimatum. The one who said you had to choose. He said you couldn't continue to, well, um, he basically said it was him or me, you couldn't keep..."

"Screwing both of you." Tony finished the sentence.

I sighed and nodded my head. Sarah fidgeted as she watched everything unfold. Her nervousness served as an indicator to me that this encounter was beginning to take a heavy toll on her. I tried with minimal success to avoid showing the effect on me. I felt somewhat calmer after I sat behind my desk and felt Edward's hands comforting me again.

"Yeah, it was the main reason we both faked our own deaths. I knew, at least I thought I knew you well enough to know you'd never divorce me. We wanted to make a fresh start in California."

"Then where is Neil and why didn't you stay in California?" I asked.

"I don't know. I came home one night after I'd been out barhopping and found him and all his stuff gone. No note or anything. Just his key on the kitchen counter."

Smart man. I wished I had been that brave when I was married to Tony. He was the master of manipulation and I was very young and had a fear of being alone in the world.

"If I'd known you were having an affair, I probably would've given you a divorce if that's what you really wanted," I said.

"Hell, if I'd known that, I would have told you about the time I slept with Sarah." I snickered at the thought until I realized he was serious.

"Oh no. No no-no. There's no truth to this, right? I mean, I thought you were gay."

"I thought maybe it was just being married to you. So I invited Sarah out for a drink one night during the semester you taught that night class before we moved to Ohio. And..."

"Stop." The thought of them together sent a deep ache through me. I stood, tried hard not to get physically ill, and turned to face Sarah. "Tell me it's not true." I waited for an answer that did not come.

That was the moment I knew I had lost all control of the meeting with Tony.

Chapter Five

I FELT AS IF everything I knew about my life was unraveling like a loose thread on an old sweater. Thoughts ran helter-skelter through my head and I spit out the first thing that materialized in a sentence.

"You couldn't even stay dead, could you, Tony?"

"When did you turn into such a sour bitch?" He replied.

"Enough," Edward said. "No one talks to my Cassandra that way."

I took a moment to regain my composure and that's when all hell broke loose. Tony yelled at Edward and Michael was yelling at both Tony and Sarah. Sarah was screaming at Tony and Michael. Edward was holding on to calm by a thread while trying to get Tony to leave. Tony was holding his own against everyone's verbal bombardment.

I stood back and took it all in. It was quite a sight, watching these people I knew, and some of whom I loved, behaving this way. Then, after a moment, I looked at Henry and Alex. They were standing on the opposite side of the room from the insanity and watching everything unfold, wide-eyed like kids at the circus. I walked over to where they were standing near the door.

"It's been a long afternoon. I think things are pretty much under control here though. Why don't y'all call it a day?" While I had only lived in Virginia for a short time, I found myself slowly slipping back into the Southern accent I had picked up while at The University of North Carolina.

Alex surveyed the ensuing chaos before responding.

"This does not look like 'under control'. You sure you're okay here, Sis?" It was the first time I had noticed he'd picked up Henry's habit of calling me Sis. I liked it. It made me smile.

"I'll be fine. Edward's here."

Henry stepped up and gave me a hug. He spoke softly in my ear, "Try to stay calm. If you need me, I'm only a phone call away. Keep an eye on Edward. He looks like he could kill Tony."

Henry kissed the top of my head and Alex gave me a hug just before the two guys headed out of the room. Alex and I were close, but Henry and I had a tighter bond. Our relationship was bound by the blood of his late wife who had been fatally shot just a month before Tony reappeared.

When Henry and Alex left, I turned and assessed the anarchy unfolding in my office. I was ready for this to stop. I had to figure out a way to rein in this circus.

"This is enough!" No one heard me or they chose not to listen.

"Listen, I said enough!" I raised the volume of my voice a second time, but still with no results. I knew what it would take to get their attention. I would have to shock them into silence.

"Can everyone just shut the fuck up for a second?!" I shouted the words at the top of my lungs and silence followed. I didn't normally swear and it took a lot to drive me to that point. These four people knew me well enough for my words to have maximum effect. "That's better."

Libby-Mae buzzed in. "Miss Cassandra, I know you said to hold all non-urgent business but Detective Hayes is here to see you. He says Mr. O'Keefe has sent him on an urgent matter."

"Thanks. Go ahead and send him in."

Brian entered in full dress uniform. I had never seen him in anything but polo shirts and khakis and it was almost shocking how much more intimidating he looked. However, when he turned to me and smiled, I saw the same sweet, caring friend I had met in the hospital's emergency room less than two months earlier.

"This is an unexpected surprise. What brings you here, Brian?"

Tony interrupted our hellos in an attempt to remain the center of attention. "Baby Girl, when did you get all first name buddy-buddy with the cops?"

Brian looked at Tony and I ignored the question and focused on Brian's comforting voice. "I ran into Zachary as I was leaving the courthouse. When he told me he needed to get these papers out here as soon as possible, I offered to bring them. I thought it might be a good idea to check on things in person as well."

He handed me a file folder with a copy of everything Zachary had given him. I flipped the file open to find the divorce papers along with a request to expedite and waive minimum residency for me. In addition, there was a copy of the temporary civil protective order and a note stapled to the front of the file. My court date was set for eight days later.

Brian walked to Tony. "Are you Antonio Scarpelli Martin?"

Tony frowned at him. "Yes?"

Brian put a stack of folded papers in his hand. "Consider yourself served. I suggest you leave now."

"I don't think so." It had been years since I heard Tony bark out a response in that manner and it made me take a step back.

As I moved backward, I found myself in Edward's arms. The touch of his body against mine calmed my mind and left me with an unwavering resolve.

"Mr. Martin, there's a protective order in those papers I just handed you. I'd hate to have to enforce it, but I will if necessary," Brian said.

Tony was fuming as he moved toward the door. He passed me but stopped short, catching everyone off guard, and tried to grab my wrist. Any sense of security I felt vanished. I was terrified. He always grabbed me by the wrist right before he hit me when we were married. It was something I still had issues with and Edward discovered quickly that it was one thing from my past relationship that I still struggled with. After a few mishaps, Edward took great care to make certain when he felt the need to grab me and hold me close that his hands stayed away from my wrists.

"I'm not done with you yet, bitch," he said. But before he could make another move, Edward grabbed his arm and twisted it behind Tony's back pulling it upward and shoving him into the wall. I had never seen Edward show such raw anger and it was an intense experience layered on top of the fear Tony had induced.

Edward's voice bellowed throughout the room as he yelled at Tony. "Come back here and I will kill you! Do you understand?!"

Edward then shoved Tony out the door. Tony laughed as he got off the floor and hurried from the building.

I was left standing in a room full of people whom I needed to talk with individually and I was lost as to how to begin. I was trying to get my thoughts together when Libby-Mae buzzed the intercom. "Miss Cassandra, I'm sorry to bother you again. Miss Vivian is on line two. She wants to remind you about dinner tonight."

"I'll take it, thanks." I exhaled, trying to calm down. "Hi, Vivian."

"Just wanted to remind you about dinner at five," she said. "We need to go over the last of the details for the wedding."

"We need to postpone dinner," I said, my voice trembling as I spoke. "Things are a little crazy right now. Edward, Brian, Sarah, and Michael are here and –"

"Well, have them come for dinner, too. I'm sure it has been a long day for everyone."

"I'm afraid so." I blinked back the tears forming in my eyes. "But Vivian, we found out a lot about each other this afternoon, and it wasn't pretty. We would not be good company at all."

"Come anyway. Everyone will still need to eat."

I hung up the phone and looked at the four people I thought I knew. They taken seats in different parts of the room and Brian was standing by the door.

"It appears we've all been summoned to the main house for dinner. There will be no arguing about this." I looked at the clock. It was quarter of five. "I think we'll leave now and I'll talk with each of you once we're there."

I shut down my computer, grabbed a bag that held paperwork, and as I reached the door Brian asked, "Rough day, huh?"

"Yeah. Thanks for coming Brian." I always found myself smiling when I spoke his name. "I really appreciate it."

I looked at the others who were waiting for me. "Why don't y'all go up to the main house and I'll catch up in a minute."

Edward did not look happy about leaving me behind with Brian but knew it was not the moment to say anything. He held my coat as I slid into it, and kissed me before joining the others as they quietly filed out the door.

"Believe it or not, though, there've been worse days."

"In your case, yes, I'd believe it," Brian said, looking at me intently. "Did I really hear you swearing as I was walking up the stairs to your office?"

'Not my finest moment. I was trying to get everyone's attention. Sorry."

"I have no problem with it. It's just unlike you. Cassandra, you look shaken. Are you okay?"

I looked down the hall, insuring the others had walked down the stairs and out of hearing range. "I've never seen Edward like that before. It was, well, disturbing."

"Don't worry about him. The only time I've ever seen him like that is when he's trying to protect you. He scared you though, didn't he?"

I nodded.

"You know, if he ever frightens you, all you have to do is call me. I can be here in a heartbeat and the Willow Creek police can't be bought."

"I know. I don't think it would ever come to that. But I had no idea Edward could be driven to that kind of violence."

"We all have our limits."

"I suppose. You are coming for dinner, aren't you?"

"I think I'll pass tonight. I need to head home and get the twins packed. They're going with my mom up to Pennsylvania to visit family. Maybe another time." Brian was a hard-working, single dad whose life aged him a decade beyond his true years. He was a tall, broad man who wore his hair buzzed short making his blue eyes his most striking feature. He lived and breathed for his twelve-year-old twin girls.

"You should be home with the girls. I'm not so important that you couldn't have sent another officer out."

"Don't worry about it. I'm on duty until five either way and you are that important. Good friends are hard to find. Why don't I walk you to the house? It's getting dark and it's probably a good idea you aren't alone. He took my bag, waited while I buttoned my coat, and then held the door for me.

As we walked, we continued our talk.

"Brian, I need a favor."

"Name it."

"It's a police favor. I know the Willow Creek Police Department really doesn't have the resources, but is it possible to have a patrol car around the Thomas Hall area for the next few days?"

"Is Tony really that stupid?"

"He'll break that protective order within seventy-two hours, I'd bet money on it. The only thing Tony ever wants is the one thing he can't have."

"And right now that's you."

Chapter Six

DINNER, ON A NORMAL night, was a talkative event at the main house of the vineyard. Politics, news, local gossip, family stories, and whatever else piqued the family's lively interest. Any topic was always up for discussion. But not that night. Silence filled the dining room. Everyone was waiting on me. They wanted to see how I had weathered the day's events. I, however, had nothing to say. Small talk was never one of my strong suits and anytime I was left to begin a conversation, I usually failed miserably. It seemed forever before I finally came up with something acceptable to say.

"Vivian, who cooked tonight? Not your usual chef. Dinner's good, but the style's a little more Italian and not quite so French."

"I don't know how you can tell the difference, dear, it's just baked chicken, but you're right. We're testing a new chef. The one who's been here for decades wants to retire in the next couple of years. He suggested I find someone he could begin to train to accommodate Thomas Hall's varying tastes."

"Well, tonight's dinner is delicious. As for knowing the differ-ence, it's..."

Edward chimed in with me. "... in the seasoning."

I was surprised he was so discerning. It was a subtle thing that you would only know if you had been professionally trained. Of course, it explained why he was such a good cook. He smiled and had a look of mild revelation and surprise about him.

"Honey, where did you go to cooking school?"

"Le Cordon Bleu in London. You?" He asked.

"Finally, something you don't know about me," I laughed. The thought of Edward knowing everything I had done in my life gnawed at me for some strange reason and the knowledge that something, *anything,* had been overlooked gave me hope that there might yet be a few surprises in store for him.

"Le Cordon Bleu Paris. I dropped out of my Master's program in the States for a semester and studied in Paris but I didn't stay long. Do you speak French?"

"No, Spanish and I'm still trying to learn Japanese." Edward paused, looking puzzled. "Sweetie, I've never seen you cook."

"That's because you always offer."

He laughed and I joined in. I wasn't about to tell him the real reason I always let him cook. I glanced over at Sarah and Michael, who both knew the truth. Michael smiled at me, seemingly relaxed, and winked, as though he was confirming my secret was safe with him. However, Sarah didn't look nearly as amused.

"How can the two of you sit here and laugh?" Sarah questioned. "The guy that used to beat the crap out of you showed up in your office today alive and you're sitting here talking about cooking schools and foreign languages. I'm not going to let you do this to yourself again."

"Do what?" I asked.

"The same thing you did when Lewis died. You walked around for a month acting like everything was fine. Then, when you finally let reality creep into that big brain of yours, Fred had to check you into that high-priced hospital until you could get your act together."

I once confided in Vivian that I had suffered a nervous break-down while working on my Master's degree. It was obvious by her expression she had not told her son and was concerned about how he might react. When she and I looked at Edward we found him un-phased by Sarah's comment. It was one more thing about me he knew prior to my arrival at Thomas Hall.

I couldn't believe Sarah had the audacity to bring up my once fragile mental state. Especially in light of what I had discovered she had done. The longer I sat, the more I felt betrayed. Not only had she slept with Tony while we were married, but bringing up my brother, whom I never spoke of, was more than I could tolerate from someone who was supposed to be my friend. I attempted to channel my future mother-in-law's grace. It took all the self-con-trol I had to slide the chair out from under me and stand up.

"Sarah, I think it's time we talked in private."

Sarah followed me to the library and I closed the heavy double doors behind us. She sat down in the leather recliner and I remained standing although I felt the physical effects the stress the day had brought.

"C.C., before you say anything, let me explain some things."

"No, I don't want an explanation."

"But, I need to tell you what happened. I really think –"

"No!" I yelled, having no restraint left in me. "No more. I can't believe this! How could you dare? Tony was my husband!"

"You've been living with Edward too long. You're becoming a control freak."

"No, I'm not." Something that had been deeply seated in my mind for the last few weeks suddenly, and without warning, I heard myself say, "Why do you hate the fact I'm happy here? For the first time in a long time, maybe ever as an adult, I'm somewhere where I'm actually happy, loved, and safe. I'm madly in love with a man who adores me. I've got a job that's fulfilling and challenging and it's a wonderful feeling. You're the only person I know who keeps finding something wrong with this. I don't understanding anything about you anymore!"

"C.C., I don't think –"

"Sarah, you don't think! I don't want to hear anymore empty words from you. You need to go!" I turned quickly and left the room.

I returned to the dining room, feeling the warmth in what I was certain was now my own red and angry face. I was on a rampage, and I was not finished yet. Everyone stopped their conversations. I stood in front of Michael. He looked up at me and smiled.

"Why didn't you tell me?" Although I tried to be calm, I felt my voice get louder. "Why doesn't anyone ever tell me anything?!"

I took a deep breath in hopes of regaining my composure. I caught a glimpse of Vivian who looked worried. I knew exactly who she was worried about too. Me.

"I know, Cassandra. I'm sorry." Michael had never called me Cassandra before and I was taken aback by it. He, like most of my friends from school and childhood, had always called me C.C. It was only the initials of my first and maiden name. I had been trying to get everyone to refer to me as Cassandra, but with very little success.

"You should have told me about this a long time ago," I said.

Vivian stood and cleared her throat. "If you'll excuse me, I think I will take my dessert and coffee in the sitting room. Why don't you join me when you're done, dear?"

"I will," I said. "Thank you."

Vivian rose from her chair and walked out of the room, pausing long enough to pat my arm.

"Do you want me to go, too?" Edward asked.

"It's up to you. Of course, you know if you don't stay, I'll tell you anything you want to know later."

He lifted my hands to his lips, kissed them softly, and then headed toward the door. He stood in the doorway and said gently, "I love you."

Edward didn't wait for a reply. He knew I had trouble saying the words aloud, even when we were alone. He often told me it did not matter that I rarely said it, that he knew how much I loved him. But in my heart, I was certain he wished I said it more often.

I turned my attention to Michael, who motioned for me to sit in a chair next to him. I took a seat and realized I must say the right thing. I knew the value of my words.

"Why didn't you ever tell me how you really felt about me?" I asked, now much calmer than when I entered the room. "I wish you had told me. If not the night we met, then later. I wish I had known how you felt ten years ago."

"At the time I didn' realize how important it was," Michael said, his Carolina accent seeming thicker than usual. I saw regret in his eyes. "I felt like you were too young and I knew I couldn' get past it. I was afraid if I told you it'd just hurt your feelings and I didn' wanna do that. When I found out you thought I didn' like you, I figured it would just be easier to let you believe that."

As I listened to Michael, I realized the reason my best friend's marriage had been so tumultuous was because of me. I didn't know what to say to Michael but words burst forth from deep inside. "Michael, the night we met, you were the one I hoped would call me, not Tony. I so wanted us to be friends. If I'd known, then maybe ..." Nothing more could be done to ease the ache and regret I now saw playing out in his expressions. I softly touched his shoulder as I turned to leave.

As I walked toward the sitting room, it finally dawned on me that Michael had been in love with me for over a decade and I had never known. And it did not even rank first on the list of things that completely dumbfounded me over the course of the day.

When I walked in the room, I served myself a slice of cheesecake from a serving cart before Victor, the family's butler, could do it for me.

Victor was a short, thin man with gray hair, in his mid-sixties. He had worked for the Baker family for over thirty years, but his distinctive Yorkshire accent was forever present in his speech. He had planned to retire a few years earlier, but decided to stay on until Senior passed away. After Senior's death, Victor agreed with Vivian that it would be easier for the family if he could stay on through the first of the year. His experience would be invaluable during the holidays and our upcoming nuptials.

"Cassandra, can I get you something to drink? Some herbal tea perhaps?" Victor asked.

"Actually, a glass of the '94 Port would be lovely." He smiled and hurried off to fulfill my unusual request. While I may have been the head of a winery, I rarely drank outside of work. But no one was shocked at my choice of drinks that evening.

I took a seat next to Edward on the sofa, patted his knee, and let my hand linger on his leg for a moment. Vivian watched the two of us until I turned my full attention to her.

"I didn't handle that very well, did I?" I said, already aggravated with myself for losing my temper. I picked at my dessert, even though I had lost my appetite long before I entered the room.

"From what my son just told me about your afternoon, I'm amazed that no one is dead or in jail. If a little yelling and screaming is all you need to do to manage this, I'd say you're handling things just fine." I smiled a bit and she continued. "Cassandra dear, I know you've had a long day, but there are still some things we need to go over for the wedding. We're less than a month away."

"I know, but I think we have a bigger problem. I'm still married." Every time I said it out loud it became more of a reality and on this occasion I found myself saying it again. "I'm still married to Tony."

I sat my plate on the table next to the sofa and calmly walked outside, passing Sarah and Michael as they prepared to drive back to D.C. I hoped the fresh air would sooth me, but when I stepped outside and inhaled, my stomach and nerves found no peace.

Chapter Seven

THE SUN WAS BARELY up the next morning when I found myself at my desk staring at the phone. I needed to know if Tony's family was aware he faked his own death. I picked up the receiver two or three times, setting it down each time, thinking how crazy this was going to sound if they didn't know.

Finally, I dialed the number from my address book. The secretary who answered was new. It was obvious she didn't want to put the call through, but I convinced her to put me on hold and check with Poppy.

"Cassandra, what a pleasant surprise." Poppy's voice was unchanged by time. Over the last decade, it had remained constant. It was deep, soft, and laced with an Italian accent.

"I wasn't sure you'd take my call." I ran my fingers through my ponytail, wrapping a few strands of hair nervously around one finger as I talked with him. "I didn't know how you would feel about me marrying into another family."

"You will always be a Scarpelli. I will always be your Poppy. Even after you remarry. Oh, and I got the invitation. Congratulations."

"Will you be coming?"

"I would not miss it for the world. But I have a feeling an RSVP is not why you called me this early in the day."

I hesitated before beginning. "Poppy, I probably should have flown to Chicago to talk to you about this, but the reason I'm calling is exactly *why* I can't leave Virginia right now."

"You have lost me. What is going on?"

"Did you know Tony is still alive?" There was a long silence punctuated by the throbbing of my head.

"Cassandra, are you certain of this?"

"Yes," I said. "I've seen him, Poppy. Talked to him. He told me himself that he faked his own death."

"When was this?" Poppy asked.

"Yesterday."

"So you know where he is?"

"Yes, he's staying at the motor lodge here in town."

"I am flying to Virginia on Friday. Could you make me a reservation somewhere for one evening? Someplace discrete."

"You'll want to stay at the family mansion."

"Interesting name for a hotel," Poppy said.

"No, you'll stay at the Baker family mansion here at Thomas Hall. It's quiet, discrete, and there's a helicopter pad on the property."

Around lunchtime, I found myself again sitting in my office staring out across the fields. The grapevines rose from the ground, tall, thick, and perfectly aligned against the cloudless blue sky. They looked as if they were fortress walls, designed to keep danger out. But they could not protect me from Tony. I knew he would return to Thomas Hall and my stomach churned.

I was thinking about my call with Poppy when the phone rang. It was the front gate. There was a delivery truck with two crates for me, shipped from Florida by an F. Clark.

"Finally," I said aloud. I had been waiting for these crates for over a week. I told the guard to send them to Edward's villa. However, I was told I needed to sign for them personally. I asked him to send the driver and I would meet him at the house.

"I don't have time for this," I said under my breath as I put on my coat. I was just about to wade knee-deep into the previous years' budget proposals and actual expenditures trying to figure out if the winery was bleeding money in a particular area. Since day one of being in charge I felt like the winery should be bringing in more money and spending less, but not at the cost of happy employees and a quality product.

I hopped into one of the many golf carts we used around the winery and headed to the house. When I arrived, I saw not only a truck and driver but my Uncle Fred as well. I barely brought the golf cart to a stop before jumping out and running over to hug him. I had only seen him once in the last year, and even then it had only been for a few hours at a funeral.

My uncle was a tall lanky man, built much like my father. Most people wouldn't know the two of us were related if they met us individually. At one point in time, we both had dark hair but Fred's had grayed prematurely. With his olive-toned skin and brown eyes, we were a study of opposites in physical features.

Most of my adult life had been spent as a woman of average height who was extremely overweight. It was only in the two years prior to my arrival at Thomas Hall that I had been able to whittle my weight down to something better suited for my height. I realized though, that I'd never be super-model thin like Twiggy or Kate Moss, but more curvaceous like Marilyn Monroe. Regardless of my weight, the green eyes and porcelain skin I inherited from my mom along with my dad's jet black hair made me an unusual-looking person, and I had never grown to like it.

Fred Clark was not only my uncle but became my legal guardian after my parents died when I was twelve. He was my last living relative, and coincidently, Edward's frat brother and best college friend. While they were friends for years before our first meeting, Edward and I were certain we had never met before the night we sat next to each other on a United Airlines flight from Seattle to Chicago.

"Fred, what are you doing here?"

"We need to talk." He led the way into the house, his voice was serious and unusually monotone. "Sit down, please, Cassandra."

My uncle never called me by name. For years he had only referred to me as Kiddo. I hated the nickname, but never really felt like I was in a position to complain. I knew what he wanted to talk about. I overheard one of the many conversations he and Edward had over the last few days and fully expected the forthcoming conversation. I just had not expected it in person.

"Go ahead. Get it out of your system." He had never reprimanded me the entire time I was under his charge and I didn't know what to expect. So I took a seat, folded my hands neatly in my lap, and waited.

"What the hell were you thinking?" His eyes looked as though they might bulge out of his head. "You should have told me the very first time Tony hit you! I can't believe you put yourself through that for two long years. Maybe I shoulda left you in that psych ward longer!"

Fred had never once raised his voice to me and I knew everything he was saying was true. Nevertheless, my lower lip began to quiver and I could feel my eyes fill with tears. "That's enough. You have no right to go there."

"Broken ribs, broken nose, dislocated elbow, black eyes. I think I have *every* right. You're my niece, damn it! I promised your parents I would take care of you! I promised them and ..." I tuned him out as tears ran unchecked down my face. He stopped when he saw the effect he was having on me. He moved closer and put his arms around me. "Oh God, Kiddo, don't cry. I'm so sorry. It's just ... it's not your fault."

"Yeah, it is. I should have told you." I suddenly wished he had stayed in Florida. I stood up and dried my face with my fingertips. "Is there anything else? Because I need to get back to work."

He allowed a small smile, fully knowing I was using work as an escape from the conversation. "Just one more thing. Where's Tony now?"

"He's staying at the motor lodge in town. Why?"

"Because it's time for him to pay for what he did to you."

"Fred," I said, not certain whether he was making idle threats or if he was about to attack Tony. "Stay away from him. I'm serious."

"Don't you get it, Cassandra? I've told every man in your life that if they ever hurt you, I'd kill them. And I meant every word." He headed for the door but I stopped him, grabbing him by the shoulders and turning him around. When I looked into his eyes I saw a fury that confirmed he meant what he had just said.

"No! Don't even think it. If you kill him, you'll get caught and end up in prison. Losing you would hurt me more than anything he can do to me alive. I can't afford to lose any more family members."

Fred looked at me and I could see that some of what I had said was starting to register with him.

"You're right," he said. "How did you end up being the voice of reason in this family?"

"I don't know. I'm not that reasonable. I'm still planning a wedding I'm not sure will even take place to a man I hardly know. That pretty much defies good logic, don't you think?"

"No Kiddo, that's love. And logic and love are two things that rarely intersect."

"Really?" I replied, not certain it was the answer I wanted from him.

"Yeah. Speaking of, where's Edward today? I was hoping to see him if he's around."

"He's somewhere around the winery. He's probably at the main house having lunch with his mom. Why don't you go up there, find Edward, and get something to eat."

"No lunch for you?" He asked.

"I'll grab something at the office. I've got a meeting soon, so I've got to get back." We walked out the front door, turning in different directions to head to our own destinations. As I climbed into the golf cart, I yelled out to him. "Don't even think about leaving Thomas Hall!"

I was shutting down my computer for the night when Henry popped his head in the door. "I'm getting ready to head out for the day. Did you need anything before I go?"

"It's a bit early for you. Got big plans?"

"Sort of." Henry looked at his watch. "I better get a shower and change or I'm going to be late."

"Going out with the guys?"

"Not exactly." He put his hands in his pockets and stared at his feet.

"A date?" I asked.

"Well, sort of. Yeah, I guess it is." Henry's response was more like a teenager than a grown man and it took everything I had inside of me not to laugh out loud.

"Who with?"

"Aren't you nosey?" He said, looking up at me.

"Fine, don't tell me. I can wait. I'll just read about it in this Thursday's edition of the Willow Creek Herald like the rest of the county. It'll be nice for *me* not to be the center of gossip this week."

Henry let out a sigh as though it had just occurred to him what he was about to do. Anyone who dated a Baker became immediate fresh meat for the carnivorous press. "It must suck to be right so often."

"Well, whoever she is, she's the lucky one." I walked over and gave Henry a kiss on the cheek.

"It's Zoe," he said, turning back toward the door.

I took a good look at Henry and smiled a little bigger. He was about to get his world rocked.

Zoe Marshall had been a friend of the Baker family for years. I didn't know what the inciting incident was, but as a teenager, Zoe's parents kicked her into the streets and told her never to come back. The Bakers took her in and from my understanding, Edward helped finance Zoe's Day Spa & Boutique.

I had only known Zoe since I had been at Thomas Hall. In that short period of time, I learned she not only liked to work hard, but play hard as well. She was constantly out drinking, dancing, raising hell, meeting men, and bedding them. So, at first, Zoe seemed like an odd choice for Henry. He was a discrete, mild-mannered, quiet man, the complete opposite of her. After some thought, I realized that maybe she was exactly what he needed. Henry's late wife, Darla, had been a controlling, manipulative psychopath who had orchestrated his life for years. Maybe it was time for him to just cut loose and have fun with someone like Zoe.

As I headed out of the office, my cell phone rang.

"Cassandra Martin."

"Cassandra, it's Zoe. I need your help."

"Were your ears burning? Henry was just telling me the two of you have plans tonight."

"That's why I need your help. I can't figure out what to wear."

"Are you feeling okay? I'm the last person you should be asking fashion advice from."

My sense of fashion was not the best in the world. For years I had lived in jeans and t-shirts. No make-up. No jewelry. It was only after I arrived at Thomas Hall did I find the need to expand my wardrobe, as my life in Virginia was much more formal than any other I had led.

"Henry won't tell me where we're going. He wants it to be a surprise. Got any clues?"

"He didn't tell me anything," I said. "Zoe, you own a clothing store. Go pick out something."

"I just wish I had some idea."

As she spoke, it occurred to me what Zoe's real problem was. "Are you nervous?"

"Terrified," she replied.

"Why?"

"I just don't want Henry to be like the rest of the guys I've dated recently. My psychic says he could be the one."

"Your psychic?"

"Yeah, there's a good one in town. You should go see her sometime."

"Oh no, I don't think so. I had my tarot cards read once in Jamaica. It was so accurate it still scares me. Anyway, why don't you wear black slacks like the ones I bought last week and the blouse that's in the window display?"

"You don't think it's too low cut."

"No, the Baker men have a thing about low necklines and cleavage." I knew this from first-hand experience with Edward.

"I just wish I had a little more cleavage to fill out the neckline of the shirt."

It was hard for me to believe that Zoe could possibly have a problem with the way she looked. Any woman I had ever met would gladly commit murder in exchange for Zoe's features. Long beautiful black straight hair, smooth caramel skin, exotic features, trim figure, and shapely legs. It was crazy how gorgeous she was.

"Zoe, I wouldn't worry about tonight too much. I mean, you and Henry have known each other for ages and he wouldn't have asked you out if he wasn't interested."

Chapter Eight

Returning home from work that night was a surreal experience. It was warmer than any evening in the two weeks prior and the cloudless sky allowed every star to sparkle. As I strolled down the path, the unmistakable smell of grilled steaks floated in the air and knew it was coming from our house. I could hear the two men I loved the most on this planet laughing and talking and I found myself completely content with my world at Thomas Hall.

As I moved further down the path, the tone of their voices shifted, and within a few more feet, I could hear what they were saying.

"Seriously though, did it have to be my niece you fell for?"

"I know, I'd say I'm sorry but I'm not," Edward said. "Do you realize that this time next month you'll be my uncle?" The two men burst into full blown laughter and didn't stop when I rounded the corner to the back of the house. As I got closer, I tripped over one of the stakes that had been placed in the ground where the pool and hot tub were to be dug, but managed to regain my footing before embarrassing myself.

Edward and I shared a common backyard with Phoebe and Henry and I suggested installing an in-ground pool. Phoebe was moving back to Thomas Hall with her two children as soon as her house was finished and I thought my niece and nephew might enjoy it. They had recently suffered through the divorce of their parents and the transition would be easier if Thomas Hall was a fun place for kids to live.

"Hey, Beautiful," Edward said as he walked out to meet me.

"Hey yourself." We met at the edge of the patio and gave each other a long, loving kiss.

Edward tasted of beer. My guess was the guys had spent the afternoon putting back beers and catching up.

He took my briefcase, if you can call it that, and carried it for me. My briefcase was nothing more than a Vera Bradley tote bag that I carried my laptop and a few files back and forth from the winery to the house, and when we reached the patio table and chairs, Fred gave me a hug.

Edward walked into the house and returned a few minutes later with a fresh glass of ice tea in his hand. He handed it to me and kissed me again before getting back to the grill. I looked at Fred who sat smiling, watching our interaction.

"What?" I asked.

"The two of you, together, it's ... well, I don't know how to explain it."

Edward turned to Fred. "What did you expect? We're getting married in less than a month."

Edward and I had a comfort level that confused most people. In less than two months our relationship looked like that of a couple who had been together for years. He never had to tell me if he wanted to go out on the town or stay home. I never needed to tell him if I wanted a glass of wine or iced tea. We both just knew. We were like old souls reunited after an eternity apart. It was as if our new selves were picking up where our past lives left off.

"I've spoken to both of you about your relationship, but this is the first time I've really seen the two of you together. I mean you're my frat brother and my niece. It's just stranger than I thought it'd be."

"In a bad way?" I asked fearfully, holding my breath in anticipation of his reply. I couldn't imagine being in the position of having to choose between the two of them.

"No, Kiddo, it's all good."

"Clark, why do you call her that?" Edward calling my uncle Clark as opposed to Fred was a carryover of the guys' frat house days together.

"What? Kiddo? I don't know. I just always have."

"It irritates me," Edward said. I was taken aback by his bluntness but stayed out of the conversation. "If there's one thing she not, it's a kid." He looked over his shoulder and peered at me with his sexy eyes in a long, lingering look that made me quiver and I exhaled sharply.

"I guess not." Fred was contemplating Edward's comment. "You got to remember. In my head, she'll always be barely fourteen and leaving to go away to college."

"So in your mind, I'll always be a fat, pre-pubescent, nerdy genius. Gee, thanks a lot."

Edward walked to where I sat, knelt down, and said softly for my ears only, "If it makes you feel any better, in my mind you'll always be the sexy, naked woman in my bed."

"Edward!"

"What did he just say?" Fred asked.

I clamped my hand over my tightly pursed, but smiling lips and shook my head from side to side.

"I guess I'm not going to get an answer from you. What about you?" He used the neck of his beer bottle to point at Edward.

"Well," Edward said as he rose to his feet. "I was telling Cassandra exactly how I remember her in my—"

"Stop right there. At the end of the day, she's still my niece and there are some things I just don't wanna know."

By eleven that evening I knew I had a problem. My uncle wasn't going to leave. He made it clear over dinner that he intended on staying until my divorce was final and Tony was out of the state.

Fred had settled into the guest room for the night and Edward and I were in bed. Edward was looking over some e-mails and I was holding open a book but my mind was elsewhere and every muscle in my body felt like a rubber band on the verge of snapping.

"Cassandra?"

I jumped when Edward spoke. "I'm sorry, did you ask me something?"

"It bothers you Fred is in the next room and we're not married yet, doesn't it?"

"No, it's not that. It's just ..." I stared at the floor. Maybe it was that. No, while I was feeling a little self-conscious about that fact, there was something more.

"Just what, Sweetie?" Edward closed this laptop, placed it on the nightstand, and laid his glasses on top of it. "You don't usually hold back with me when something's on your mind. What's going on?"

"I don't know. I just feel unsure about everything. I feel like I did..."

"When you were married to Tony?"

"Uh-huh." I could feel my chest tighten.

"First thing, breathe. You look like you're going to pass out." Edward pulled me close to him. "Now, what can I do to help you?"

"I don't know."

"Sure you do. Close your eyes and tell me."

I followed Edward's suggestion. I closed my eyes and inhaled deeply. He lightly brushed kisses onto both of my eyelids. "Now, my love, tell me what I can do."

"Convince Fred to go home."

"Really? That is the last thing I expected to hear."

I opened my eyes and looked at Edward. "Don't get me wrong, I love him more than you'll ever know. But right now I cannot deal with anyone else's issues. I really believe he'd kill Tony if he had the chance and I just don't have the energy to babysit him right now. I'm sorry."

"Don't apologize. God, I haven't had to say that to you in weeks. I hate the head trip Tony has on you." I stared at the foot of the bed and bit my bottom lip until I tasted blood. Edward was right. Tony was screwing around with my life, and it needed to end soon.

I walked out of the bedroom the next morning to find the two guys drinking coffee and Fred's suitcase next to the front door. Edward went into the kitchen and fixed my hot tea and toast. He brought it out to the living room and gave me a sweet good morning kiss after he handed it to me. I sat for a few minutes, drinking my tea and trying to wake up a little before I said anything.

"Going somewhere?" I asked.

Fred smiled. "Yeah, I'm going to take the helicopter with Edward to D.C. and catch a flight home."

"Why the sudden change of heart? You seemed so determined last night to stay."

"The more I thought about it, the more I realized that you're not a kid anymore. You don't need me hovering over you or trying to protect you. Edward will take good care of you, but it looks like you can take care of yourself these days."

"You really mean that?" I asked. Fred nodded his head and drank his coffee.

I turned and looked at Edward as he read the day's Wall Street Journal and wondered if he had convinced Fred to go home or if Fred had come to this conclusion himself. I didn't care either way. The final result suited me.

"Honey, are you coming home tonight or staying in D.C.? I know you'd planned on working from here tomorrow, but you've been away from work a lot lately. If you need to stay in the city tonight, I'll understand."

Fred piped in, interrupting our conversation. "*Honey*? Really?"

"No *Sweetie*, it will be late, but I'll be home." I knew he had emphasized the nickname Sweetie for Fred's sake. "I don't like the idea of you here alone with Tony hanging around town."

It wasn't long before the guys headed out the door. I nursed my second cup of tea and stared at the two oversized wooden crates that were on the truck Fred had arrived with. I had taken the day off to go dress shopping with Vivian, but she wasn't coming until lunchtime. Since the crates weren't going to unpack themselves, I decided to dig into the task at hand. Plus, I had a strong suspicion that something I'd been trying to find might be in one of the containers.

The crates were three feet wide by five feet long and stood about three feet tall. I pried open the first crate. It was the one I packed when I sold the house in Ohio.

"This one won't take long," I said to myself.

It was mostly photo albums, yearbooks, pictures in frames, diplomas, that kind of stuff. I put the books and albums on one of Edward's empty bookshelves. The pictures in frames were wrapped in my great-grandmother's tablecloth and matching napkins. I rubbed the linens between my fingers before putting them into the laundry hamper. I remembered the last time they were used and felt a stream of emotions bubble up within me. "No, I'm not going to do this."

Swallowing hard, I regained my composure and walked around the house, finding places for most of the pictures. I took the remainder of the things, along with the diplomas, and put them in my closet until I could figure out what to do with them.

The bottom of the crate was scattered with loose pictures and my stuffed Winnie-The-Pooh, whom I had slept with from the time I was a baby until I was fourteen years old.

Edward had claimed early on in our courtship he wanted the bear's job. I carefully placed the bear on Edward's bedside table with a note.

> *Mr. Baker, Have decided to retire due to wear and tear. Want my job? Please apply with Ms. Martin as soon as possible. Sincerely, Mr. Bear*

It had only taken me an hour to get through the first crate. I took a break and had a glass of water before cracking open the second box and peering inside. It all looked vaguely familiar but I didn't immediately recognize any of it. I knew I hadn't packed it. As I went through the box I began to understand why Fred sent it. It was the box Fred packed for me when he cleared out my parents' house after they died. Most of the things, I had no clue what to do with. There were, of course, more pictures. Some were in albums, others in envelopes with labels on them like "Cassandra's First Birthday" or "Lewis at the Little League World Series", but most were loose. The albums I stuck on the shelf with the other photo albums. Like an archeological dig, the deeper I dug the more value the items held. However, it wasn't monetary value, it was memories. As I opened a small box of Christmas ornaments, I thought about the last Christmas my family shared together. Each ornament brought forth a different memory of Christmas' past. I closed the box and pressed my lips together tightly. I knew someday I would hang the ornaments on a tree, but felt this year would be too soon for me to consider it.

My father's high school class ring and an antique camera my mother received as a birthday gift from her father brought back memories as well. However, when I discovered the baby blanket Lewis and I had both used, the emotions I quelled earlier rose to the surface. I lifted the blanket to my face and inhaled deeply. The blanket smelled faintly of apples and cinnamon and it reminded me of home. Every house I spent my childhood in always smelled of freshly baked apple pie and the memory was overwhelming. Teary-eyed, I gently folded the small green blanket and tucked it into the bottom of the blanket chest, in hopes of using it for a child of my own someday.

If the crate had not been almost empty, I probably would have given up and stopped for the day. However, I was nearly finished and had yet to find the reason I was going through the crates to begin with. At the bottom of this crate, I spied two white boxes, the kind dry cleaners use to preserve heirloom clothing. Each box had a little ribbon secured door that untied and revealed the clothes through a cellophane window.

"Ah-ha." I said aloud, even though I was the only one in the room. "Jackpot!"

The first door revealed my baptismal gown. It still looked as beautiful as it did in the pictures the day I wore it. Being all of eight weeks old at the time, I had no memory of the event, but seeing the tiny lace trim and puffed sleeves, made me long to sift through the photos in search of that day's event. I resisted the urge though, thinking it best to wait until I went through the pictures and put them in some kind of order.

The moment I opened the door to the second box, I knew I was close to finding what I was looking for. I wondered if I should even bother taking it out of the box, knowing it probably would be a wasted effort, but soon couldn't resist. When I laid it across the sofa I was filled with happiness and then a feeling of sadness. It was my mother's wedding dress and veil. It was perfect. The dress I'd dreamt about. After so many years, tainted with so many tragic events, I didn't even know if I would be able to find it and was over-joyed that I had. The dress was simple, yet elegant. The ivory-colored material, while wrinkled from over three decades inside the box, formed a princess, off-the-shoulder, A-lined, full-length dress with a short, square chapel length train. The zipper in the back was covered by pearl buttons and loops. I thought about how long Edward would stare at those buttons before giving up and ripping the dress off of me.

The problem was my mother was four inches shorter and who knows how many pounds lighter than me. I knew her dress wouldn't fit me, but that wasn't what I was in search of. It was the veil. However, when I picked it up, it began to disintegrate in my hands. All this effort, only to find the short, ivory lace veil had not survived the test of time.

I was still staring at the wedding dress when I discovered Vivian standing beside me.

"I knocked but no one answered. I hope you don't mind that I let myself in."

"Not at all. I mean, technically you do own the house."

"It's your home now, not mine, " she said. "I see you found a dress. It's perfect. Are we still going shopping this afternoon?"

"Shopping? Oh yes, but the dress isn't mine. It was my mother's. It won't fit me. I'm too tall and busty compared to her for it."

"Why don't you just try it on?" Vivian examined the dress, looking at the seams, and then held the dress up to me. "Yes, you should try it on. It might work."

"Vivian, I can't." I looked at the dress and thought of my mother. The tiny, rail-thin woman who I found myself missing more as the wedding day crept nearer. "I would just be setting myself up for disappointment and I've had enough of that for one day." I held out the crumbled piece of veil, still in my hand.

Vivian then did something that confused me at first. She started turning the top half of the dress inside out, carefully examining each seam. The longer she looked at it, the more she smiled. "This will fit you, dear. Take a look. When the dress was taken in for your mother the seamstress didn't remove the extra material. See, there's at least four inches of extra material through the bust and waist." She flipped the dress upside down and looked at the hem.

"Oh good," she continued. "There is at least six inches of extra fabric hemmed in the bottom. You have to try this on."

I blew out a deep breath and took the dress from her. "Okay, but I'm going to need your help."

She followed me back to the bedroom. I put the dress on the bed and took off my yoga pants and t-shirt. Within moments she was helping me into the dress. I stood in front of the full-length mirror and looked at myself when Vivian had zipped it as far as it would go.

It was hard to believe my mother had gotten married in this dress. It seemed so much bigger than I remembered it being. It had been so long since she died, my memories of her physical features and the reality of her were no longer the same.

I smoothed out the front of the dress with the palms of my hands as Vivian circled me carefully examining every inch of the dress. "Cassandra, if you want to wear your mother's dress, I know someone who can let it out. Of course, the decision is yours."

Emotions I hadn't anticipated began to take over my ability to speak. I nodded my head and knew it was time to get out of the dress. I reached back and unzipped the partially done zipper. I carefully took the dress off and handed it to Vivian. She laid it across the bed and followed me to my closet, where I was trying to figure out what to wear on our trip to Richmond. Shopping with Vivian required more than just jeans and a sweatshirt. As I pulled a black skirt and fluffy pink sweater out of the closet, Vivian struck up a new conversation.

"Cassandra, dear, I need to ask you about something."

I turned in her direction and her smile was her silent approval of what I had chosen to wear. "Sure, what it is?"

"It's about a rumor I heard the other day in town."

"You mean the one about me and Brian?"

"So you've heard it?" She walked over to the vanity where I was seated and brushing my hair. I had been told by almost everyone that I had beautiful hair. However, I wasn't very good at managing it. Vivian knew this and always helped me whenever she was around and I was trying to get it to behave.

"Sooner or later, all rumors get back to the parties involved."

"I hate to ask," she said, sounding almost embarrassed. "But what exactly is your relationship with Brian? The two of you seem to be quite close these days."

I looked into the mirror, making sure she could see my eyes as I answered the question. My father told me once that the truth always showed through my eyes and I wanted to make sure she could see them. "We are close, but trust me, it's strictly platonic. He is a really nice guy and a good friend. That's all." I paused for a minute, thinking about how the rumor seemed so ridiculous at first, but the more times I heard it, the more I understood why people would make such an assumption. Brian was a single, smart, and somewhat attractive guy. It was then I thought of a way to crush the rumors about the two of us. "But I think we need to find him a girlfriend. One who likes teenage girls too, because I think he's going to have his hands full in a couple of years."

Chapter Nine

THE TRIP TO RICHMOND started pleasantly enough, just as the ones to D.C. to see Edward, but I had made those trips alone. Vivian wasn't thrilled when I fielded two calls from Libby-Mae. However, all of them warranted a call and I was glad to be kept in the loop, even though I was only an hour away from the winery. Spending so much of the previous year traveling alone, I had nearly forgotten what it was like to travel with others and had to keep reminding myself to be social and to leave the reports and laptop I'd brought in my bag alone.

Since we no longer needed to find a wedding dress, Phoebe met up with us at two-thirty for an afternoon of completing my wardrobe. As much as I hated to admit it, both Vivian and Phoebe were right. If I was going to live in Edward's world, I was going to need a fuller closet and larger variety of clothing. Zoe's Boutique had provided me with a great start but she ran a small town shop with limited inventory.

The first store was managed by a friend of Phoebe's. She called ahead and her friend greeted us at the door upon our arrival. She hugged Phoebe and closed the door, locking it behind her and hung a sign reading, "Closed for a private event. Store will re-open in one hour. Sorry for any inconvenience."

Two women stood behind the counter watching us. One was young, college-aged, and the other was in her thirties. The older woman seemed vaguely familiar to me and I subtly tried to get a look at her gold and white name tag.

"Sally Hamm? Is that you?" I asked.

"Have we met?"

She may not have remembered me, but I remembered her. My sophomore and junior years of high school were spent at Williamsburg High School. Before my father died he was a professor at William and Mary, so we had settled in Williamsburg, Virginia. It had been difficult to be eleven and twelve years-old in high school, especially with people like her talking about me behind my back. Fat baby brainiac had been her favorite description of me and I had come home from school on more than one occasion in tears because of her cruel words.

"We went to high school together. Cassandra Clark? Don't you remember, the little child genius?" Her plastered-on smile turned downward and I watched the blood drain from her face, leaving it a pasty shade of white.

"Oh, of course, you've changed, a lot."

"Well, you haven't." It was a generous lie. Her once perfect complexion now seemed uneven and her hair displayed the remnants of a cheap bottle of red hair dye. Time had not been kind to this once perfect high school cheerleader.

"Are you a friend of Phoebe Foster?" She asked.

"Well, I hope so," I said, smiling and trying hard not to gloat. "After all she's going to be my sister."

I had never called Phoebe my sister before and it made Vivian's smile grow.

"Wait a minute; you're Edward Baker's fiancée?" Sally asked.

"Yes, yes I am." I felt a little guilty for enjoying the moment so much. I had never been one to rub my good fortune into someone else's face, and Edward's affection certainly qualified as good fortune, but I just couldn't help myself. Phoebe seemed to understand the situation and chimed in with a question in order to add fuel to the fire.

"Have you seen the ring? You have got to show her the ring." She grabbed my hand and all but pushed it into Sally's face.

I turned my hand slightly from side to side so the light would reflect off the center stone of my five and a half-carat diamond ring. For the first time, I was thankful to Zoe for forcing me to keep my nails and hands looking nice. She had put some kind of artificial nails on my fingers, with a French manicure that would not chip or come off, even with polish remover. Zoe always rolled her eyes when I told her to make them shorter, but I was happy with the way my hands looked while showing off the ring. Edward had it custom-made for me just after the death of his father. It was a beautiful platinum ring with a huge emerald-cut diamond center stone surrounded by smaller diamonds.

"Wow," Sally said staring at the ring, along with everyone else in the room.

"Yeah, but the guy who gave it to me is the real wow," I said as I pulled my hand back, smiling. I remember thinking I needed to thank Edward again for buying me this outrageous piece of jewelry. While I originally balked at the frivolous expense, it had been worth every penny for its effect that afternoon.

I turned, still smiling as Sally began to speak. "Let us know if you need anything. We'll be around."

As I began to weed my way through the racks, Phoebe struck up a conversation. "What was that like, being so young in high school? How did that even happen anyway? Normal people just don't skip that many grades."

"Well," I said, pausing to think about how to explain it. "I didn't really skip that many grades. I only went to a traditional school until I was in second grade. No school my parents put me in knew what to do with me. I was always getting in trouble because I was bored. So my parents decided to homeschool me. The problem was, about the time I hit high school material, my mom's career really took off. She couldn't be flying off to photograph movie stars and supervise my education, so I volunteered to go to high school."

"But what was that like?" Phoebe posed her question again.

"I didn't think it would be as hard as it was. My parents made an effort to make sure I spent time with kids my own age but I wasn't prepared for what teenagers were like. I found my way after a while though. I ate lunch in the library every day, tried to stay out of the way, and aced all my classes."

"Okay, that sounds miserable."

"It wasn't so bad. I'm really glad I did it though. Mom had an amazing career. She wouldn't have lived long enough to enjoy that kind of success if she had waited until I was in college." There was a long silence as Vivian and Phoebe both stopped looking at the clothes and stared at me. "What?"

"No wonder he loves you so much," Vivian said. I dropped my head pretending to not hear her and looked at the dresses in front of me.

I had never quite figured out why Edward was so crazy about me. Every day after I agreed to marry him, he told me a half a dozen reasons why he loved me. He loved me for my body, mind, and soul and made no apologies for any part of it. He told me once he had felt that way since the first night we met, but I just didn't get it. I knew I was getting the better deal in this relationship. It seemed like I was the only one, with maybe the exception of Phoebe, who saw it that way. Sometimes I wondered if it was all too much too fast, but I knew better than to turn away from good fortune when life sets it in front of you. I was thinking about my recent run of good luck and love when I realized Vivian was speaking to me.

"What do you think of this suit?" She said. She held up a lavender wool skirt and jacket that had some potential and I nodded my head.

"I can't believe you two are getting married in just three weeks," Phoebe .

"Yeah," I said half-heartedly. "It's getting close."

Vivian stopped her search through the racks and looked at me once more. Her wrinkled brow sent up an alarm that my response concerned her. "Cassandra, is everything okay? You don't sound very excited."

"Oh no," I said quickly, hoping she would understand the nature of my previous response. "It's just that there is so much going on right now. I'm trying to not let it get the best of me but ..."

As I thought about it all I could feel the strain build within and Phoebe must have seen it as she was quick to steer the conversation back to more frivolous things. "You know what you need, a sexy cocktail dress. Like this one." Phoebe held up a short, silver sequined cocktail dress that had a very sixties retro look to it. I wrinkled my nose in response.

"What? Edward would love it," she commented.

I took a closer look. No buttons, lots of cleavage, bare arms, and lots of leg showing. She was right, he would love it. "Fine. I'll try it on, but I think it shows a little too much skin for me."

Vivian and Phoebe each pulled a few more outfits of varying nature and shipped me off to the dressing room. I came out to the viewing room and showed them each look. By trip number five out of the dressing room, I was ready to go home. Nothing I tried on quite seemed to work. It either didn't fit or just looked plain ridiculous on me. I walked into the room to show Phoebe and Vivian the cocktail dress Phoebe had pulled off the rack. I wasn't sure if it was the wrong size or if I was just too self-conscious for a dress that revealing, but I felt as though I could expose myself at any moment.

When I looked at myself in the oversized three-way mirror, my frustration finally got the best of me and I looked at Vivian. "Can't I just wear jeans and t-shirts and never leave Thomas Hall again? I could be one of those eccentric women married to a billionaire who never leaves the house."

As I stepped down from the pedestal in the center of the viewing room, I could hear Sally and the other salesgirl chatting somewhere in the back. They had big voices and it was obvious they were unaware as to how their voices carried. I turned for the dressing room when Vivian gently touched my arm to stop me.

"Cassandra, dear, what's wrong? You seem determined not to find anything new to wear. Are you sure about this?"

"About what?" I asked, already knowing where the conversation was headed, and it had nothing to do with clothes.

"Are you sure you want to get married so soon? It just seems like you went from 'It'll be a long engagement' to 'We're getting married in nine weeks' overnight. And I've noticed you're a little anxious about the big day arriving."

She was right. That was exactly what happened, but it had been no ordinary night. The evening Darla died I had almost died too. I had never spoken to anyone about what really happened that night. The police knew what they needed to know and Edward knew the one detail I had created to keep Henry safe. But the toll it had taken on me had been more than I was willing to admit. The fragility of my existence had forced me to push the date as close as humanly possible. But I had begun to wonder, as well, if this was all too much, too soon. I shook the thoughts of that night and avoided answering Vivian's question by focusing on the task at hand.

"It's just that none of these outfits are quite me."

"Are you sure?" She asked, pushing the subject.

"Yes," I said and then in a quick moment everything that was weighing heavy upon me came spilling out. "It's just that my dead husband isn't dead, I'm not divorced yet, and Edward is being stubborn about signing the prenup."

"I didn't think Edward wanted a prenup," Phoebe said.

"He doesn't, I do."

"Oh," Phoebe replied, sounding surprised.

"I called Zachary's office and had him draw one up. It's really simple. If things don't, well, you know, work out, we'd both walk away with what we started and split any joint assets."

"What about children?" Phoebe asked. While I'd never mentioned it to her, I was certain Vivian had told her Edward and I had decided not to wait until we were married to actively try to conceive. I had always dreamt of a big family and with Edward being two decades my senior, we both agreed there was no time like the present to begin.

"There's a provision for them. Edward would provide reasonable child support, medical, and education." I could hear the two salesgirls continue to talk about my engagement. I hated being the center of gossip.

"That sounds reasonable," Vivian said. "What's the problem?"

"He says we don't need it. He says we won't be one of *those* couples." I turned to my newly divorced sister-in-law and bit my lip. "Sorry."

"It's okay," Phoebe said. "Do you believe him?"

"Of course, one-hundred percent."

"So why have it drawn up if he doesn't want one?" Vivian asked.

"Listen to them talk in the back of the store." I continued back to the dressing room to change as we all listened.

"... and, oh my God, did you see her when she walked in? How the hell did a mousy girl like that land a guy like Edward Baker."

"Believe it or not, she looked worse when she was younger. She was fat. I mean like Goodyear blimp fat."

"Yeah, and did you see the gossip section of the paper? Apparently, her first husband showed up this week and she's been telling everybody he was dead."

"Man, she must have nailed that Baker guy good to get the ring then. After all, sex is the way a gold digger gets—" The conversation came to an abrupt halt as if someone had hit the power button on a radio.

This time when I walked out of the dressing room I was wearing my own clothes, although there were still several items left in the room I hadn't tried on. I picked up my purse from the chair only to find Vivian, Phoebe, the manager, and Sally with her partner in crime standing near the door.

Vivian, who was usually the definition of calm elegance, was scolding the two women as if they were puppies who had just chewed on her favorite pair of shoes. "Exactly who do you two think you are? This poor girl has been through a hell you'll never even understand. And now that she's found happiness, you have the nerve to gossip about her while she's in the store. I hope you realize that you've lost a big sale today. In our family, the sky is the limit when it comes to what Cassandra wants, and we might have very well bought the entire store out. You two should be ashamed of yourselves."

Phoebe stood just behind her mother, mouth slightly agape. My expression soon followed that of my future sister-in-law's.

"Vivian, it's okay, really. Let's just go." I turned and faced Sally who could not bring herself to look me in the eye. "I was right, you haven't changed at all. You're still the same miserable girl you were in high school. I'd have thought after all this time you would've found some real happiness." I looked down at my ring and thought of Edward. "I'm just glad I did."

As I opened the door I discovered my face full of camera lenses. My guess was Sally had called and tipped off the press in hopes of her own fifteen minutes of fame. I closed the door and turned around. I looked at the manager. "Back door?"

"Of course," the manager replied before turning to Sally and the young clerk. "And you two, you're fired. Pack your things and go." Sally seemed to be shocked that her behavior caused her to lose her job.

Phoebe called our driver and within moments we were shuttled out the back entrance and into the limo.

"Now where?" Phoebe asked.

"Home. I'm done."

Phoebe's cell phone interrupted our conversation. I could not tell whom she was talking to but there were a lot of uh-huhs and oh-nos. As she listened she whispered to me. "Do you have your laptop?" I nodded and retrieved it from my bag. As I powered it up, she yanked it out of my hand as she said goodbye to the person on the phone and started clicking away.

"Damn."

"What's wrong?" Vivian asked. Phoebe looked at her and turned the laptop in her direction but kept the screen out of my view. When she looked at the screen she gave out a heavy sigh.

"What?" I asked as I looked at Phoebe, but she was already back on her phone. I turned to Vivian. "What is it?"

"It's just tabloid trash. Nothing you need to worry about."

I motioned for her to hand the computer back to me and she did so reluctantly. I felt nauseous when I read the online tabloid on my screen. "Wedding or No Wedding? Baker bride-to-be holds out for better prenup." It had been posted five minutes earlier and I was certain that this was not the only website that stating, "... an unnamed boutique employee overheard Cassandra Martin discussing her prenup with Edward Baker's mother and sister while shopping. The same source implied there were threats between Mrs. Vivian Baker and her son's fiancée that involved postponing the wedding ..."

I slammed the laptop shut and threw it into the floor with enough force to potentially damage it. Just then my phone rang.

"Hi, Beautiful." It was Edward.

"Have you seen it?"

"Yes, I just got off the phone with Phoebe. Don't worry, I'll take care of this."

"Don't. It'll just fuel the fire. Remind me again why eloping in Vegas is a bad idea."

When Tony and I married, we went down to City Hall and, with Sarah and Michael as our witnesses, tied the knot. It had always been enough for me, but Edward felt I had missed out on some great life experience by not having a big wedding with all the trimmings. I wasn't thrilled about the idea of being the center of attention for an entire day, but at some point, we had compromised what we both wanted with a small church wedding at the Catholic Church and a reception at Thomas Hall.

"Sweetie, I will put a stop to this and you'll be glad we didn't elope when it's over," he said.

"No, I won't. You know how I feel about being the center of attention. However, I know a proper wedding is important to you. I guess I'll just have to save Vegas for the next husband." I sighed and everyone, both in the limo and on the phone, started to laugh.

On the way home, Vivian tried to assure me the gossip about Edward and me would eventually die down, but we both knew better. We were almost to Thomas Hall when I remembered the invitation I extended to Poppy for Friday night.

"Vivian, I hope you don't mind, but I invited someone to spend the night at the main house this Friday."

"You know you're always welcome to have your guests stay with me. Do you mind if I ask who?"

"It's actually Tony's Grandfather Scarpelli. He wants to talk to me before he sees Tony and he's the type of person who likes to keep a low profile. I thought it would be his best option."

"I'm surprised you'd want him in the same state with you. You gave me the impression once that you'd cut yourself off completely from his family after he died, or at least when you thought he was dead."

"Poppy's different. He's always been nice to me, even when the rest of Tony's family thought I wasn't pretty enough or good enough for him. Sometimes I forget he's Tony's grandfather and not mine."

"Cassandra, did you say Poppy, as in Poppy Scarpelli?"

"Yes Ma'am. Is that a problem?" I cringed as I asked the question, worried I had overstepped my place in the Baker family by inviting him.

"Well, if anyone had ever told me a Chicago mob boss was going to stay at my house, I'd have told them they were crazy. But if he's smart enough to see how beautiful you are and you love him, then he's welcome at Thomas Hall."

Chapter Ten

As we approached the gate of the winery, Vivian buzzed the driver's intercom. "Don't worry about dropping Cassandra at her house. She'll be going with me to the main house. Thank you."

"I will?" I asked, unaware that I was expected there.

"I need you to look at the place cards for the reception. I can't make up my mind which ones to use."

The moment she used the words "can't make up my mind" I should have known something was amiss. Vivian was one of the most decisive women I ever met, but somehow her sudden indecisiveness did not register as unusual.

"Vivian, I'm sure either will be fine."

"Please, just humor me. You could stay for dinner too."

"Ah-ha, the real reason." I smiled and she smiled back. Since her husband's death, Vivian had adjusted quite well to living alone, except at dinnertime. She and Senior had not been apart for dinner in years and to not have someone to share her evening meal with often left her feeling lonely. I made it a habit to conveniently be at the house on Tuesdays and Wednesdays just before dinner and Henry would go as often as he could. Edward and I usually had Sunday dinner with his mom and the rest of the family would be there whenever possible as well.

When we reached the house, we stepped out of the car and walked through the beautifully carved double doors. I found it odd that Victor was not there to greet us and take our coats. It was dark in the foyer as I followed Vivian to the dining room.

I suddenly had a very uneasy feeling and, for a brief moment, wondered if Vivian would dare to do something I had explicitly asked everyone not to do. As I reached the entrance to the dining room, I realized that was exactly what she had done. I was immediately met with a high-pitched squeal. "Surprise!"

The dark cherry wood dining room had been transformed into a spectacle of pale pink and white, with flowers, ribbons, and balloons everywhere. The smell of the fresh-cut flowers was perfectly complemented by the vanilla-scented votive candles that numbered in the hundreds. In the corner was a small table stacked high with elegantly wrapped gifts, all with large bows.

The dining room table was covered in a beautiful white linen tablecloth and pink napkins. Surrounding it were Phoebe, Zoe, Libby-Mae, Kelly, and Kelly's companion Margie.

At the beginning of our engagement, I had been a little jealous of the tight relationship Edward had with his assistant Kelly. She was a beautiful woman with long auburn locks, lightly freckled skin, and closer to Edward's age. One night, I confessed I was worried someday he might come to his senses and run away with her. His answer was laughter followed by a kiss. Kelly had been in a committed relationship for over a decade with a physician at a hospital in the D.C. area. The two women had flown to California the first time same-sex marriages became legal and were married before a justice of the peace in San Francisco.

In addition to those five women, Dr. Rice's wife, Evelyn, and Judge Smith's wife, Candice, were in attendance. They were old family friends of the Baker family and while I didn't know them well, they were always sociable when I ran into them in town. Vivian once told me they were thrilled that Edward had ended up with such a sweet girl.

The guests were rounded out with a couple of Phoebe's friends from Richmond. I had spent the afternoon having lunch and shopping with these ladies one Tuesday in October.

Phoebe came forward first and gave me a hug. "You really didn't think we'd let you get married without throwing you a bridal shower?"

"Well, I was hoping."

"Don't be silly," Libby-Mae chimed in. "It'll be fun."

The only person in the room who seemed to understand how much I hated being the center of attention was Zoe. She walked over and handed me a glass of wine. "Sorry, I tried to stop them." However, she smiled the whole time she spoke and I wondered exactly how hard she had really tried to prevent this event from happening.

As I gulped down the entire glass of Chardonnay, Vivian put her arm around my waist and guided me to the table. In addition to the linens, the table had been set with gold-rimmed white china at each seat, all thirteen of them. I was amazed by the number of chairs at the table. I wondered if I even knew thirteen people in Virginia.

Each seat had a place card and a menu card was gently laid across each table setting. I looked at Vivian who appeared to be anxiously awaiting my response. It was as if at that moment she realized why I requested that no one host a shower for me.

"It's all so beautiful, but so much work. Vivian, you really shouldn't have. I mean, you've done so much already."

"Well, I did," she said. "So try to enjoy yourself."

Everyone took their seats, but there were gaps at various points around the table. Phoebe turned to her mom, who was seated to my right. "Who's missing?"

"Well, let's see," Vivian said. "I thought your friend Patty was coming?"

"Oh yeah. I almost forgot. She called on my way up. Her husband's out of town and the babysitter got the flu. She couldn't find anyone else to watch the kids on such short notice. But there are still two empty chairs."

Just then Victor entered the room and handed Vivian a note. She read it, smiled, folded it and tucked it under her plate. "My sisters just called. They send their regrets. Everyone's fine but there was some sort of minor emergency they've been asked to assist with that couldn't wait. So that's everyone then."

Libby-Mae looked at Vivian and then me. "Wasn't Sarah invited? I know I mailed her invitation."

"I called and uninvited her," Vivian responded. "Considering the circumstances, at the moment, I thought it would be for the best."

"Oh," Libby-Mae said, not knowing of our recent estrangement. "But isn't she your matron of honor?"

"She was supposed to be," I said. "Maybe I just won't have one. Do I really need a matron of honor?"

"No dear," Vivian said. "It would be nice if there were the same number of bridesmaids and groomsmen though. But we don't need to worry about that tonight."

As we spoke, Vivian placed her hand on mine. She knew how close Sarah and I were, and how heartbreaking the situation was for me. The comfort she provided was just enough to make me smile. As I turned my attention back to the party, the first course of dinner was being served.

There were four simple, but elegant courses. I was surprised at the menu. I never realized Vivian paid so much attention to my likes and dislikes. It made me happy to know she thought so much of me. The first course was crab stuffed mushrooms, followed by a pear and blue cheese salad with a walnut and raspberry vinaigrette dressing. The main course consisted of steamed lobster with drawn butter and asparagus, followed by chocolate mousse.

Several conversations intertwined throughout the meal, but as dessert was served, the main conversation turned to my upcoming nuptials.

"So tell us about the wedding," Mrs. Rice said.

"Yeah," continued Phoebe's friend Jessica. "What does your dress look like?"

"It's the same dress my mother wore. Vivian arranged for the alterations today."

"Isn't the wedding in just a couple of weeks?" Jessica asked.

"I know. I'm cutting it close but the dress had to be dug out of a crate that was in storage in Florida."

"Well, what about the bridesmaid's dresses?" Mrs. Smith said. "Surely those have been taken care of."

"Oh yes, Ma'am. Vivian found these beautiful emerald green dresses. They're simple, elegant, classic. Perfect for a small wedding."

"They are gorgeous mom," Phoebe said turning to her mother. "We had our final fitting late last week. They fit beautifully."

"Oh good," I said. "I kept meaning to ask you how they turned out."

I was immediately bombarded with another question. "What about the flowers, Miss Cassandra? I haven't heard you say anything about them." I think Libby-Mae found it odd that I rarely spoke of the plans when I was at work.

"Um, Vivian, are there flowers?" Everyone laughed, thinking I was joking, but I honestly didn't know if the flowers had been ordered.

"Yes, dear. White roses and pale pink orchids, just like tonight. But if you don't like them, it's not too late to change them."

"No, this is perfect. Don't change anything. I like the candles too."

"Maybe we'll add more then."

It was becoming more and more obvious to everyone in the room that I had very little to do with the planning and execution of my upcoming nuptials. It was then that Margie, Kelly's companion, looked at me. "Cassandra, how much do you even know about your own wedding?"

The truth was, not much. I was a terrible party planner and Vivian had volunteered to help with the plans. In the end, I willingly let her take it over in almost every detail.

"I know it starts at five," I said.

Vivian smiled as she walked back towards the table with a handful of the gifts I had noticed earlier. "Actually, we moved it to four."

"We did?"

"Father Tennelli had a scheduling issue."

"Oh, what time do the invitations say?"

"Don't worry, they're correct. Why don't you start opening your presents?"

Presents. I loved receiving gifts, but I couldn't think of a thing in the world I could possibly need. However, my party guests knew better. Dr. Rice's wife gave me a beautiful garter to wear on my wedding day. She had hand-stitched every piece of it herself, lace and all. Libby-Mae found an antique frame and had a mat cut so that the wedding invitation fit neatly in it. Kelly and Margie gave me a gift certificate to their favorite gourmet market in Fredericksburg. Mrs. Smith gave me a copy of two of the local churches' cookbooks, and Zoe had wrapped up half a dozen pairs of my favorite silk stockings. The stockings were one of my few indulgences and if she hadn't owned the store, I would have protested due to the cost. Phoebe's friends had all chipped in and put together a "honeymoon" basket with satin sheets, candles, edible body powder, and a very skimpy piece of lingerie that made me blush when I held it up.

I hoped that Vivian and Phoebe had not bought me a gift, as the shower I begged them not to give me, had turned into a beautiful evening that was better than anything material I could ever receive. The smiles and laughter the evening brought were the perfect therapy to counter-balance the events of the last few days. However, there was still a package, beautifully wrapped, from the two of them.

I was just untying the ribbon when I saw Jessica look towards the window. "Who's the hot guy walking up to the house?" At Thomas Hall, that statement could have applied to any number of men. Edward, Alex, and Henry were all good-looking. I leaned over and as soon as I saw the shadow of the man, I knew who it was. I wanted to jump up and run to Edward, but I knew it would be rude to race out of my own bridal shower. So, I impatiently waited for Edward to walk down the hall into the room. However, by the time he had reached the threshold, my self-control was gone. I all but leapt across the room and flung my arms around him.

"Miss me, Sweetie?" He asked.

"I didn't think you were going to be home until late."

"I thought the party would be over by now. I guess I'll let you ladies finish up." He pushed a stray strand of hair from my face and tucked it behind my ear. I'll meet you at home in a bit, okay?"

I wanted to yell at him, "No, it's not okay!" I guess my expression said it for me because Vivian was quick to speak up.

"Why don't you stay for cake and coffee?"

He looked at the ladies and then at me. When our eyes met, the smile on his face started to grow even larger. "Maybe I should. My wife is getting that pouty look she gets when she doesn't get her way."

"I really enjoyed myself tonight, but it would have been nice to have a little warning," I said as I walked out of the bathroom and began changing into a nightgown. "How long did you know about this?"

"Not until yesterday. Mom told me over lunch." He kissed the back of my neck and headed to brush his teeth and get ready for bed.

It took a long minute before the light bulb moment hit me. "Oh, so that's why Fred was in such a hurry to get out of here this morning."

I heard the muffled laughter from the bathroom as I crawled into bed. I opened the book I was reading while I waited for Edward. I was re-reading Shakespeare's Macbeth for the umpteenth time. I liked reading Shakespeare. He was one of the few classic writers who could create characters with lives more insane than my own.

"You're the only person I've ever met who reads Shakespeare for fun," he said as he walked into the room and crawled into bed beside me.

I closed the book and put it on the nightstand. "I get Will, or at least his characters."

"Speaking of, any word on the missing teenagers, you know the 'Romeo and Juliet' kids?"

"Nope. Pretty sad too. Their parents were on the local news again this morning pleading for information about their kids. I think they just want to know where the two are, whether they're dead or alive." As I watched the news that morning, I considered the odds. Odds were they had already been dead for over a week.

"Thoughts?" Edward asked, probably already knowing what was going through my mind.

"It's just sad, the whole thing." I slid under the covers, rested my head on Edward's chest, listened to his heart beating fast, and fell asleep within seconds.

After an uneventful morning at the office, I went back to the house for lunch on Edward's insistence. When I opened the front door, the aroma of curry and spices bombarded me. He had spent the morning making a delicious Indian meal for us, complete with curried cauliflower and potatoes, and sugared pumpkin balls rolled in shredded coconut. However, an hour later, when I should have been sitting back at my desk, I was naked and snuggled up to

Edward under the down comforter of our oversized bed. He was tracing the length of my body with his fingertips. As he reached the inside of my thigh, his touch caused goosebumps to rise above the surface of the pale skin of my leg.

"Oh, my," he said, inhaling deeply. I pretended to push him away from me but did it with so little force he didn't move.

"You know you have that effect on me. Why the surprise?" I reached over and planted soft, light kisses along his shoulder and neck.

"You always surprise me."

I stopped and looked into his eyes. He had the most beautiful brown eyes that always took my breath away. "I don't see how. You know so much about me."

"What do you mean?" he said. "It seems like I learn something new about you every day."

I had always been annoyed by his extensive knowledge of my past, and I often wished he would tell me everything he knew. "Edward, when you had the private investigator look for me, what did you find out about my past?"

"Hiding something?" I shook my head and smiled. I had my secrets, but they were ones I would tell Edward in due time unless he already knew about them. "When the lead private investigator came back the first time with what he had found, he started with your life at college."

"Lead?" I asked. "There was more than one?"

"There were four. I remembered you said you graduated from UNC so they started there. Going backward in time was easy. Your parents, your brother, all of that was public record. But after your freshman year of college, you started to slip off the radar. It was just an apartment address and college enrollment. Then you married Tony and got a job at the University of Ohio. But after Tony died, for all intents and purposes, you just vanished."

"So for the last two months, you've known all these things about my past and haven't asked me a single question about it?"

"I know your past is hard for you to talk about. Besides, it's sad and I hate to see you unhappy." He touched the back of his hand to my cheek and I could feel my body temperature rise. I suddenly had a great desire to kiss him, rip all his clothes off of him, and make love to him. Again.

"You know you can ask me anything," I said. "I'll tell you whatever you want to know."

"You had a brother, right?"

I turned away from him and pulled the covers up to my chin. "Anything but that. I don't talk about that."

"Okay," I could hear a mild twinge of frustration punctuate his voice. "I'll try again. You were the only survivor of the car wreck, weren't you?"

"Yeah. When the car stopped rolling, my dad and I were the only two still breathing. He bled to death waiting for the ambulance."

"Oh, Sweetie." He pulled me to him so we spooned, our bodies pressed close. He knew it was one of my favorite places to be. It was my happy place. The one place where I felt completely safe and loved.

"You're the only person alive who knows that. I told everyone else he died on impact, like Mom did. The EMT at the scene knew I was lying, but I think he knew why. I didn't want the people who loved my dad to know he'd suffered."

"How long did he live?"

"I don't know, but it seemed like an eternity waiting for help to come." I relived the entire night in an instant. "We were out in the middle of nowhere. Dad talked to me the first five or ten minutes then he stopped talking, but I could hear him breathing. Then I heard nothing."

"What did he say?"

"I guess my Dad knew he was dying. He told me he was proud of me and that he loved me, that I was special and must remember that always. He said he wished he could live long enough to see ..." I had a hard time getting the last words out but Edward held me closer. "To see me graduate, walk me down the aisle on my wedding day, play with his grandchildren."

"How old were you?"

"I was finishing my junior year of high school. So, twelve, almost thirteen."

"What else did he say?"

"He told me family was everything. He made me promise to tell my brother that he and my Mom loved both of us very much and that we were going to have to take care of each other." I knew I had said the word 'brother'. It was part of what he wanted to know. I just wasn't certain I could bear to tell him the rest.

"Your brother wasn't in the car?"

I paused for a moment. "No, I had been invited to tour Yale that weekend and he had a baseball tournament. He was at home."

"I thought he died in that accident Cassie."

"No, he died a few years later. Fred and I buried him next to my parents, but you already knew that, didn't you? They're all there together and if it weren't for me they'd all probably still be alive."

"You don't really believe that do you?"

I closed my eyes and took a deep breath. "I have to because it's the truth."

"Did you have other siblings?" I wondered why he asked because I was certain he already knew.

"No, just, just…" I wanted to say his name. I hadn't said his name in over a decade and I knew if I could say it, it would help release me from the guilt somehow. I just didn't know if it was possible. I took a deep breath. "Just me and Lewis."

It was like a tidal wave of emotions crashed down on me. Guilt, sadness, grief, and somehow relief. They were all there, along with other emotions that I could not attach words to nor describe. Tears began to course down my face and I turned and looked at Edward. I prayed he wouldn't ask any more questions.

"Lewis Clark?" I knew he wanted to laugh. If you thought about it, it was funny. But he wiped away my tears instead.

"Lewis Newton Clark. Lewis N. Clark. My parents thought it had character. I thought they were crazy. He didn't get it."

"Oh, come on. He had to get the explorers' references. He couldn't have been that clueless."

"He was the star athlete. Baseball, football, wrestling, water polo, soccer; if it was a game that could be won, he was out there winning it. But he struggled to keep his grades up enough to play. Twice I rewrote his term papers after he went to bed so he wouldn't fail classes. He never even knew I'd done it. I hate to say this about my brother but he was the stereotypical dumb jock. He was only a year ahead of me by the time I went to high school."

"You aren't going to tell me how he died, are you?"

"Edward, I can't. It's just too ..."

"Then tell me something about him that makes you smile."

"He's the only other person, besides you, who's ever called me Cassie."

Chapter Eleven

It seemed like only moments later I was dressed in a new red silk blouse, tea-length black, wool pencil skirt, and red heels. My hair was pulled up and I was wearing my mother's gold crucifix. Edward was retying his tie for the third time.

"Are you certain you want me at this dinner?" He untied the crooked knot and started again.

"Yes, Poppy will want to meet you." I walked over, took the tie from him, and retied it, getting the knot right on the first try. "I've never seen you this nervous before."

"Well, it's not every night someone shares a meal with a mafia don who's the closest thing your beautiful wife has to a grandfather."

He constantly referred to me as his wife. In Edward's mind, we were husband and wife the day he got down on his knees and held my ring in his hands. His mindset worried me. We weren't married yet and it looked like Tony wasn't going to make it easy.

"A word of advice, go light on the mob talk and heavy on the grandfather talk. He doesn't like to talk about his job, but family, he'll talk about them all night long."

"Okay, good to know." Edward walked to the window and looked out at the darkened skies. "It's raining. Why don't you take the golf cart up to the main house and I'll go meet Mr. Scarpelli at the helipad with an umbrella. I don't want you catching a cold. I'll have no sick brides on our honeymoon."

Fifteen minutes later, I was pacing in the foyer when Edward and Poppy walked through the front door, comfortably talking and laughing.

"Well, well, what do we have here? Two happy men arriving for dinner this evening?"

Edward held up Poppy's bags. "I'm going to get someone to take these up to the Elizabeth Suite."

"No, have them put in the Roosevelt Suite. The Elizabeth is 'wedding central' at the moment."

He smiled and leaned down, pressing his lips against mine and I felt my entire body become tense knowing Poppy was standing just feet away for us. I pulled away from Edward feeling slightly embarrassed.

Poppy looked the same as he had the first time we met. Gray hair, slicked back, bright blue eyes, and as round as he was tall. He was dressed as if he had come straight from the office, but that was the way he always looked. Today his custom-tailored suit was black, although he had dozens of suits to choose from. The three-piece business wear had been completed with a crisp, white dress shirt and a green silk tie.

"You look well, Poppy. You haven't changed a bit."

"You have. You look much thinner," he said as Edward stood beside me. "How much weight have you lost since I saw you in Chicago last year?"

"I don't know, about sixty pounds, maybe a little more."

"Hmm." I could tell Poppy wanted to say something. I was not certain if he was happy for me or shocked at the drastic change in my appearance. It was only after I thought Tony was dead that I managed to pull my life together and begin to follow my dreams. In doing this, I felt better about myself and managed to get down to a healthy weight. Regardless of what Poppy was thinking, I decided it was probably best to change the topic.

"Thanks for coming. I know how busy you are."

As we talked, the three of us moved to the sitting room. A table filled with cheese, crackers, fruit, and wine glasses awaited us. Vivian assumed it would be a long evening. Cheese, wine, and then move to the dining room for a five-course meal. I appreciated that she was not trying to rush through dinner. It had been a long time since Poppy and I had spent an evening together and I was looking forward to it.

"I need to understand everything that is going on before I go see my grandson tomorrow morning. I know your take on things will be of great help to me."

I heard the click of heels behind me and knew Vivian had entered the room. I turned to find her looking radiant and regal, as always. She was a petite woman and wonderfully slim, despite rapidly approaching seventy, giving birth to three children over a dozen years, and never setting foot in a gym. Her hair, which she usually wore in a classic bob, was pinned back in a French twist and every strand of hair was perfectly in place. She was wearing a light gray skirt, navy blue blouse, and matching colored heels. Her pearl necklace and earrings completed her classic look.

"Poppy, I'd like you to meet Vivian Baker, Edward's mother. Vivian, this is Poppy Scarpelli...my, well, Tony's grandfather."

"Pleasure is mine, I am certain Mrs. Baker." He reached for her hand and gently kissed it. For a brief second, I thought I saw Vivian blush.

"Oh please, call me Vivian. Why don't I get a drink for everyone? Cassandra, what do you recommend?"

"The newer Pinot Noir, Special Reserve, I think would do nicely."

Edward looked at me. "I'll go to the cellar and get it."

"Honey, carefully." He nodded, understanding what I meant. It had been less than two months since his father had been murdered and I had nearly been beaten to death in the same cellar by his now deceased sister-in-law. Every time Edward went to the cellar he would get angry. I recently discovered he blamed himself for my injuries that night. He thought that if he had not taken the phone call from Kelly or had walked down with me, he could have deterred the attack.

Poppy raised a single eyebrow at me. "Something dangerous down there?"

I thought back to that night and every detail replayed in a fraction of a second. "Not anymore."

Poppy nodded. It was something he did when he had heard or seen enough on a topic to understand all he wanted to know. His eyes scanned the interior of the house. "Is this where you live now? It's very nice."

As we talked, Edward returned looking unusually calm to have made the trip to the cellar. He walked to the small table and set the bottle down. Within seconds, Victor arrived, pouring wine and fixing everyone small plates of fruit and cheese.

"No, this is the main house. Edward and I have a home together just down the path."

"Together?" He asked.

I felt heat rush to my face. In my past life, the one I shared with Tony, I would have never lived with a man I wasn't married to. Vivian seemed to understand where the conversation was headed and knew the embarrassment would kill me, so she intervened on my behalf.

"Yes, it just seemed silly to have her settle in here to turn around and uproot the poor child again a few months later. Besides, I think she prefers her privacy."

"I really do." I remarked, sitting on the love seat. Edward joined me and Vivian gestured for Poppy to take the larger of the two chairs close by, while she chose the other one. "But I like it when Edward's home on the weekends, too."

Poppy's face showed his confusion as he turned to Edward. "You don't live here?"

"I have a place near my corporate headquarters in D.C." He paused to look at me. "But I don't have a life until I get here."

I could feel my face warming again. I stared out the window, but only for a brief moment before I felt Edward's hand under my chin, gently guiding my face back to his. "You know it's the truth."

I looked into his eyes, took a deep breath, and smiled. No one had ever made me feel the way he did. I leaned in close, closer than was probably appropriate in front of others and intertwined his fingers in mine.

Edward knew small talk wasn't my strong point and tried to keep the conversation moving. "Are you retired, Mr. Scarpelli?" As soon as he said it, I could tell he remembered what I had told him about avoiding shop talk and his eyes widened.

"I keep trying to," Poppy said, with a slight chuckle in his voice. "But I constantly find myself right back in the middle of things. At the moment, I am dealing with grandchildren whom all think they should be in charge of the family business even though they would probably destroy it within a year."

Vivian smiled. "My late husband, Senior, had a cure for that. He left Cassandra in charge."

"Really?"

"Yes, and she's doing an excellent job."

"Maybe I am going about this all wrong." He turned from Vivian to me. "How would you like to take over –"

"Poppy, you'd better be joking or I swear I'll have you committed." We both began to laugh and the rest joined in.

"You would do a good job, but I don't think you would enjoy the work," Poppy said, sounding almost serious. "I think you might be more suited to this profession." He held up his now empty glass. "This is very nice. I'm surprised you remembered that Pinots are my favorite."

I hadn't remembered; I had just been lucky. I made a mental note to have Libby-Mae ship Poppy a case of the Pinot on Monday. It could be an early Christmas gift. As I stood to refill everyone's glasses, Victor entered and announced that the first course was ready at our leisure.

Edward and Vivian lead the way and Poppy and I followed. While we walked he softly asked, "Cassandra, tell me, how did you find Tony?"

"I didn't. He found me."

Poppy didn't nod his head again that night.

Edward and I walked to the main house the next morning to find the subtle flirting that began at dinner between Poppy and Vivian had not stopped. The entire evening had been strange for me, watching my surrogate grandfather and my future mother-in-law behave in such a way. However, they were enjoying each other's company so much that I could not help but be happy for them and their newfound friendship.

After breakfast, I gave Poppy a tour of the grounds and buildings, including the home that Edward and I shared, which he referred to as a cute little dollhouse. By ten o'clock Poppy was ready to leave and get to the matter at hand.

We all knew where Poppy was going and whom he was going to see. I wondered what the outcome would be, so I asked Poppy to give me a call when he returned to Chicago. He promised he would and as he walked out the front door of the main house he turned and kissed Vivian gently on the lips. My mouth was still wide open when Poppy's car drove away.

Needless to say, the afternoon was comparatively quiet. We spent most of it at the main house. Edward perched himself in front of his late father's desk and tried to get some work done. I think he was trying to avoid looking at his mother as well. Seeing that kiss rattled me, so I could only imagine the effect it had on him. My guess was he had never seen a man, besides his father, kiss his mother on the lips. However, Vivian acted as if it were no big deal and insisted we go over the seating arrangements for the reception.

I tried hard to continue as if nothing unusual was happening in my world, but I felt as if some kind of fog had engulfed me. A fog that would never lift. It was a suffocating feeling. Everything seemed to take longer. Making decisions, expressing opinions, and answering questions all required more effort than these things ever had before Tony's arrival in Virginia. And it was exhausting.

Around four-thirty my cell phone rang.

"Cassandra, it's Poppy."

"You're back in Chicago already? That was a quick visit."

"Yes, yes it was," he said. His voice was harsher and sharper than I had ever heard it. "I am sorry you were ever married to Tony. He is truly a bottom feeder. I am ashamed to call him my grandson."

"Poppy, what happened with him? He's your family."

"I would rather not discuss it but I will tell you this when he faked his death, he stopped being a member of any family."

"Oh," I said, a little surprised by his response. One of the reasons he and I had always gotten along so well was because of our unwavering loyalty to our families.

"Cassandra," he continued. "I want to make something very clear to you. Something I should have said last night. You will always be part of my family and I am very happy with how you are choosing to live your life."

Chapter Twelve

By the time my conversation with Poppy was over, the sun was making its way beneath the horizon. Most evenings Edward and I took a long walk. It was a nice wind-down from a busy day for both of us. Most of the time, we hardly spoke. We just walked, hand in hand and enjoyed each other's company. The only thing that normally stopped us was bad weather. I knew within the next few weeks though, the combination of early nights and cold days would steal our time among the vines. Some evenings I didn't focus on anything at all, but that particular night I thought about what we would do when it was no longer good walking weather.

As our house came into view, I noticed the living room light on. When we left earlier in the day, all the lights in the house were off.

"Someone's in the house," I said to Edward and we stopped abruptly.

"It's probably just the household staff sneaking in to clean while we're out."

"No, I have an arrangement with Victor. The staff only comes while I'm at work during the week and no one comes on Fridays, Saturdays, or Sundays unless I call."

"When did that happen?"

"About a week after our engagement. I couldn't get used to having people in and out of the house all the time and I don't want anyone bothering us on the weekends."

"I'm a little surprised you've set so many limits on the staff," Edward said, touching my arm, leading me toward the house.

"You've got to remember, I've never lived like this before. It takes a little getting used to. Don't get me wrong, the staff here is great, I mean really great, but sometimes it's all a bit much."

"Well, you'd never know it. Everyone keeps telling me how well you're fitting in. Like you've lived here all your life." As we reached the front porch, Edward faced me and brushed my cheek with the back of his hand. "Wait here and I'll go see who it is."

I had recently purchased a small patio bench and positioned it against the wall on the porch. I took a seat and fumbled through my jacket pocket until I felt my cell phone and clutched it tightly. I had spent a year traveling the world without any means of personal communication whatsoever. In that time, I never worried for my safety. However, since moving to Thomas Hall, my cell phone had become a security blanket and I never left the house without it.

The moment I saw Edward walk in the front door I realized who was in there. Edward's voice bellowed across the vineyard. "I told you, if you came back here, I'd kill you!"

I raced through the door, finding Tony pinned to the wall by Edward, his hands circling Tony's neck.

"Stop it! He's not worth it." Edward looked at me and loosened his grip. "Besides, I don't want Tony's blood in our house."

Tony glared at me and raised a single eyebrow. "You've shacked up with him? Baby Girl, you have changed."

"Why are you here?" I asked. "I can have you thrown in jail."

"Don't humor yourself. I didn't know you'd be here. I came to see the old guy. I wanted to take him up on his offer."

Edward snickered. "You mean the offer where you never see Cassandra again. That offer's come and gone."

"I could fight this divorce next week. I could stretch it out for months, years even." Tony walked over to the small bar, opened the cabinet, and helped himself to a scotch. "Or I could agree to it all and be gone Wednesday night."

"What do you want?" Edward asked.

"Same as before. A million a year for ten years. First million in hand before I leave this 'blink-and-ya-miss-it-town'."

"Done," Edward said, wasting no time in his decision. "You'll have the money the morning of the court date."

"No."

Both men looked at me.

"No, Tony. I am sick and tired of you! You're stupid and arrogant and I'm done with you. You could've taken the money and run, but you blew it. And now, maybe for the first time in your life, you're going to have to accept the consequences." Only at that moment, did I realize how truly angry I was about everything concerning Tony. "You want to fight me in court, go ahead. I have an unlimited source of lawyers at my disposal now. I can blink and have the press involved in a heartbeat. Then every member of your family will know you're alive, not just Poppy."

"You're responsible for that? You little bitch."

"I can make it worse."

"You wouldn't dare."

I pulled out my cell phone and pressed the speed dial for Brian's phone.

"Hello, Brian? Yeah. Do you remember when I said Tony would break the protective order in seventy-two hours? I was a day off. Yes, our house. Thanks." I hung up the phone and looked at Tony. "The police are on their way. Anything else?"

"No." Tony's eyes held a flame I knew all too well. He wanted to hit me, but he had never done so in front of witnesses. He set down his drink and moved toward the door. He turned to face me with, "Do I want anything else? Actually, yeah, I do."

He reached back, clenched his fist, and swung. I closed my eyes and flinched, waiting for the impact. I heard a crunching sound, like that of a hard pretzel pressed under the heel of a dress shoe, but was completely unharmed. I opened my eyes to find Edward standing over Tony, who was stretched out across the floor, holding his own arm.

"Holy shit! You broke my arm!" The fracture of Tony's left radius bone hadn't broken the skin but the ragged edges were pushed against his tightly drawn flesh.

Edward stood, shocked by his own ability to do what he had. "I told you, if you showed up here again, I'd kill you. Cassie's right. You really are an idiot."

We all stood motionless for a moment before the doorbell rang. To the best of my memory, it was the first time anyone had ever used it since my moving in and it took me a second to figure out what the sound was. I opened the door and two Willow Creek police officers walked in, followed by Detective Brian Hayes.

"This son-of-a-bitch Baker just broke my arm!"

The two officers helped Tony to his feet and walked him toward the door. The first officer looked at Brian. "Should we take him to the emergency room?"

Brian looked at me and I nodded my head. He looked at Tony's arm. "Yeah, take him to the ER and then to jail. Don't forget to read him his rights, too." The two walked Tony out and put him in the back of the patrol car. I closed the door as they drove away, and then leaned on the inside of the carved wooden mass. The room began to spin and instinctively I slid down until I was sitting on the floor.

"Oh my God. What have I done? I couldn't keep my big mouth shut and now ..." The tears began to flow down my face and within seconds both men were on either side of me, trying to convince me this wasn't my fault. That was when I finally understood that my life was falling apart, along with our plans for a December wedding.

After Brian left, Edward and I settled in for the night. I curled up next to Edward, trying to focus on something to talk about besides Tony.

"Edward, where were we going to go on our honeymoon?" I traced a map across his chest with my fingernail. He probably didn't know it, but it was the island of Santorini.

"You know it's a surprise. And you're not going to find out just because Tony showed up tonight."

"I hope it was someplace warm. I'm sick of this cold weather and it's only November. I would have liked a nice tropical getaway on some island paradise."

"Nice try, but I'm still not telling." It was not until we laid in silence, holding one another, did he realize that I was speaking in the past tense. "Sweetie, we *will* get married come the first of the month."

"Um-hmm."

"You don't believe that, do you?"

I closed my eyes and shook my head from side to side.

"Since when?"

"I don't know. I guess I'm just starting to realize how difficult this is going to be."

"Divorcing Tony?"

"Getting a divorce from Tony." He pulled me in closer to him and I shifted my head from the pillow to his chest.

"It *will* happen, Sweetie."

"I know. But if it doesn't, I mean, if we can't get married in December, can we still go away for a while? If we postpone the wedding, the press is going to go crazy. I don't want to be here when they do."

"I promise you, no matter what happens, December second, we will get on a jet and go away for a while, okay?"

"And it will be someplace warm?"

"Yes, my love, I'll make sure it's someplace warm."

I was still and quiet, listening to his heart race at a near frantic pace. I lifted my head, resting my chin on his chest. "Are you feeling okay?"

"Yeah, why?"

"Your heart. It seems like it's beating a lot faster. I thought maybe you'd been taking some cold medicine or something."

"No, I'm fine." He ran his fingers through my hair and I found it soothing. "But with a beautiful woman like you laid across my chest, it's no surprise my heart's beating a little faster these days."

"You know, I used to go to Mass on Sundays," I said smiling at him. It was ten-thirty in the morning and I was still in bed, snuggled up to him. We had been up for over an hour, just not out of bed. I was wearing a nightgown when I fell asleep the night before, but that had been on the floor for over an hour as well.

"Are you implying that I'm steering you down a path to Hell?" Edward's Cheshire Cat grin stretched across his face. We were both in better moods than the night before and there was nothing foreseeable that could change our current state of mind.

"No, it's just strange not going to church on Sundays. It's okay though, I go on Wednesday mornings now."

"I didn't know that," he said, still smiling, but serious now. "Did you want to go on Sundays? I mean, we can if you want."

"No, Wednesday is good. I know Catholic Mass isn't high on your list of fun and we get to spend so little time together as it is. It just works better for me to go during the week."

The fact that he even thought to ask if I wanted to go to Mass, and even offered to go with me, was a testament to his eternal devotion. I had never had a man center his life around my needs. In the beginning it was overwhelming, but as time passed, I began to understand that he was his happiest when he was making me happy.

"It's just really different than the church services I grew up attending. I'm sure you've noticed my family isn't big on Sunday service."

"That's fine. So, since we missed Mass while you were giving me a guided tour of the sin that will probably land me in Hell, what do we have to do today?"

Edward found the humor in my comment and laughed before answering. "Actually, nothing."

"Nothing? No wedding this, or reception that? It seems like that's been our Sunday every week for the last month."

"Not today, we're taking the day off. I've turned the ringer off on our cell phones, told everyone not to bother us unless the house catches on fire or someone dies. So the question is, what do you want to do today?"

"Wow, I can't remember the last Sunday we had to ourselves. Come to think of it, we've never had a Sunday completely to ourselves. I don't know. Is there something you'd like to do?"

He kissed me passionately before replying, with a big smile on his face. "There's a lot we can do today."

"I meant after we drag ourselves out of bed," I said, playfully pushing his face away from mine. He started tickling me and for about five minutes we wrestled with each other, kissing, tickling, and rolling around. When I finally begged for mercy, he stopped and kissed me again.

"You never answered my question," I said.

"I would like to watch the Redskins at Dallas game this afternoon."

"We could do that. I wonder if we got a New York Times today."

"Sweetie, we live at Thomas Hall. Of course we did. I'll go get it." Edward got up, pulled on some boxers, and returned a few minutes later with his coffee, and my favorite tea, ginger peach. In addition, he had warm cinnamon rolls with cream cheese frosting and a New York Times, all on a teakwood tray.

"Okay, that's impressive looking. How did you manage all of that in less than five minutes?"

"Before you woke up this morning, I called the main house and asked them to send down some kind of pastry and a paper. All I had to do was warm the rolls and ice them." He picked up a roll and gently put it in my mouth, forcing me to take a bite and eat it.

"Yummy. Practicing for the cake cutting at the reception?"

He laughed and kissed me. As we ate, we dug into the Sunday paper. He started with the business section and I read the comics. When I was done I moved on to the book reviews and entertainment. That's when Edward opened the food section.

"This looks good," he said as he nudged me, so I would look at his paper. "Pork stir fry. We should make this. It would be fun to cook with you."

"Yeah, sounds good." I looked at the overly complicated directions and planned to "lose" the recipe as soon as he headed back to D.C.. I loved Edward's cooking and I loved a good stir fry, but cooking with him would reveal my most embarrassing secret. Before I could even blink, he was on the phone with the chef at the main house, requesting for all the ingredients to be sent down to our place for us to cook today. After he hung up, he turned to me. "Everything will be here in about an hour. Why don't we make it for lunch today?"

My first thought was to say no because I was going to have to tell him the truth. He'd find out sooner or later.

"What about an early dinner?" I asked, stalling for time. "We just ate."

"A cinnamon bun and tea does not constitute eating breakfast."

"It does in my world." This was a favorite line of ours. Our worlds were different, and sometimes merging our lives was like trying to mix oil and water. I had grown up in a typical middle class neighborhood, and a lifestyle to match. Edward, on the other hand, had been brought up in a world most people can only dream about. Cars with drivers, private planes, multiple homes, nannies, and a live-in housekeeping staff had been at his disposal since the day he was born.

I was slowly adapting to the lifestyle change. It wasn't as easy as people might think. It was a mindset. I had always lived simply and switching gears to match Edward's life was hard for me, but I had no intention of making him change. He thought nothing of flying to New York for dinner if there was a certain five-star restaurant on his mind. As for me? I would give serious consideration before making the fifteen-minute drive into Willow Creek for lunch at my favorite sandwich shop. From the beginning, I knew it would be years before I would feel completely comfortable living in Edward's world.

But our very different worlds were not my biggest problem that morning; my secret was.

"What do you mean you can't cook? Sweetie, you went to Cordon Bleu."

"Right, I went. I was there for just over three weeks before..." I purposely let my voice fade away. Edward's expression changed when he realized what I'd been trying to hide.

"Three weeks. That's when the first practical takes place. Don't tell me you flunked out."

My face turned what I am certain was fire engine red. I held up my left hand, flipped it palm-side up, and showed it to him. As I spoke, I ran the index finger of my right hand down a faint but visible scar that crossed over two fingers. "What's the one thing you can do that will guarantee failure on a practical cooking exam?"

He lifted my hand to his lips and kissed the scar on each finger and then put his arms around me. I looked into his eyes, despite my embarrassment. "Oh Sweetie, what were you trying to cut and how many stitches did it take to sew you back together?"

"Squash and twelve."

"So I'm going to have to teach you to cook, huh?"

"I'm a lost cause. I can't cook. I mean, I can barely microwave popcorn. What if I just watch?"

"No, I'll teach you. It will be fun. I promise." I was certain the next hour of my life would be about as much fun as a root canal. I raised an eyebrow, and then accepted the fact that I was about to have a cooking lesson, whether I wanted one or not.

He turned me around and walked me back to the counter where I had confessed my lack of cooking skills. In front of us were the carrots I had abandoned. He watched as I clumsily arranged the carrots and picked up the knife. As I began, Edward encouraged me. "You're doing great. I want to show you something, but I'm going to have to wrap my hands around your wrists. Is that going to work?"

"I think so." I could feel my palms start to sweat and shake slightly. He knew that holding my wrists was the one thing that freaked me out. In what seemed like a different life, being held like that was a precursor to violence. It was something I never quite gotten over, and Edward was well aware of it. I assumed it was the only way he could show me what he needed to be done. So I nodded my head and took a deep breath. He gently laid his hands of top of mine and wrapped his thumbs around my wrist. I waited for the panic to set in, but it didn't come. I smiled just a little, surprised by my own sense of calm. "Okay, show me what I'm doing wrong."

And for the next hour, he showed me how to chop, slice, sauté, and stir fry. I didn't cut off any fingers, burn the pork, or mutilate the vegetables. And while we watched the game, we devoured the best stir fry I had ever eaten.

Chapter Thirteen

Monday morning's early alarm left me in an odd mood. I was uncertain if it was related to the recent insanity or if it was from rising so early. However, I was determined to spend a few extra moments with Edward before he headed back to D.C., even though I felt less than talkative. The silence over breakfast was broken only when Edward spoke.

"What's wrong? Besides the whole Tony thing. Something's bothering you this morning."

Edward was right, there had been something on my mind for a couple of days, but I had not brought it up the day before in order to avoid Edward's reaction. "You don't want to know."

"Try me."

"Prenup." After I said it, I drank some of my hot tea. I knew I didn't need to elaborate and I clearly saw that the word had provoked the reaction I had fully expected. There was a long stretch of silence before Edward said anything.

"This is important to you, isn't it?" I nodded my head. "Why?"

I shrugged my shoulders and pursed my lips. It was enough for him to know I wasn't going to have this conversation again.

"Okay, I'll get it looked at today, but why don't we go to your office first."

As we took the long way around to the production building he tried to convince me that he really didn't need to go to the corporate office, all the while holding on to me like his life depended on it. However, I had spoken to Kelly the day before and knew better.

"Honey, you can't skip out another day. Besides, isn't there a board meeting today?"

"I know, you're right," he said. "I do need to be in D.C. today, but I hate leaving you here with all that's going on. Hell, I just hate leaving you."

I smiled and he slowed his pace, holding me a little tighter. The sun was deceiving, as the icy wind blew across the path, but it did not seem to bother Edward. I could hear his heart still racing quicker than I felt it should when I leaned back and rested my head against him.

It made me reconsider the suggestion he made over breakfast that I spend a couple of days in D.C. with him. I liked the idea of being close to him, but I knew I would not be going. I had an appointment that I could not cancel. The state alcohol control agent was not fond of people rescheduling appointments, and I had already done it once.

It was an unsettling feeling, to worry about someone's health. I never worried about anyone's health except for Senior's, and then only for a very short time. The people I loved never seemed to live long enough to die of natural causes. However, I found myself in a position of genuine concern and had no idea what to do about it.

As we walked, we noticed Henry cutting across the lawn to join us so we stopped and waited for him. He had just finished breakfast with his mother. He and Edward drummed up a serious conversation. Although most of it was about me, I chose to let the two brothers talk and only listened.

"Why isn't B&B Security available?" Henry asked.

"Brick is at some security convention and Bubba's recovering from knee replacement surgery."

"Well, if B&B isn't available, who do you plan on hiring to watch over Cassandra?"

"That's the problem, there is no one else to hire around here and the places in D.C. won't keep their mouths shut to the press, no matter what they promise."

"I'm no bodyguard, but I could keep an eye on her if you'd like. I'll just stay at Cassandra's place tonight," Henry said. "I know I'd feel better if my future sister-in-law wasn't alone with that psycho running around town. You know it's only a matter of time before he figures out how to make bail."

"Yeah, I know. If you don't mind, and it's okay with Cassandra, I know I'd feel better about leaving her here. And when did you start calling the house Cassandra's?" Edward asked as a small smile formed on his face for the first time that day.

"Oh, about a week after she moved in," Henry replied. The two guys looked to me for approval of their plan.

"It sounds fine to me. I'm curious to hear about your date with Zoe anyway."

"You went out with Zoe?" Edward said, now sporting his famous grin once more. "Oh man, I can't wait to hear about that one either."

After work that evening, Henry and I went straight from the production room floor to the main house to have dinner with Vivian. However, I really wanted to go home and crawl into bed, but I knew I would be just as depressed about Edward's absence there as I would be anywhere else.

I spent most of the day wishing I were closer to Edward. It started the minute he left Thomas Hall and it had not ended. I never told him, but I hated the ever-so-practical arrangement we had for our jobs that required carefully juggling our schedules to be together. I knew it was greedy of me, but I wanted him home with me every night at Thomas Hall and the recent events in my life had only increased my secret desire to have him close to me all of the time.

Vivian had the chef-in-training whip up a French pork stew, fresh bread, salad, and fruit with cream for dessert. About halfway through the meal, Henry broke my thoughtless trance.

"Anybody home?" Henry asked.

"I'm sorry. Did you say something?"

"Cassandra, dear. Are you okay?" Vivian asked. "You seem a little distant tonight."

"I'm sorry, I just," My cell phone interrupted my thought. The caller ID told me it was Edward. "Excuse me." I stood and walked from the room as I took the call.

"Hi, Beautiful." Edward's cheerful voice radiated a tone as to the type of day he had experienced.

"Hi."

"That's not a very happy hello. Maybe I should come home tonight."

"No, I'm, I'm okay. Just tired." I missed him so much it took everything I had not to say "Get on the helicopter and come home". I had never loved anyone the way I loved Edward and sometimes it scared me. I struggled a little to come up with conversation, but finally remembered something I wanted to ask him. "Oh, um, did you get a chance to have your lawyers look over the prenup?"

I could hear his sigh before he answered. "Yes, they all agreed that it was far too generous, in my favor."

"I, I know." I paused for a moment, trying to get the words in my head out of my mouth. "I wish you would just sign it."

"Sweetie, you sound like you're struggling just to talk. This is all starting to take its toll on you, isn't it?" I didn't answer, so he continued. "I'm coming home."

"I know you could be here in less than an hour, but ... I'll be asleep by then." I wasn't about to tell him I had not slept through an entire night in the last week. "You should really stay in D.C. You have a big meeting early tomorrow morning and you'll need to be ready."

"You know, I hate it when you're right."

I laughed a little and listened as he told me about his day. We finished our conversation and I returned to the dining room. Henry and Vivian's dinner conversation had turned to the still missing local teenagers and the reported rise of missing people in the area.

Since settling into life at Thomas Hall, I had gone from having episodes of insomnia to sleeping like the dead. However, the last week had been different. With all that was happening, it was no surprise to me that I found myself waking up every three or four hours. When I woke up at one in the morning, I went to the bathroom and got a drink of water from the sink. As walked back to bed, I heard sounds coming from the living room. I figured Henry had fallen asleep watching television. I opened the door to the bedroom, intending to turn off the television and cover Henry with a blanket.

The room was lit only by the dim glow from the television. It was on one of the movie channels, but I didn't recognize the film. Two vampires were discussing something about bloodlines. I grabbed the softest, fuzziest blanket we owned from the chest next to my bedroom door and walked around from the back of the sofa as I unfolded it. When I looked down to see how to place the blanket, I found Henry was sitting up, with no clothes on, in a very compromising position with Zoe, half naked on her knees in front of him. The whole scene came very close to looking like what I imagined would be the makings of a bad porn flick. Not that I had actually seen any.

It took me a second to grasp what was going on. When all the pieces fell into place, I quietly gasped. They both froze when they saw my shadowy figure next to them.

"You know, we have a guest room. Feel free to use it." I said, trying hard to pretend I wasn't embarrassed, for either myself or the two of them. I turned around and went back to bed. No one should ever see their brother-in-law naked.

There wasn't much on my calendar Tuesday, so I decided to work from home. Libby-Mae and the guys knew how to reach me if anything urgent arose. I just didn't feel like sitting at my desk reliving everything that happened in that office just over a week ago. It had become a daily event for me ever since my meeting with Tony and I couldn't bring myself to relive it yet again.

I warmed some water and made myself some tea before I sat in the living room, intending to read the latest issue of *Virginia Wine Lover Magazine*, which had shown up on my desk the day before. That's when I saw the multiple shoe boxes of photos still sitting on the coffee table.

Tossing the magazine on to the side table, I moved to where the boxes sat, dumping all the pictures out and placing the empty boxes in a row. I designated them for early childhood, pictures of Lewis, graduations and award ceremonies, family, and I don't know who this is. I also made a pile on the floor for out of focus pictures and another for duplicates.

The whole sorting process took less time than I thought it would. Within an hour, all the loose pictures had been sorted and I was down to a series of labeled envelopes. I opened each, checking for duplicates and out of focus pictures.

The hardest envelopes were the ones of Lewis playing baseball. In those pictures he was everything a big brother should have been. Not the bloody, mangled corpse I had to identify at the hospital near Boise State University. Every day I tried to erase those images from my mind, along with the events that followed, but I knew they would be engraved in my brain forever.

The last envelope was labeled "Fred's Graduation Weekend". When I opened it and slid the pictures out, the first was of Lewis running across a green field with campus buildings surrounding it. He couldn't have been more than four or five years old, so I knew any pictures of me in this group would be of me as an infant. As I continued to look there were pictures of Dad, Fred, Lewis, me and even the odd picture of Mom. Being a professional photographer, she rarely made an appearance in front of the camera.

Most of the pictures, though, were of Fred and his friends. Some of the guys I recognized as frat brothers but others were complete strangers to me. Mingled in with these young college guys was Lewis clowning around.

It didn't take long to find a picture of Edward and Fred sitting on the front steps of the Kappa Sig Frat House. They were both so young, with no gray hair, no wrinkles around the eyes. The two looked like boys and not the men they had become. They were laughing as if one had just told the other an inside joke. I'd never seen this picture before. I wasn't certain anyone had. While it was over twenty-five years old, it looked as if it had just been printed.

I wanted this picture in a frame now. I walked around the house, looking for a frame I had reluctantly set out a few days earlier. It was a picture of me and Sarah taken when I received my Ph.D. When I found it, I picked it up off the bookcase and traced the outline of the two of us with my fingernail as I sadly shook my head. I felt the same empty pit inside of me I did whenever someone I loved died and it broke my heart. I slid that picture out of the silver frame and inserted the one of my two favorite men in their youth.

Around two, Victor called and asked if I was going to be at the house for a few minutes. There was a package for me and he thought he would drop it off. About ten minutes later, I sat with a large gold-foiled box on my lap. The card was small and plain. It simply read, 'Love, Edward.' However, it wasn't his handwriting, which was very unusual. Edward always signed the card himself.

I untied the green bow and lifted the lid with giddy anticipation. While I never needed a gift from Edward to be happy, the fact that he took the time to arrange for me to receive something special always left me feeling loved and appreciated. However, when I looked inside the box, I was disappointed with its contents. Why in the world would Edward think I would want this? Was this supposed to be my wedding gift? I picked up the phone and dialed and he answered his phone like he always did when he knew it was me.

"Hey, Beautiful! What's up?"

"Got your present."

"You don't sound excited. Most women would be acting like they won the lottery. You don't have an ethical problem with it, do you? Oh God, I never even thought to ask."

"No, it's not that Honey," I said. "And thank you, I appreciate the thought."

"But ..."

"Well, it's just so, so Darla." Darla was Henry's late wife and the opposite of anything I ever wanted to be. She was self-centered, manipulative, vicious, controlling, and had tried to kill me twice in order to get what she wanted. So, whenever I felt like something was just extremely self-indulgent, to the point of being ostentatious, I came to refer to it as being Darla. It didn't help that the box's contents were similar to something I knew had once belonged to her.

"Sweetie, I see where you're coming from, but this wasn't exactly my decision. It's a tradition thing. My great-grandfather gave my great-grandmother a full-length white mink coat on their wedding day. They married on what was an incredibly cold New Year's Day, at least that's what we've all been told. Ever since, the men on my mom's side of the family have always given their brides a white mink coat as a wedding gift."

"So basically, you're telling me I either have to tell your mom I hate it because it reminds me of Darla or suck it up and take one for the team."

"Pretty much."

"I suppose there are worse things I could have to do."

"Does it fit?"

"I don't know." I said. "I haven't taken it out of the box."

"You should try it on and make sure it fits. If not, the furrier told me he could deliver a different one."

We talked a bit longer about bits and pieces of things. Loose ends that needed tying up, winery decisions I needed his input on, and his work schedule between now and the first of the month. While we talked, I gently took the mink out of the box and slid into it. I had never worn a fur coat and had no idea what to expect. It was soft, warm and much lighter in weight than I thought it would be. It fit beautifully and made me feel cocooned in luxury. It was only then that I began to understand the appeal of owning a mink coat.

The coat was full-length, with the bottom edge at the base of my calves. It was the color of snow with barely visible vertical lines, where the mink pieces had been stitched together. The sleeves were fingertip length, barely exposing my hands and the collar lay perfectly along my neckline.

"Cassandra? Did the alcohol bureau agent give you the packet of forms you needed?"

"What? I'm sorry. I was distracted."

"By what?" He asked.

"Your wedding gift. I'm wearing it."

"Well? What do you think?"

"I swear I'll deny it if you tell anyone, but I could learn to like it."
I said, smiling.

"I can't wait to see you in it when I get home. As a matter of fact,
don't bother wearing anything else."

"Nothing at all?"

"Well, you could wear those purple high heel shoes you own.
And some jewelry."

"I'm not sure that qualifies as clothing."

"It does in my world."

Chapter Fourteen

Tuesday afternoon Edward wasted no time making his way back to Thomas Hall. When he arrived I was waiting at the front door in a purple lace see-through bra and matching panties, the heels he liked, along with a long string of pearls I received as a gift during my travels, and my wedding gift. I had every intention of fulfilling my fiancé's request, but in the end I was too chicken to go completely bare underneath.

When Edward walked through the door he knew, without a word spoken between us, what I thought I needed. I had never been a demanding person in bed. On the contrary, I tended to be almost subservient. I may have been an adventurous traveler before arriving at Thomas Hall, but when it came to sex my experience had been very limited before my engagement to Edward. I knew I loved everything that he and I had ever done together, but after listening to Zoe's escapades I was aware that I still had a lot to discover. I decided to take my education into my own hands that afternoon.

I pushed him onto the bed and took off his clothes, not bothering to unbutton his dress shirt but just popping buttons as I went. I knew what I wanted and made no apologies for it. I found words like 'more', 'faster', and 'now' flying from my lips. I didn't ask him for what I wanted, but acted as though I was ordering dinner in a restaurant. This was a far cry from a normal evening of making love, an evening when we usually took our time, talked, laughed, and cherished each other.

We both knew what I was doing and it had absolutely nothing to do with connecting as a couple. It was about forgetting everything that was going on around me. Forgetting friends who had betrayed me. Forgetting a dead husband who was very much alive. Forgetting about the divorce I was about to finalize. Forgetting all the dead relatives I had buried. To a certain point it was about forgetting who I was. I was desperate to feel anything that would make me forget my world, even if it was for just a moment. However, when we were done, I felt no different than I had before. I was no more relaxed, no happier, and I had managed to escape nothing that haunted me.

We lay next to each other for a long while. Not in the spooning, loving position we normally took, but flat on our backs and silent. I was still staring at the ceiling when Edward rolled onto his side, looked at me, and finally broke the silence.

"Exorcising demons?"

"I'm not sure I understand the question." Actually, I did. I was just avoiding the answer.

"Don't get me wrong, that was pretty amazing," he said. "But the woman I just had sex with was not my fiancée."

I looked at him with furrowed eyebrows, thinking about what he said. I thought for a moment before I responded. "I don't know if I should be flattered or insulted."

"Cassie, I know things aren't normal right now. I don't expect you to act like your usual self, and if the last forty minutes or so is the outcome, I don't mind you not being yourself every now and then."

I smiled at him and quietly laughed. He looked back at me, his expression one of deep thought.

"What?" I asked.

"I've been trying to tell you something for about a week now and I think you need to know before you walk into court tomorrow."

"Sounds serious." A flash of panic tore through me, and then horrible thoughts raced through my head. Someone was ill. No, dying. It always ends with death in my world. Oh God, it was Edward's heart! It had to be. It had been racing so fast lately, even when he was sleeping. But none of my thoughts prepared me for what I was about to discover.

"When I hired the private investigating team to find you," Edward began. "I had them look into Tony, too. I wanted to know as much as I could about you and that meant finding out about him. I wanted to know it all. What he liked for lunch, who his first girlfriend was, whether or not he ate paste in kindergarten. I don't know exactly why, but I was determined to know everything. About a month before Dad died, the lead investigator called me with an update. You had disappeared somewhere in Northern India about five weeks earlier, again. One day you'll have to tell me why you liked India so much. Anyway, after he told me you're last known location, he told me he'd traced Tony's death certificate to a coroner who had been falsifying death certificates in exchange for cash. Then he gave me the name Tony was using in California and his address there. I already knew he was still alive when Brian discovered who was making those prank calls."

I could not make what Edward was saying register. All I could think was that I had not heard him right. He could not have known Tony wasn't dead all along. But he had, and when it finally clicked in my brain, I began to feel as if with each breath I was inhaling anger and rage. It was a sensation I had never felt before and had no idea how to control it, let alone stop it.

"Wait a minute? You knew? You knew this whole time. And you didn't tell me!"

"I figured if he was serious enough to fake his death, he'd make sure he never saw you again. I was just trying to protect you. I didn't want you to have to go through all of this."

"No!" I said, "You were just..." I struggled in my anger to find the words. "You were just trying to make sure you got what you wanted."

"I just thought –"

"No, you didn't think! What if Tony hadn't shown up until after we were married?" Little switches were going off in my head, leading me to new realizations but it was the last one that crushed me.

"Oh my God! You were ready to marry me knowing it wouldn't be legal!" I felt the air being sucked out of my lungs as I processed everything I had just learned. "Get out!"

"What?"

"Get out of my bed and out of my house you sorry son-of-a-bitch!" I couldn't believe the words I heard coming out of my mouth.

"Excuse me? Did you just call me a –"

"You heard me! Get the hell out now!" I picked up the pillow beside me and threw it at him and he caught it just before it hit him in the face.

"I, I … okay. I'll go up to Mom's for the night." He continued to stutter out incoherent words as he climbed out of bed and threw on sweatpants and a shirt. "I can't believe this. You've got to at least try and understand."

"Understand what? That you are too controlling of an ass to not tell me the truth?"

"I was just trying to protect you."

"There is no way! Just leave."

"You can't stay here alone, it's not safe."

"Then I'll hire someone to stay with me. Just go."

"Cassie, please take a minute and think."

"Don't you dare 'Cassie' me, you sorry bastard! Out! Now! Right now!"

As soon as I heard the door close, I climbed out of bed and headed for the shower, stopping only to make one phone call.

I was barely out of the shower, dressed in yoga pants, tank top, and a sweater when I heard voices outside the kitchen window. I walked over and cracked the window in order to hear the conversation. I poured myself a fresh glass of tea as the cold night air blew through the opening.

"Hey Brian, what are you doing here? Delivering pizza on the side now?" Edward had waited outside the whole time. He knew it was not safe for me to be alone and had parked himself on the front porch, waiting patiently for his relief. And in this case, it was Brian Hayes.

"Cassandra called me. She said B&B Security wasn't available and wanted to know if there were any off-duty cops who might be interested in making some money doing security for the night. The twins are away, so I decided maybe I'd better come. She'd be well protected with any of the guys on the force but I don't know if they would keep their mouths shut to the press." Brian paused for a long moment before continuing. "I'm guessing you told her you knew Tony was alive before the calls started."

"Yeah, and thanks for letting me tell her. I know you wanted to say something the second I told you last week."

So Brian knew and he hadn't told me either. My first thought was to be furious with him too. Then I realized not only was it not his secret to tell, but he had promised Edward he would not say anything. The men continued to talk.

"As for the pizza, I had not eaten dinner when she called and I figured she might not have either."

There was another long pause before Edward spoke. When he did, his voice shifted and the tone sounded even more serious. "You know I still blame you for everything that happened. Hell, we don't even talk. So tell me, how did you end up being my fiancée's best friend?"

"You know Cassandra," Brian said. "She just draws people to her, like a magnet. She doesn't even know she's doing it. And then, poof, the next thing you know you're her best friend, or in your case, soon-to-be husband."

"I'm really worried about her Brian, but I promise you I won't make the same mistakes twice. It's just the way she's dealing with everything that keeps making me think she's going to skip town before I get her down the aisle." I wondered what Edward meant about blaming Brian and making the same mistake twice, but I didn't linger on the thought.

"So, you don't like the way she's handling things," Brian said sarcastically. "That's no surprise. This might be breaking news to you, but you have control issues, you always have."

"I know," Edward said. "But I'm not sure she's handling things at all. With the exception of Tony's appearance here the other night, she's walking around like nothing unusual is going on. I mean she's a little jumpier than usual but she's gone into the office every day, unpacked boxes from storage, gone shopping in Richmond. She's trying to act like this isn't even out of the ordinary for her."

"Well, if you don't mind me saying, it sounds like her whole life has been far from ordinary. Maybe it was just how she was raised. You know, when all hell breaks loose, just stick with your regularly scheduled program and everything will work out." Brian was trying to reassure him, even though there was a certain level of friction between the two of them that I never understood and the recent rumors had only magnified it. "Try not to worry too much. I'll keep an eye on her tonight."

"Yeah, that's what I'm afraid of. But I know she needs someone to protect her and she won't let me so …" I could hear the creek of the bench as Edward stood up. "Be careful what you say tonight. I mean, she kicked me out of my own house. She's really emotional, and not in a sweet Cassandra kind of way. She's angry and totally illogical."

Brian chuckled. "Edward, she is a woman and they've been known to be emotional, you know. I don't think they ever pull girls aside when they're teenagers and tell them how to deal with a dead husband showing up alive three weeks before their wedding."

Less than half an hour later, Brian and I sat at the kitchen table and talked about his girls as we ate the pepperoni pizza he had brought. I liked the twins and they thought I was the best thing that ever happened to Willow Creek. I met them in mid-October and we were becoming fast friends.

"Cassandra, what am I going to do when the girls are teenagers? I don't know that I'm going to be able to handle the dating thing."

"I bet you thought you couldn't handle toddlers and diapers when you started either."

Brian had been a single father to the girls since their second birthday. I didn't know all the details and never asked. From what I could piece together, Brian and the girls' mother weren't together when he picked up the girls to celebrate their birthday. She was supposed to pick up the girls the next morning and never showed up. Brian found out not long after that she left town. No one had seen her since, but he never complained. He loved his girls and was doing a good job raising them.

I walked toward the sink to put my dinner dishes in their proper place. "Don't worry, you'll find your way."

I turned from the sink to find I was standing face to face with Brian. "You really think so?"

"Yeah, I really do," I said.

Nothing in a million years could have prepared me for what he did next. Brian placed one arm around my waist, pulled me towards him, and softly pressed his lips to mine. My first thought was to push him away but found myself doing nothing to stop him. It was almost as if I had subconsciously wondered what kissing him would be like all along, even though the thought never truly crossed my mind until the moment our lips touched.

I'd be lying if I said I didn't enjoy it and found myself wondering what life would be like with Brian. No conference calls on date nights, no last-minute business trips, someone sleeping next to me every night, no paparazzi, and I knew I would always be safe. The thought of living out of the D.C. gossip columns was very appealing as well.

The one thing I was certain of where Brian was concerned, was that he never held back information. If he thought I needed to know something, he told me. He never made the decision of whether or not I should know something, claiming to be doing what was best for me. Of course, he did not know half of my past either. Maybe that was a good thing too.

As for his twins, an instant family, would just be icing on the cake. It was no secret to anyone who had known me for more than five minutes that I wanted to have a big family. His beautiful pre-teen girls would make a great start.

At some point, I put my arms around his neck, lifting myself slightly to his face. He pulled me closer to him but kept our kiss soft and slow. Brian's hand moved from the back of my head and brushed down the side of my body, hugging every curve as it went. His touch was like wearing silk pajamas, light, soft, and comfortable. As his hand made its way slowly to my hip, I realized the problem. This was different from the way Edward and I kissed. It lacked passion. It lacked the desperate desire that Edward and I shared. Brian may have been my best friend and a really good kisser, but I was not in love with him.

I ended our kiss, lowered my arms from his neck, and stepped just out of his reach.

"You know, I think you're a great guy, but you know how I feel about Edward, too." I spoke quietly and calmly while my heart raced. "And yes, I'm angry with him right now. I'm angrier with him than I've ever been with anyone in my entire life, but if I walk away from a relationship every time something isn't perfect, I'll end up alone forever."

He took a step closer and wrapped his hand gently around the back of my neck so I was staring into his eyes. "You don't have to end up alone."

For a brief moment, I thought about what he was saying, even contemplated it, and then shook my head slightly from side to side. He took his hand off my neck and let his arms fall to his side.

"I'm sorry. I guess I shouldn't have kissed you now."

"Now? You've thought about it before?"

"I've wanted to kiss you since the moment you called me at home to talk about Senior's murder last month."

"Oh," I said, standing motionless, somewhat perplexed by what had just happened and fighting off the start of yet another migraine. "So now what?"

"I guess we could forget this kiss ever happened unless someday you decide to leave Edward."

"I'm not sure you should count on either of those things from me, but I think I can keep my thoughts to myself."

"Fair enough," he said, pushing a stray hair away from my face. "You look exhausted. Maybe you should try to get some rest. Tomorrow's going to be a long day for you."

I looked at the clock. It was nearly ten. "I could try, but I doubt I'll sleep."

"Then what do you want to do?"

"Hop on a plane to Bora Bora. You'd like it there. It's beautiful, sunny, and warm. Wanna come?"

"Nobody's stopping you. After what I just did, do you even need to ask?"

I didn't bother answering the question. I just smiled, turned on my heel, and went to bed.

As I lay under the warm comforter, I replayed the whole strange evening in my mind and wondered two things. Would I ever be able to forgive Edward for keeping Tony's existence from me and had I made a mistake rebuffing the advances of the man in the next room?

Chapter Fifteen

EDWARD SHOWED UP AT the house a little after eight the next morning. He silently relieved Brian of his guard duties having already showered and shaved. He didn't have a suit at the main house and had come home to get one. As he worked his tie effortlessly into a Windsor knot, I finished a phone conversation I was having with our bottle label designer.

"I'm sorry. I won't be able to proof the labels today. I have to leave Thomas Hall for the day in about ten minutes. I should have the proof sheet edited and back to you late tomorrow. Great. Not a problem. Thanks, you too."

Edward looked in my direction. "Still mad?"

I remained silent.

"Okay then. I'll just finish get dressed for court."

"Why?" I asked, staring blankly at the paperwork, in order to avoid making eye contact with him again.

"We're going with you. Me, Mom, Henry, Alex. Phoebe's on her way up from Richmond."

"Then call and stop her. No one's going with me."

"No. Our family pulls together when something like this happens to one of us. We're all going."

"This isn't a family thing. It's something I need to handle myself," I said.

"No, you don't. And besides, I don't want you alone with Tony."

"I won't be. There will be lawyers, judges, and police officers. It *is* at the courthouse after all."

"I'm going, Cassandra. End of discussion. We all are."

I blew out a deep breath before answering. "Fine."

"Fine?" He was surprised I caved so easily. When we argued I tended to dig in and hold my ground, but I was in no mood for a fight.

"Yes, of course. It was crazy for me to think you would ever let me do something the way *I* wanted." Whether or not Edward was being controlling or caring, the memory of the previous evening's confession tainted my opinion. "But I need a few minutes alone first. Why don't you go up to the main house and have breakfast with the family? I've already had tea and toast. You can have the car pick me up on the way out."

Edward noticed the photo I'd found the day before.

"Oh my God, I remember when this was taken. It was the weekend Fred and I graduated. Clark's sister-in-law was taking pictures like crazy that weekend."

"Great picture, huh?"

He looked at the photo, then at me, and then the photo once more. "Of course, Clark's sister-in-law was your mom. This was one of her photographs, wasn't it?" I nodded and he continued. "But wasn't there a picture of you and Sarah in that frame?"

"Yeah. It was time to let it go."

"The picture or the person?" He asked.

"I don't know," I said sharply, not in the mood for that conversation either. Come to think about it, I wasn't really in the mood to talk about anything with anyone.

Edward put his arms around me and I shrugged them off. I amazed myself with my own ability to hold on to the anger his confession had created within me.

He faced me, cupped my face in his hands, kissed me on the forehead and said, "I am sorry, really I am." Then he headed out the door before I could think of anything to say.

As soon as he was gone, I picked up my cell and dialed Victor.

"Good morning Cassandra. What can I do for you, dear?"

"I need a favor."

When Victor brought my car around from the garage, I knew I wouldn't have more than a twenty-minute lead on the others.

"Where are we going?'

"I'm going alone Victor."

"No my dear. It will be an emotional day. If you want to go without the others that's fine, but I'm going to drive you. You might not feel like driving home afterwards."

"You're probably right. I just don't want you to get in trouble with the family."

"You're part of the family too. Now, where to first?"

"Mary Magdalene Church."

The fifteen-minute trip never seemed as long as it did that day. I sat in silence, no cell phone, no radio, no conversation. When we arrived at the church, I asked Victor to wait in the car and quietly slipped inside.

I stopped at the single door that lead into the church and glanced down the aisle. The same aisle I had hoped to walk down in a couple of weeks. I took one step into the chapel when I saw Father Tennelli walking between the pews to meet me.

"Ms. Martin, I'm surprised to see you here today."

"I was hoping you'd be here Father. Do you have a minute to sit and talk?"

"If I'm not here for my parishioners, what's the point of being a priest? Is here okay?"

I nodded and we sat in the first pew we came to.

"Father, I suppose you know why I'm in town this morning."

"It's been the gossip all over town. Your husband not being dead. Is it safe for me to assume the rumor about you having a court date today is true?"

I stared at the floor and nodded.

"Are you sure this is the solution? Have you given any consideration to trying to make the marriage you're currently in work?"

"It's not an option, Father. He has no desire to be married to me and hasn't for a long time, maybe ever."

"And you."

"I still want to marry Edward, I think. That's why I'm here. I need to know." I didn't bother elaborating. Father Tennelli already knew my question. Could he still marry us if I was divorced and not widowed? While I was hopeful, deep in my heart I already knew his answer.

As I looked up, he shook his head from side to side and placed his hand on my shoulder. "I'm sorry Cassandra, but no, if you divorce I won't be able to marry you in this church. I hope you understand. It's not personal. It's the church's position on divorce. You could try to get the Church to declare the marriage invalid, but that could take a while. If you're determined to get married next month, maybe you could use Mr. Baker's church. I know the Anglicans are more flexible on the subject of remarriage." When I did not respond he stood up and walked along the pew and out the side door toward the office.

I sat for a few moments longer, saddened by the news I had just received. I prayed for strength and perseverance, knowing I would need it for what was about to transpire.

I slipped out the back door and made the short walk in the cold, windy air to the courthouse, leaving Victor waiting in front of the church.

The press was so certain I would arrive by car, they didn't notice when I slipped through the crowd of cameras and onlookers and walked straight into the courthouse. I entered the larger of the two courtrooms to find Zachary O'Keefe waiting for me.

Zachary had been the family's personal attorney for a couple of years before I arrived at Thomas Hall and I found him a difficult man to figure out. He could slip in and out of a small group of people without being noticed, but was a dominating presence in a court room. He was a man of average height, average weight, medium brown hair, medium skin tone, and dull brown eyes. He was that guy who looked like someone you knew but couldn't quite place. However, when Zachary entered a courtroom, he became a different person. He was a larger-than-life presence during a trial with a booming, distinctive voice not unlike that of James Earl Jones, only less formal and more southern. He spoke eloquently when pleading a case and moved around the courtroom effortlessly, charming lawyers, witnesses, and jurors alike.

"Cassandra, where's Edward?" Zachary asked.

"I left the Bakers at Thomas Hall."

"That's not going to go over well with the family," he said.

"This isn't a family matter."

"To them it is."

"Zachary, you worry about this huge mess and I'll deal with the family. Okay?" I was slightly annoyed with the fact my attorney was siding with my fiancé, but managed to keep my emotions in check. "Can you approach the judge and ask for a closed courtroom? I don't want the press in here. For that matter, I don't want anyone in here."

"Let me talk to Tony's attorney, but I don't see where it will be a problem. Judge Smith is presiding today."

"Can he do that? I mean, I know Judge Smith pretty well. He's a good friend of the Baker family."

"Welcome to small-town life. If Judge Smith excused himself from every case where he knew someone, he'd be unemployed."

"Oh, okay, but if Tony gives you any problems remind him that the statute of limitations for domestic abuse in Ohio hasn't expired yet," I said.

"Something you need to tell me?" Zachary asked.

I didn't really feel up to elaborating so I simply replied, "I think I just did."

The hearing lasted what felt like an eternity. The stenographer overslept and was twenty minutes late getting to the courthouse. Tony was late, too, but that was no surprise to me. He was rarely on time. He even made the bailiff who went to pick him up from the jail wait. When he entered the courtroom, I noticed the bright blue cast on his left arm.

The legal jargon dumbfounded Tony and his lawyer kept asking for a moment to re-explain things to him. Occasionally, Zachary would slide a legal pad in front of me with a comment or question scribbled on it in a print style that looked like it had been lifted off a blueprint. Not having any legal background, I was surprised to find the proceedings easy to follow.

About halfway through the hearing, he slid the yellow pad in front of me.

Are you doing okay?
Just bored out of my mind.

I scribbled with my sloppy handwriting and pushed the pad back toward him and within seconds he pushed it back.

You should have gone into law. You'd have been good at it.

My response summed up my emotions about the whole morning, not just his statement.

And live in this hell on a daily basis? I don't think so.

Just as I thought the nightmare was coming to an end, Judge Smith announced the hearing for the dissolution of my marriage would be held over until next Wednesday. I could feel the saline fill my eyes and my whole body tense up.

Zachary leaned over and put his hand on my shoulder. "Don't worry. This is just a formality. He's got to make sure he does this right."

I had intended to respond, but the judge began to speak again.

"The next item on the docket is the Commonwealth of Virginia versus Antonio Martin. However, Ms. Martin, I'd like you to stay for this as well. I may need your assistance and you may need your lawyer if Mr. Martin tries to defer fault to you."

I nodded my head in agreement, but the feelings of panic and terror washed over me. I kept telling myself this wasn't happening, but I knew it was. I turned to Zachary and whispered. "I don't understand. What does he mean *assist*?"

"Don't worry. I thought this might happen. He's going to try to nail every charge he can on Tony and he wants to make sure Tony doesn't try to blame you for any of this."

I immediately focused my attention back to Judge Smith, who wasted no time reading the charges as Zachary continued to rest his hand on my shoulder in an attempt to help me remain calm.

"... So, Mr. Martin, while it is not illegal to fake your own death, other actions associated with this act are against the law, and you are hereby charged with the following: insurance fraud, mortgage fraud, obtaining falsified death certificates, obtaining falsified birth certificates, providing false information to the Social Security Administration, illegally obtaining a California driver's permit, illegally obtaining a U.S. Passport, ..."

It sounded as if he would continue this laundry list of charges for an extended period of time and I wasn't certain how much more I could take before it made me sick. I found out it didn't take very long.

Chapter Sixteen

BY THE TIME VICTOR and I were at the front gate of Thomas Hall, I could no longer stand the confinement of the car as my body begged for fresh air. I had Victor stop the car and let me out about halfway between the gate and the main house, but not before thanking him for driving me back and forth to town. The sun had finally made an appearance, peeking through the scattered clouds floating across the sky but it brought no extra warmth to the day. Despite the weather, I leisurely walked down the center of the drive and when I came to the fork in the road I decided not to go home and deal with Edward, but instead turned left and headed up the slight incline to the main house.

When I reached the footpath, I could see Phoebe standing in the doorway, tapping her foot and trying to look intimidating. However, in her red sweater and black slacks, Edward's tiny sister looked more like an angry ladybug than a woman in her thirties. I knew better than to laugh, though. It was time to pay the piper for leaving everyone at Thomas Hall earlier in the day.

I was about four yards away from her and was beginning to wish I had just let everyone come to the courthouse. "How much trouble am I in?"

"That depends."

"On what?" I asked.

"On whether or not you have the time for lunch. I didn't make the trip up from Richmond not to spend some time with my future sister-in-law."

"I think I can manage that."

As we walked into the house, Edward appeared. He heard my voice when I entered the house and made his way from the library to meet me. He was not happy and looked as though he expected me to be remorseful. But when I didn't say a word and kept walking, he spoke up.

"I want a word with you."

"You want a word? Here's one – No! I don't want to talk to you right now."

"Too bad. Because I have a few things I want to say to you." I stopped and turned back to face him. Phoebe walked back toward the sunroom and Edward continued to speak as he walked toward me until his face was within inches of mine. "Do you know what I did this morning after you left? Well, let me tell you. I drove down to the courthouse, had to deal with the damn press only to find out you requested a closed hearing. Then I had to deal with the press on the way out and all of their questions about why I wasn't in the courtroom with you."

"So?" I knew the reply was rude, but I was still too mad at him to care. "You didn't tell me Tony was still alive."

"How long am I going to have to pay for that?"

"Until I'm through being mad!"

"Fine," He said.

"Fine," I repeated, turning to catch up with Phoebe. When I entered the sunroom she was standing at the window. She watched as a construction crew rebuilt her home on the foundation that once held her tiny vineyard cottage.

"How's the rebuild coming?" I asked.

"Slowly, but surely," she said as we walked to the table and took seats across from each other. "What's going on with you and Edward?"

"Hard to explain, but basically we're mad at each other."

"I already figured that part out." When I didn't respond, she seemed to realize that whatever it was, it was too private for me to talk about, at least with her.

In front of us were salads with grilled chicken, apples, walnuts, blue cheese, and a warm bacon vinaigrette dressing. I picked up my fork and began to play with my food as Phoebe ate. After a couple of bites, she set her fork down and looked at me.

"Things didn't go well today, did they?" she asked.

"It could've gone worse."

"Mom's right. You are way too optimistic for your own good sometimes. I don't know how you do it. Divorce isn't fun, even when it's simple."

"And this one's definitely not simple."

Phoebe took another bite of her salad and I forced an apple chunk and some blue cheese into my mouth.

"It should be simple. I mean, you have no kids and no joint assets. So, what's the problem?"

"Neither of us is a resident of any state. I traveled long enough not to have state residency anywhere and Tony wasn't even considered legally alive until today."

"Cassandra, doesn't one of you need to be a Virginia resident to file for a divorce here?"

"Yes," I said. "Judge Smith was helpful with that. Because of my professional status in the county, he waived the one-year habitation requirement for residency."

"So what's the problem?"

"He wouldn't grant residency and a divorce in the same hearing. I've got to go back next week."

"That's cutting it very close to the wedding, don't you think?"

"I know. I'm beginning to wonder if, maybe, well, if we shouldn't think about..."

My cell phone rang and I was happy to answer it. I wasn't sure how to finish my sentence.

"Hey Sis," Henry said. "You okay? I thought you'd come see me when you got back."

"I'm so-so, but I'll live. Actually, I'm having lunch with Phoebe. Do you need me at work? I can be there in about fifteen minutes."

"No, all is good here. I did see Edward earlier though. What happened with you two last night?"

"What do you mean?"

"He wasn't himself this morning when he was at the main house for breakfast. He seemed agitated for lack of a better word."

"Well, he deserved it," I said sharply.

"Okay, this is obviously none of my business. I just wanted to check on you. I'll let you get back to lunch."

"Thanks. Henry, I'm sorry about today. I should have let you come to the courthouse this morning." When Phoebe heard that it was Henry on the phone, she rolled her eyes.

"Yeah, you should have. But I'll get over it."

I had barely pressed the end-call button on the phone when Phoebe chimed in.

"What did my slacker brother want?" Phoebe sounded annoyed.

"What do you mean slacker? I thought you adored your brothers."

"Oh I love them both, but Henry's just so un-ambitious. It's hard to believe those two men are related sometimes."

"I think your wrong about Henry," I said. "He's got plenty of drive. He loves what he does and he's good at it. Just because it doesn't translate into dollars and cents, doesn't mean he's not successful."

Phoebe stared at me as if she were sitting across from an alien. "How in the world did you and Edward end up together? The two of you have such different ideas on what constitutes success."

"Yeah, I'm discovering we have different ideas on a lot of things." I felt myself clenching my teeth as I spoke. I tossed my fork on my plate, having lost any desire to eat.

"What happened between the two of you?" she asked. "I couldn't imagine what Edward could have done that would be that bad."

I did not want to tell her. I liked her and I trusted her, but I could not tell her what happened. Phoebe made it clear to me early on, that even though she liked to tease him, she worshiped Edward and something like this could knock Edward straight off the pedestal she'd put him on. I wasn't going to be responsible for that. She would never forgive me.

"You're right, you couldn't imagine."

The sinking feeling that I should have let the family come with me to court continued to hang over me after lunch when I went to find Vivian. She was in the greenhouse, tending to some young rosebushes when I finally caught up with her.

"Cassandra, come over here, dear. I want to show you something. It's called a Gourdault rose. Beautiful, isn't it?"

"It is. Is it a double rose, or just really full?"

Vivian smiled. "I'm always amazed by your wide range of knowledge. It is a full, double rose. How did you know?"

"My Aunt Molly, Fred's wife, loves roses. She has them all over their yard." I paused and enjoyed the silence. "Can we sit and talk for a second?"

"Of course, my dear." She used a pair of pruning shears to cut the flower and handed it to me. I lifted the delicate bud to my face and inhaled. The fragrance from the rose made me smile. We made our way to a cement garden bench inside the greenhouse and sat. "How did it go today?"

"I'm still married to Tony, at least for another week." Vivian frowned and a little pout formed. "But on the upside, I'm now a resident of the fine Commonwealth of Virginia."

Her usual smile returned to her face. "You can find an upside to anything, can't you?"

"Almost anything," I said, reflecting on all that had transpired the night before with Edward. "Vivian, I'm pretty sure I owe you an apology."

I bit my bottom lip and could feel the tears start to fill my eyes. "It's been pointed out to me by both of your sons, in less than subtle ways, that I was selfish about the hearing today. Everyone wanted to go, and I know it's because everyone cares about me, but instead I—"

"You don't owe anyone an apology, but I hear you've been handing them out like candy at Halloween," Vivian said. "I knew you wouldn't let us go with you today. Edward, as smart as he is, doesn't get it. You're trying hard to keep your life with Tony separate from your life now, aren't you?"

I nodded. Finally, someone understood. With the exception of Poppy, I wanted nothing from my old life with Tony to overlap with the life I was building with Edward but both men were making it hard. When I spoke, tears streamed down my face. "I'm not doing a very good job, am I?"

Vivian put her arms around me pushing my head to rest on her shoulder. It had been fourteen years since a woman held me like that, and that woman had been my mother.

"Cassandra, we will get this straightened out. I promise. No matter what it takes."

I walked the long way around the circular path back to our house. I didn't want to go home and possibly have to face Edward. So I decided to stop by the office and check my messages. The sun was already setting. The days were getting shorter as we approached the start of winter. The orange glow from the late-day sun washed over the grapevines, giving them a magical, happy, sparkle all their own. I hoped a little of that happy magic would wash over me, too. But it stayed just out of my reach, tucked into the vines.

When I reached the office, Libby-Mae and Alex were talking quietly and I heard her giggle. I knew that sound. Alex was trying to pick up Libby-Mae.

Libby-Mae saw me, cleared her throat, and stood up straight. Alex turned around.

"Sis, didn't expect to see you today."

"Alex. Office. Now." He strolled into my office and I followed him, closing the door behind me. He sat on the sofa by the window.

"What's up?"

"No dating Libby-Mae."

"What? We were just talking."

"She's only eighteen. You can't use her like a little plaything and throw her aside. She deserves better than that. I know now that I did. And besides, she's an amazing assistant and I don't want to lose her. So I'm telling you. No, I'm ordering you. No dating Libby-Mae."

"It's not like that. I don't have any plans to make her my 'flavor of the month' as Henry calls my girlfriends."

"Good, keep it that way."

I picked up the messages on my desk and took a look through them. There was nothing that couldn't wait until morning so I tossed them back onto my desk.

I followed Alex as he left my office and I stopped at Libby-Mae's desk.

"Miss Cassandra, am I in trouble?"

"No dear. Why do you ask?"

"You just seem angry about something. I wanted to make sure it's not my fault."

I took a deep breath and leaned against her desk. "What do you think of Alex?"

"What do you mean? As a winemaker? I really don't know much – "

"No," I interrupted. "I mean, what do you think about *him*?"

"Oh, well, he's alright I guess. I mean, I get why women find him so charming. He's good-looking, successful, and a sweet talker. He's got the whole great boyfriend material thing goin' on."

"And you think he's charming?" I asked, somewhat worried about the answer I'd get.

"Yes, but I've known guys like him. They just end up breakin' your heart. Is that what all this is about? 'Cause I have no intention of gettin' mixed up with him. You don't need to waste your energy getting upset about that."

Libby-Mae was right. I was angry and upset. I had yet to process the last twenty-four hours of my life, and I had no clue how to do it either. Libby and I talked for a few minutes longer about the uneventful day at the office before I headed home, fully expecting to find Edward, and another argument, waiting for me.

When I stepped out the door of the production building I caught a glimpse of Zoe's car pulling up to Henry's house. She saw me as I walked in her direction.

"Hey girl!" She said as she stepped out of the car.

"Hey, Zoe. Spending the night at Henry's?"

"Yeah, um, about the other night ..." Zoe's face filled with a soft, warm blush.

"It's okay. I'm just glad somebody's enjoying themselves."

"Cassandra, you're supposed to be getting married in less than three weeks. What happened?"

I tried to compose myself. "Edward knew Tony was alive before I moved to Thomas Hall and didn't tell me. I'm trying not to be angry with him, but I just don't know how not to feel betrayed."

"Are you sure he knew? I mean, who told you?"

"Edward came clean last night."

"What did you say?"

"I did a lot of yelling and screaming, used a few four-letter words, and then I kicked him out of bed and out of the house. I think I might have thrown something at him too, but I don't really remember."

Zoe pursed her lip tightly, trying hard not to laugh at the thought of me throwing things at Edward. "You what?"

"You heard me," I said, staring at the rapidly darkening sky.

"What are Vivian and Phoebe saying about all of this?"

"I don't know. I didn't tell them." I sat in the swing on Henry's front porch and Zoe joined me. "Zoe, what am I going to do?"

"What did Sarah say?"

"We're still not on speaking terms."

"When did that happen anyway? I didn't want to ask the other night at the shower. How am I so out of the loop on all of this?"

"You've been, um, busy with Henry."

"Oh yeah, I guess I have," she said, smiling. "Well, I know the two of you love each other. You're probably just gonna have to forgive him."

"But what if I can't? Then what?"

"Cassandra, he's a man. He's gonna do stupid stuff. He's hard-wired for it. It might be the first dumb thing he's done, but I'd be willing to bet it won't be the last."

"It's not even the first. He managed that within forty-eight hours of our engagement." I heard the front door creak and turned to see Henry step out of the house.

"Sorry to interrupt, but Edward's looking for you."

"Let him look," I said.

"Should I tell him you're here?"

"If you want." Henry looked at me, clearly upset by my callous attitude toward his brother, and then disappeared back into the house with phone in hand.

"Look, I know you love him," Zoe said. "You might just have to dig a little deeper to forgive him this time. But good God, he knew and he didn't tell you? How did he even try to justify that one?"

Before I could respond, I saw Edward rounding the corner. The moment he could see me clearly, he raced over, took off his coat, and put it around my shoulders. I had left mine at the main house.

"Sweetie, you're going to catch pneumonia out here with no coat on." When I looked up at him, his beautiful eyes stared back at me and behind them, I saw a sadness I had not seen since his father's funeral.

Chapter Seventeen

WE WALKED HOME AFTER an awkwardly silent dinner with Zoe and Henry. I knew Edward was freezing because I was wearing his coat and the wind ripped through me like icicles. Neither of us said a word until we turned the corner and Henry's home was out of sight.

"You know," Edward said. "You're pretty amazing."

"Hmm. Why would you say that? Nothing special here." I had purposely added the last comment to aggravate him. Until that moment, I had never said anything to intentionally irritate him, but I was miserable and it is true, misery does love company.

He pretended to ignore my comment. "I just don't know how you've managed to hold it all together with the hell that's broken loose around here."

"I have no choice," I said, stopping to look at him. "If I think about it, really think about it, even for a second, I'll go insane. I mean, I've discovered my dead husband is very much alive. So

I'm divorcing him, which is something I swore I'd never do, but since I can't be married to both of you, he's got to go." I wanted to stop there but the words flew out of my mouth involuntarily. "I met you, fell in love, got engaged, almost got killed twice, and inherited controlling interest of a winery that I don't know the first thing about running." The pace at which I was speaking rapidly accelerated until I sounded frantic. Edward tried to interrupt but I kept going.

"This week alone, I've had to deal with a missing bottle shipment at the office, a husband who's suppose to be dead but isn't, divorce lawyers, and two calls from my best friend's husband, whom I just learned has been in love with me for years." I dropped down and sat in the middle of the driveway as if the weight of all these things would no longer allow me to stand.

"And if that isn't enough, Sarah told me last month she plans on leaving Michael after the holidays. Oh, and she slept with my not-so-dead husband before we all thought he was dead but *after* we were married." I tried to stop my litany but felt like I'd explode if I didn't continue. "Oh, and just to top it all off, you knew Tony was alive the whole time and didn't tell me."

Edward tried to say something, but I didn't give him the chance.

"We're supposed to be getting married in less than a month, which may or may not happen at this point. So, no. I am not okay."

I looked at him, waiting for him to say something. I knew there was nothing he could say to fix this mess, but I had gotten it all out for him to absorb the magnitude of my world. He sat down on the driveway beside me and held my ice-cold hands. He took a deep breath before blowing out a puff of chilly air that was visible even in the darkness.

"Ok, let's work in reverse," he said. "I should have told you about Tony. I really did believe I'd be able to spare you all this. If I had known for a minute he would show up here, I would have told you when you first came to Thomas Hall."

"It shouldn't have been something you had to think about, Edward. How am I suppose to share my life with you if I'm always wondering what you're hiding from me?"

"Look, I'm not perfect, but I love you. I know you're not going to like the way I do things sometimes, but you've got to believe that I'm trying to do what's best."

"By keeping things from me?" I asked. "How is that best?"

"I wasn't the only one withholding information," he said, his voice still as calm as when I began my rant. "Were you ever planning on telling me about ending up in a Chinese prison?"

"Not if I could help it. But it looked like you already knew so I wasn't really withholding anything at all, was I?"

"By the time I found out you were there, Michael had already gotten you out. My guess is you were probably in Istanbul by then." He waited as though he were trying to decide what to say next. "So, Michael's in love with you. Did you have any idea?"

"No. For so many years I thought he hated me. Then over the last couple of months, we've gotten to be such good friends. Just last week he and I had lunch together, just the two of us."

"It sounds like both Michael and Sarah are going to have to deal with some big issues. Whether they stay married or not is a decision only they can make." Edward looked into my eyes and I knew what his next question would be. "While we're on the subject, how are you feeling about divorcing Tony?"

To most people this would probably seem like an odd question, but Edward and I had often talked about the institution of marriage and he knew how strongly I felt about divorce. After all, I stayed in an abusive marriage for over two years and one of the reasons was because I felt divorce was wrong. I still did. And yet that was exactly what I was doing. I closed my eyes and leaned my head back. I couldn't find anything remotely close in the six languages I spoke to match my feelings.

"Sweetie?"

"I don't want to talk anymore." I stood up and he followed my lead back to the house.

"We need to –"

"No, you want to. We don't *need* to." For a brief moment, I had forgotten why I was angry with him, but Edward trying to tell me what I needed agitated me once more. "Why are you even here anyway? Aren't you still mad at me?"

"No, I'm not mad anymore. I just think you might feel better if –"

"Well, I am still angry! This whole thing is just crazy and I can't do it anymore! It's just all too much."

I was so tired. I felt like my whole life, all twenty-six years of it, had moved in fast-forward and I needed a minute to catch up.

It took everything I had in me to put one foot in front of the other and walk. Edward stayed a few paces behind me as we silently finished the trip home.

Our house was a beautiful two bedroom Mediterranean style villa. It had an Old-World Tuscan feel to it. The design included lots of windows that provided a light airy feeling along with walls that were painted in rich shades of vanilla and chocolate. Vivian had been insistent on building the home for Edward long before we met, but he never spent much time in it until I moved in. Maybe that's why I always felt like it was our home and not just his. Edward often commented that the house belonged more to me than him, since it was my full-time residence and he was only there on the weekends. A few weeks into our engagement, I had worked hard on making the house into our home. I had a member of the staff help me bring Edward's video game collection, books, and a few odds and ends from the main house to ours. He arrived home that weekend thrilled with the changes I had made.

I walked into the bedroom and looked at my dresser. I was so mentally spent I could not remember which drawer held my nightgowns. Two months ago I didn't even own a nightgown and now it seemed I had a dozen silky, lacey, flimsy things to sleep in. Edward found great pleasure in bringing me a new one almost every weekend. If not a nightgown, there would be panties, bras, stockings, or robes. I could not have cared less what I slept in, and for years had just slept in a t-shirt. But it made Edward happy to see me in all these beautiful things, as though I were a present for him to unwrap. However, I was so drained, both physically and emotionally, that I couldn't remember where any of them were.

Edward sensed my inability to function, opened a drawer, and retrieved a long purple silk gown. It was his favorite and one of the few I had actually purchased.

He laid the nightgown on the bed and began to undress me. He unbuttoned the waistband of my black skirt and slid it down my legs and off my body.

"Don't!" I snapped. "I'm supposed to be mad at you. Quit trying to help me."

"Does it make it harder for you to stay angry? When I try to help?" he asked as he peeled off the black tights I had worn beneath.

I sat on the edge of the bed and rubbed my eyes.

Edward lowered himself to his knees and brought his face eye level with mine. "I won't leave you alone tonight. I'm sure Tony's figured out a way to make bail by now, and he's out there somewhere, probably pissed as hell with you." His voice was no louder than a whisper. "I know you're still angry. I get it. I'm not sure how to fix it, but I will find a way. I love you too much not to."

I wanted to yell at him, scream at him, kick him out of the house again, but I did not have the strength. Plus, part of me wanted him here with me. The scared little girl who had married Tony wanted that knight in shining armor to save her, even if it was only from herself.

He put his arms around me and lightly kissed my hair. Then he lifted his head and my bra was in his hand. I had never quite been able to figure out how he undressed me so effortlessly. It was obvious that he mastered the art of stripping clothes off a woman long before we ever met.

He slid the gown over my head and I progressed in a zombie-like manner to the bathroom, where I washed my face, brushed my teeth, and brushed out my hair. When I returned to the bedroom, Edward was sitting on the edge of our oversized bed. He stood up, put me into bed, and kissed me.

"I know you'd rather I go to the main house, but I'm going to sleep in the guest room tonight." He walked toward the door and I cleared my throat before trying to speak.

"Don't go." I had said it so quietly, he didn't hear the words but knew I had said something and turned around.

"What?"

"Stay here."

"Okay." He pulled off his clothes and let them fall to the floor. Then he slid his chiseled body into black pajama pants and a black t-shirt and crawled under the covers.

The moment he took me in his arms it felt like a freight train had collided with me. I knew this feeling. It had attacked me once before and my salvation had been a private hospital just outside of Miami. I promised myself years ago that I would never let this happen again. But I wasn't sure I knew how to stop it, or if it was even stoppable.

"No." I wasn't even aware I had said it out loud until Edward responded.

"What, Sweetie?"

It wasn't until Edward placed his finger under my chin and lifted my face to his did I give up the fight. I had spent every ounce of available energy I had holding myself together emotionally over the last week and there was nothing left. Maybe it was the safety of being in his arms that gave me some unspoken permission to let go.

"What *don't* you want Cassandra?"

In my head I could list a thousand things I did not want as I began to sob, and sobbing was one of them. I did not want to break down. I did not want Tony to be alive. I did not want to know the things I knew. When I tried to answer Edward, the only sound my body would release were the little gulping noises that bubbled out.

"I know. It'll be okay." As he spoke, he held me tightly against his hard, warm body and stroked my hair.

How did he know it would be okay? There was no way he could. I was still fighting what was now a battle I knew I would lose, and the strain of it was beginning to cause physical pain in my neck, shoulders, chest, and stomach.

Somehow, I thought if I could stop crying, for just a few seconds, maybe I could push back the avalanche that had already begun. I closed my eyes, took a deep breath, and held it, hoping I would not be able to cry while I held my breath and this feeling would pass.

Holding my breath only partially worked. For a moment, I stopped crying. However, the feeling did not pass. If anything it intensified the pain. I must have held my breath for longer than I realized because the next thing I remembered was opening my eyes to find Edward's face only inches from mine. He looked petrified.

"Cassandra, breathe. Cassie, come on Sweetie, you have to breathe."

I inhaled as deeply as I could, then let it out and began the process of breathing again. Had I held my breath so long that I passed out? I wasn't sure. I was shocked there were any tears left in my body to fall and yet they continued.

I continued in my state of hysteria until exhaustion overtook my body and I drifted into a restless sleep. I do not know how long I slept, but when I opened my eyes, I was still sobbing. It took a second for me to realize that Edward, who still had one arm securely around me, was on the phone. I could not hear everything over the sound of my own crying, but Edward's voice exuded panic.

"So what do I do?" Edward asked. He followed whatever the other person was saying with a lot of quick "yes" and "no" answers.

I was wondering what he was talking about when I heard him say, "Fred, was it this bad last time?"

He was on the phone with my uncle. And they were talking about me. I was still sobbing. I wished he hadn't called my uncle, but couldn't find a voice inside of me to speak. Then he mumbled something about waiting until tomorrow before doing anything.

I drifted in and out of consciousness throughout the night and when I awoke I heard voices, but they were always fuzzy and I could only make out the one that belonged to Edward. The last time, I woke to the sound of someone screaming, only to realize that someone was me. I sat up and found myself alone in the room, but not for long. Edward ran into the room with someone following him. Was it Dr. Rice? I was confused and unsure. I heard the person tell Edward, "If this doesn't help, you'll have to take her. I'll leave the card on your desk. She'll be fine there. It's one of the best hospitals in the area. Really."

"No. This will work, it has to." I felt Edward get into bed. "Cassie, sweetheart, this will help. I promise."

I shook my head, but I did not know exactly why. Then I felt something pinch my arm and a sound, other than crying, escaped my throat. Within moments, my whole body relaxed. And when it did, I stopped the hysterical crying and drifted off into a peaceful slumber.

Chapter Eighteen

I OPENED MY EYES to find myself nose to nose with my fiancé. The sun was climbing through the windows of our room and for a brief moment, everything seemed as it should. As I examined his face, eyes closed, muscles relaxed, and hair tousled, I saw everything that could ever be important to me. But the empty pit in my chest where I felt like he reached in and ripped my heart out still remained.

I rolled out of bed, put some water on for tea, and started the coffee maker for Edward. I wondered what time he needed to be in D.C. so I picked up my cell phone from the kitchen counter and looked at the time. It was nearly nine. Something wasn't right. Edward was always in Washington by now, even on the days he lingered at home, claiming he had no early appointments. However, I didn't want to wake him either, so I called Kelly, his assistant. I knew she would be at the office as she always arrived promptly at seven-thirty, whether Edward was there or not. "Hey Kelly, it's Cassandra."

There was a long pause. "Hi. I'm a little surprised to hear from you today. Is everything okay?"

"Yeah, it's just that Edward's still asleep and I was wondering what time he needs to be in D.C. today."

"He has nothing on his schedule until Monday." Her voice was slow and deliberate.

"He cleared his schedule for the next two days?"

She seemed to hesitate before each sentence. "Cassandra, tomorrow is Saturday. He only cleared his calendar for today. He planned it a couple of weeks ago so the two of you could finish up last-minute wedding details."

"Did you say tomorrow's Saturday? That's impossible, I went to bed Wednesday night and just woke up a few minutes ago."

"I talked to Edward several times yesterday. Apparently you had a rough night Wednesday?"

"Yeah." I said, embarrassed that she knew about what had transpired that night.

"He had Dr. Rice make a house call at about five on Thursday morning and gave you something to calm you and help you sleep."

"Really?" It was Dr. Rice. I hadn't imagined it.

"Yes, Edward was so worried about you. The last time he sounded that bad was when his father died. He kept telling me everything was his fault. I told him Dr. Rice needed to give him something as well."

"So, it's really Friday, huh?"

"All day," Kelly said.

"Okay. I guess I'll let him sleep and I'll go to work. Now there's a role reversal for you."

Edward and I led a somewhat strange, but functional commuting relationship. Nearly every Monday morning I would wake up to find Edward gone, as he would always let me sleep in. So the thought of being out the door before he woke had a certain sense of irony about it. We both laughed and said our goodbyes. I liked Kelly. She always knew exactly how to tell me news I didn't want to hear in such a way that I handled it well.

I had just lost an entire day that was scheduled to the brim. So, I did the only thing a girl could do. I drank my tea, took a shower, threw on my favorite pair of jeans and a sweater, and walked to the office despite the frigid temperature. It would have made more sense to drive one of the golf carts but the extra time in the fresh air and the exercise was invigorating.

I was just turning on my computer and assessing my backlog of work when Alex strolled into my office. When he saw me, he came to a complete halt.

"You okay, Sis? You look like hell." I had noticed it too. When I stepped out of the shower and looked at myself in the mirror the dark circles under my eyes were in such strong contrast to my fair skin, it looked as though they were drawn in with a marker.

"Rough couple of days. It looks like Libby-Mae did a good job of holding down the fort for me, though." Actually, she had done a great job. In my absence, she had handled everything on my calendar with the exception of one meeting, which she rescheduled, and the approval of the next year's labels. She left me with almost no backlog to deal with.

"Yeah, she's pretty amazing."

"So, what brings you by to see me?"

"I was wondering if you've talked to Henry this morning. He's late and I need some invoice numbers from him."

"Did you call the house?"

"No answer. And his cell phone goes straight to voicemail."

"Do me a favor. Call the guard shack. See if he came home last night."

I pulled up my e-mail and started deleting the junk. I figured it was the quickest way to deal with three days worth of e-mails.

"Henry left at six-thirty last night and hasn't been seen since," Alex said.

All I could do was let out a small laugh. I knew exactly where to find Henry. I picked up the phone and called Zoe's apartment. Henry answered, sounding groggy and agitated.

"What?"

"You're late for work," I said.

"Cassandra, is that you?" I could hear him fumbling with something in the background. "Oh crap, I'm late."

"It's okay, just come in once you're moving. Oh, and tell Zoe for me that if she plans to do this to you on a regular basis, you need to finish the night at your house. You have to be at work earlier than she does."

"I'll pass along the message."

Less than twenty minutes later, my cell phone rang.

"Where are you?" Edward asked, his voice brimming with concern.

"Work. You know, that place where people go to accomplish things away from the house."

"I am familiar with the concept. Maybe too familiar." He chuckled slightly as he spoke, but then his voice turned serious. "You okay, Sweetie?"

Was I okay? I did not know. I just knew that life would go on, with or without me. And I still wanted to be part of it.

"Of course I am. I'm just a day behind. I had yesterday's schedule packed because I was gone the day before that. It's going to be a busy one."

"Well, don't push yourself too hard." I knew he was thinking about yesterday and how much or little it would take for a relapse. The line was silent and I knew I needed to say something about my behavior.

"Edward, about Wednesday night ... I guess what I'm trying to say is thanks for taking care of me yesterday. I ..., I ..."

"It's okay. As long as you feel better today. You *do* feel better though, don't you?"

"Yes, it's just that Kelly gave me the impression I was kind of an ugly mess. I guess what I'm trying to say is I'm sorry."

"No, don't be. I'm glad I was there. You may have been a mess, but you're always beautiful."

"I guess I should call Dr. Rice today and thank him for making a house call."

"He did tell me he'd like to talk to you when you felt up to calling. He's worried about you. We all are."

"I know. So what are you doing today?" I asked hoping to change the subject.

"I was going to go into town and take care of a few things. But I'm thinking I should probably just stay here."

"No, go do what you need to do. I'm just going to be at the office all day anyway."

He thought about it for a long moment. "Okay, but promise you'll call me if you need me. I can be back in a heartbeat."

I hadn't been off the phone with Edward for more than ten minutes when Vivian called. I was beginning to feel like it was Grand Central Station in my office and would be glad when Libby-Mae came in after lunch.

"What are you doing at work today?" The tone of her voice was such that she could have been my own mother calling to scold me.

"I have a ton of things to do, Viv. I mean, I've been out of the office since Monday, and the work didn't stop piling up." It was a bit of an exaggeration, but I was certain it was the only way to avoid a lecture.

"Cassandra, you should be resting today. I was shocked when Edward told me you were at the office. Are you really okay?"

"As okay as I'm going to get for now. I'll feel better when the divorce is final."

"I might have something that will cheer you up. Can you come up to the house around two?" I didn't feel like being around people, but the last time I saw her I cried all over her favorite roses and the concern in her voice was so overwhelming I agreed to come up to the house.

It was a mere moment after I hung up the phone that it began to ring again, but this time someone else answered it. The door to my office was open and I could hear Libby-Mae's voice handling the call.

I walked out to her desk as she hung up the phone. Libby-Mae was wearing jeans and a Thomas Hall Winery sweatshirt, her hair was pulled back into a ponytail, and she wasn't wearing any make-up. While this was the norm for me, she was usually very fashion-ably dressed with every hair in place and light makeup. I had never seen her like this and on closer examination, I realized that her eyes were bloodshot and filled with tears.

I sat in the chair next to her desk and took her hand. "Lib-by-Mae, what's wrong? Why aren't you at school?"

"My best friend, Mandy, didn't come home after the end-of-sea-son bonfire for the football team last night. Nobody knows what happened to her. She and her boyfriend had a fight at the bonfire about Susie Nelson and she insisted on walking home. But she never showed up. Detective Hayes is worried it might be like the other people who've disappeared lately." She started to cry, so I did the only thing I could think of to do. I wrapped my arms around her and held her until she was done. "I know I should've gone to school, but I just couldn't. So I came here instead."

"Does someone besides me know where you are? I don't want people to worry that you've disappeared, too."

"Uh-huh. I told my Uncle Dave and he called the school for me. My mom was too drunk this morning to care." Libby-Mae's family life was dysfunctional at best. I was just glad that she had some family that truly cared about her as much as everyone at Thomas Hall did for our newest employee.

"Are you sure you want to be here today? If you want to take the day off, it's okay," I said.

"I need to do something, Miss Cassandra. And I certainly don't wanna be at home."

I thought about what she said. "It sounds like we're in the same boat. You work as long or as little as you'd like today. Okay? And keep me posted on Mandy."

When I walked into the main house Vivian was smiling, seemingly happy, chatting away with Tony. I could feel the agony squeeze my body like a vice. I had not expected to walk in on the two of them and I was not strong enough to be the confident, powerful woman I needed to be around him.

They were standing in the foyer when they noticed my arrival.

"What are you doing here?" I asked. "Shouldn't you still be behind bars?"

"Nope, Vivian here was kind enough to make bail for me."

"God, Tony, no more lies. It's bad enough you spent our entire relationship lying to me, but now you want to bring my future mother-in-law into this. Can't you just leave us all alone?"

"Don't worry baby girl, I was just leaving."

"Quit calling me that. I am not a baby nor am I your girl."

"When did you start talking back to men?" He turned from me to Vivian. "Your son needs to put her in her place."

When she silently nodded and smiled, I felt like I had stepped into an old episode of The Twilight Zone. I took a moment in an attempt to figure out who this woman was because she was not the Vivian I knew and loved. It looked like her and it sounded like her, but I couldn't get past the fact she was agreeing with Tony.

Tony headed out the door. As he did he turned back to Vivian. "Thanks again for lunch. You're a really good cook."

Vivian put her arm around me. It should have felt comforting, but instead I felt confused.

"You look upset, dear." she said as she waved good-bye to Tony. "Don't be, we won't see him at Thomas Hall ever again."

I turned and faced her. "Vivian, what did you do?"

"I gave him what he came to Virginia looking for, a nice fat check."

"And what do you get in return?"

"Your peace of mind, dear," Vivian said.

"How much money does that go for these days anyway?"

"Not as much as you'd expect."

"You know, Edward tried to do the same thing the night after we learned Tony was in town."

"Did he now?" I couldn't tell if she was honestly surprised or if Edward had already told her. "How are you today, really?"

"I look that bad, huh?"

"I've seen you look better, dear. I just know you scared my son to death."

"I know, I didn't mean to. I really tried—"

"Oh, I didn't mean to imply you did it on purpose. I just know it must have been bad. He was more upset than he was when you were in the hospital. He kept telling me that it was his fault."

We continued up the stairs as we spoke. Vivian's arm never left me and I now found her presence comforting.

"That's what he keeps telling everybody, but it wasn't just him. It was just, everything." A wave of despair fell over me and I had to stop moving for a second. "It's just all too much at once."

She squeezed her arm a little tighter around me. We continued to move again and within a second we were at the Elizabeth Suite. When I walked into the room, it was full of everything imaginable for a wedding. Centerpieces for the tables, guest books, party favors, the works. In addition, two short, plump, identical looking gray-haired ladies, who looked vaguely familiar to me, sat chatting away. Usually Vivian would have properly introduced everyone, but she fell short of the norm.

"Cassandra, I want you to go put on the dress that's on the bed. It should fit."

On the bed laid a wedding dress. It was my mother's wedding dress, but it wasn't. My mother's dress was some satiny, synthetic blend of material, but this was pure silk. This was longer in length, broader across the bust, and a slightly different shade in color. It was more a champagne color and less ivory. It was though, in essence, my mother's wedding dress. But it had been made for me.

This was *my* wedding dress. Next to it, packaged in a keepsake box, was the dress my mother wore.

I sat on the edge of the bed and ran my hand down the length of the silk. I picked up my dress and hugged it, wanting to jump up and spin in circles like a child. At some point I found myself squealing with delight like a kid on Christmas morning.

I quickly slipped out of my clothes and into the dress, praying it would fit. And it did, almost perfectly. The only issue was the length, which I quickly discovered was not hemmed at all.

When I walked out of the bedroom one of the gray-haired ladies walked up to me and took my hands into hers, in much the same way Vivian often did. Vivian was at the bar, opening a bottle of Champagne.

"Oh, it does look beautiful on you," the woman said.

"Vivian, shoes?" the other asked.

"They were on the bed too."

"I'm sorry. I was so stunned by the dress that I guess I didn't see the shoes."

The second gray-haired lady was already headed out the bedroom with shoes in hand and within moments had placed the perfectly fitting footwear on my feet.

The two ladies worked in tandem perfecting the fit and within moments they were finished and looked up at me from the floor where they had been adjusting the un-hemmed silk that formed a creamy puddle on the floor.

"There, all done," one of the women said.

"Wait, it needs one thing," Vivian said. "Stay put. I'll be right back."

Vivian hurried out of the room only to return a few minutes later with a white, square box tied with a matching ribbon.

"Something old," she said smiling. "But only if you like it."

I untied the ribbon, which hadn't been touched in years. Upon opening the box, I discovered a beautiful cathedral-length single-layer veil adorned with tiny crystals and pearls that were hand sewn in an elaborate design.

"Vivian, it's amazing. But wait, this looks vaguely familiar."

"Yes, I'm wearing it in the wedding portrait in the foyer."

"It's amazing," I repeated, examining the tiny, elaborate details. "I've never seen anything like it."

"And you won't," Vivian said, pausing to point at the two women. When she did, I noticed the two women had strikingly similar features to Vivian. "It's one of a kind."

"The two of you made this?"

"It was the first veil we ever made. The first of many."

Vivian removed the veil and placed it on my head. The two combs sewn into it to secure it on my head were cracked, but it made no difference. The moment I saw my reflection in the mirror, I felt the way I thought a bride should and wondered if I should even be letting myself feel this way. I felt the smile melt away from my face and my eyes turn watery.

"Okay, dear, it looks like it's time for you to get out of your dress. Then the four of us will have a little chat while we drink a bit," Vivian said.

"Oh, I can't stay. I've got to get back to work."

"That's one of the things we need to talk about," one of the women said. "Just put the dress on the bed."

When I came out of the bedroom in my own clothes, the three ladies were sitting, sipping champagne and chatting away as if they'd known each other a long time. Vivian handed me a glass along with a plate of finger sandwiches. She knew it was the one drink I would never turn down and had probably figured out I had blown off lunch.

"Cassandra, I just realized I haven't introduced you to my sisters, Virginia and Violet."

"Are these the sisters you have lunch with on Wednesdays?" I now understood why I could not tell them apart. Vivian's sisters were twins, and my guess was that they were identical.

"Yes, and we've decided you're going to start having lunch with us every Wednesday as well," one of the sisters said. "Viv's worried you're turning into a workaholic."

"You are?"

"When Senior left you in charge of the winery, I don't think he intended for you to be in the office every day of the week," Vivian said smiling. "He did it to make sure Edward wouldn't lose track of you again."

"The winery's a mess, Vivian. As soon as I get things in order, it will get easier. And like you, I know exactly why Senior left the winery in my hands. And some days, if he were alive, I'd have to kill him for it." The four of us laughed. I took a moment to eat one of the sandwiches before continuing.

"Ladies, about the dress, do you know someone who can do the alterations?"

"Well, since we made the dress, we'll be doing the alterations," one of the sisters said. "We should probably explain why we made you a new dress. When we began to take the first seam out of your mother's dress, we discovered the material was beginning to dry rot. The dress wouldn't have survived the alterations."

"I hope you don't mind the few changes we made. We thought it would be a little more flattering for your body type." The other sister continued. "Your mother was built a little differently than you, wasn't she?"

"Yes Ma'am." For a brief moment my thoughts drifted away to my mom, and I wished she were there with us. However, I was brought back into the moment by the voice of one of Vivian's sisters.

"Well, the alterations will be done by midweek at the latest. But why such a rush to get married?"

"You're not pregnant, are you?" the other asked, eyes opened wide.

"I wish." I glanced at Vivian, who looked up and smiled.

I turned my attention back to the twins. "I'm impressed you can even do the alterations yourselves, let alone make a wedding dress. I'm not even sure I know how to thread a needle."

Virginia and Violet looked at each other, appalled by what I had just said as though I'd just confessed to some gruesome crime. Vivian would later tell me they had been well-respected wedding dress designers in their twenties, but gave it up after about a decade to raise families of their own. Occasionally, they still made the odd dress for family members and friends, but only upon request.

I could not tell which one spoke first, but their banter was quick, hysterical, and reminded me of the three fairies from Disney's Sleeping Beauty.

"We're going to have to fix that. Everyone should know at least how to sew on a button." The comment made me blush, but they continued as if they were unaware of my embarrassment.

"Right away."

"No, not right away. After the wedding."

"After the honeymoon."

"No, after the holidays. We'll start with cross-stitch."

"No, embroidery."

"Needlepoint would be best."

"Excellent."

I looked at the twins, then at Vivian who was grinning from ear to ear. I had never seen the expression on her face, but at that moment I knew exactly where her son had gotten his Cheshire cat grin from. As I thought about everything these women had done to make my wedding dress perfect, one fact loomed large. Edward and I would not be getting married in December.

Chapter Nineteen

EDWARD RETURNED FROM HIS trip to Willow Creek just before four and joined Vivian and me in the library. It was cold and dark in the room. The built-in bookcases full of novels and the soft leather furniture gave the room a homey feeling, but the silence that filled the space weighed heavy upon all of us. Vivian and Edward stared at me, as I had been the one who requested we sit down and discuss the wedding. I had never done so before and I'm sure they both knew why. I struggled to find the words no one wanted to hear.

"I think we should postpone the wedding." I could hear my voice cracking with each word. But, all things considered it seemed like it might be a good idea. I needed more time. More time to divorce Tony, and more time to make sure I was doing the right thing marrying Edward.

Edward and Vivian sat motionless. I'm certain they wondered if this was from the breakdown or if I was getting cold feet. I continued to be the voice of reason, although I had no desire to be.

"The ceremony is two weeks away and my..." I choked on the words as I continued. "My divorce isn't final yet."

"You don't think Judge Smith will grant you a divorce in time?" Edward asked, somewhat confused.

"Even if he did, Father Tennelli can't marry us. Catholic priests don't marry divorced Catholics, especially to non-Catholics. So even if my divorce is finalized and we get a new marriage license in time, there's no church and no one to officiate."

"Cassandra, dear, I can take care of finding someone to preside over the service."

"Vivian, I can't ask you to do anything else. You've done so much already." I knew she would offer to fix everything, but I wasn't sure she could or if I even wanted her to make the wedding happen. "Letting us have the reception here at Thomas Hall, the invitations, the flowers, the caterers, my dress, and now this. It's too much work."

"Nonsense. I'm enjoying every minute of it." She ignored my suggestion, in hopes that I would reconsider postponing. "But there are a few details I need to go over with you. You still need to make some choices about –"

"Postpone or cancel?" Edward interrupted his mother and he looked at me as though my reply could destroy him. "I know I should have told you but—"

"Just stop," I said. I was emotionally drained and did not have the energy to relive the night I found out Edward knew again. "I'm trying to let it go, but I can't if you keep bringing it up."

"What happened?" Vivian asked.

She didn't know what Edward had confessed to me and I wondered if she even knew at all. He looked at me for guidance, but I answered the question for him instead.

"Edward knew Tony wasn't dead when I first arrived at Thomas Hall for Crush Weekend and neglected to tell me until the night before my court date."

Vivian gasped in horror as she looked at her son with her eyes wider than I had ever seen. "Edward James Baker, Jr.! You knew? You knew and you didn't tell her!" She shifted her eyes to me and her fiery gaze softened. "No wonder the last few days have been so hard for you. I'm surprised you haven't killed my son yet."

"It has taken a great deal of restraint."

She focused her attention back to her son. "What were you thinking? I know I raised you better than that. You're lucky she hasn't left you and Thomas Hall at this point. You know it wouldn't take but a phone call for Sarah to drive down here, pack her up, and move her in with the two of them."

"I don't know about that," I said. "I'm still not exactly on speaking terms with Sarah."

"Cassandra, you never answered my question," Edward said, completely ignoring his mother.

I looked into those eyes I loved so much. I wanted to tell Edward how much I loved him. I wanted to reassure him everything would be fine. That I would be fine and we would get married in December, just like we'd planned. But that was not what came out of my mouth.

"I wouldn't be divorcing Tony if I didn't want to marry you." I stood up and Edward rose from his seat before I could stop him. "Stay here with your mom. Vivian, if you would, please come up with a plan for postponing the wedding and the last possible date we have to make that decision."

"I'll take care of everything, dear, don't worry."

"Sweetie, where are you going?" he asked.

"Back to the office. I've got some work to do."

"Can't it wait? You look upset."

"That's why I'm going to work. At least there I expect things to be total chaos."

Chaos. It was my favorite word to use on those assessment quizzes in magazines or the ones doctors ask you to fill out. 'Describe your life in five words.' I could usually do it in one.

Two hours later I sat in my office, staring at the phone. I had finished my paperwork, cleaned out and organized my desk drawers, returned phone calls, hung the diplomas I brought from the house, and updated my calendar through the end of the year. There really was not anything else left to do. I always kept things on my desk as up-to-date as possible and Libby-Mae was turning out to be such an asset that missing a couple of days from work was not as big of a deal as I made it out to be. It had just been my excuse to escape.

I shifted my gaze to a photo on my desk. It was of Sarah, Michael, Edward, and me the evening of the Harvest Ball. It had been a magical night. I looked at the smiling faces staring back at me and wondered how the magic of that night could disintegrate with the arrival of one person and the secrets he held.

I was not even sure I wanted to resolve things with Sarah. However, I found myself picking up the phone and dialing in hopes of finding something worth salvaging.

"Hello." It was Michael. I had hoped he would not answer the phone. The whole thought of him being in love with me left me feeling uncomfortable and more awkward than usual.

"Hi."

"Cassandra, how ya doin'?"

"Not so good," I said.

"I'm glad you called then."

"I didn't call to talk to you." I paused for a moment and thought about what I said. "Wow. That came out harsh. I'm sorry. I know it's no excuse, but I haven't been myself lately."

"I would imagine not. I'm pretty sure I deserve it though."

"No, you don't. I'm just trying to handle one thing at a time and today it's dealing with your wife."

"Sounds logical." I could not think of a response so we just sat, listening to the silence at the other end of the receiver. "You wanna talk to Sarah?"

"I'm not sure, but I guess I should."

I could hear Michael and Sarah's muffled voices as they passed the phone from one to the other.

"Hey C.C."

"Hi." The moment I heard her voice, I knew calling had been a mistake and I fought the urge to hang up the phone. We sat, both completely silent for what seemed like hours, before she spoke.

"What do you want me to say? I'm sorry? If you want an apology —"

"You really think an apology will fix this? You slept with Tony while we were married. I thought you were my friend."

"I am." The tone of her voice indicated she thought she could talk herself out of this indiscretion. "I was only trying to protect you."

"There seems to be a lot of that going around."

"I really didn't think you'd ever —"

"Sarah, I wasn't finished. I didn't need you to protect me. I needed you to be a real friend, someone I could trust."

"You *can* trust me," she said.

"Not anymore." The heartbreak of the situation bubbled to the surface and filled my voice. "I just need to know why. Why did you do it?"

"Ever been married to a man who's in love with someone else?"

"Yes. Yes, I have. And he went so far as to fake his death to escape our marriage." The long silence on the other end of the line indicated her acceptance of my understanding this fate.

"Well, I guess it's just how I cope," she said.

"That doesn't even make sense. Your marriage was falling apart so you coped by sleeping with your best friend's husband?"

"You shouldn't be talking about disastrous marriages. If your marriage hadn't been such a train wreck he wouldn't have wanted to sleep with me."

I did not know what else to say. Her words stung, but she was right. My marriage to Tony was miserable. We sat in silence yet again. It was a strange occurrence as our phone conversations were usually talkative events with no breaks in the conversation.

I knew then, without any doubt now, that it was over. She and I were done. My only girlfriend from college, and I was letting her go. I knew I should have felt sad, but I didn't. Maybe it was because the friend I was giving up was not the same friend I thought she was for all of those years. There was nothing left for me to say, so I simply ended the call.

The door to my office silently opened as I hung up and Edward made is way across the room and sat in the chair in front of my desk. His half-hearted smile as I put the phone down told me I was not finished with hard conversations. "I told Mom I was coming up here to find out if you wanted salmon or tilapia for the fish at the reception."

"But ..."

"But the truth is I had to get out of there before Mom killed me. The last time I saw her that angry at me was when she found out I'd gotten a tattoo."

Even though I felt a smile creep onto my face, I knew Edward was avoiding the reason he had actually come to my office. "And?"

He looked into my eyes, pausing briefly before he began. "I want an answer to my question. Do you want to cancel the wedding?"

"Do you?" I snapped and then pursed my lips together. I hadn't intended to sound so curt, but didn't rush to apologize either.

"Why would you even ask me that?"

"Because you keep asking me," I said, standing. "I told you earlier, I wouldn't be divorcing Tony if I didn't want to be with you. I'd just let it sit in limbo. I know this is horrible to say, but I wish he were still dead. I wish I just didn't know he still existed." I could feel tears well up in my eyes. "I wish he had just stayed away. Life would have been so much easier." It was then I finally understood. This was what Edward had tried to protect me from. He knew how crushed I would be by the weight of it all and not even he could have anticipated the domino effect Tony's reappearance would have on everything and everyone in our lives. He had wanted to keep me from having to live through this nightmare.

But I still needed to figure out a way to forgive him.

I pressed the menu button on my cell phone until the glowing green light confirmed it was two-eighteen in the morning. When the light timed-out, the cool living room was again swallowed in darkness and I was no closer to finding a way to forgive Edward than I had been three hours earlier when he went to bed. I was sitting in the same position I had been then, curled up in a ball, on the sofa, wrapped in my favorite blanket.

It had been a long evening of trying to work through so many issues that rattled around in my head. I found myself coming back to the same question over and over again. "What am I doing here?" There was no reason I couldn't walk away and it seemed that ever since I came to live in Virginia, the death, destruction, and mayhem that plagued my life were all at a record high. But I loved Thomas Hall and loved the Baker family as well. And most importantly, I was too in love with Edward to run away.

"You might have to dig a little deeper," Zoe's voice echoed in my head. I wanted to find a way to forgive him, but I just couldn't get past the core issue. Edward had known Tony was alive before I arrived at Thomas Hall and he did not tell me. I was going to have to dig a hole halfway to China to dig deep enough to forgive him for that.

I tried reverting back to the historically logical me. The one that disappeared the day I arrived at the vineyard. How bad was it that he did not tell me? What would have happened if he had?

Before I could ask myself the question, I knew the answer. I would have stayed the weekend, so not to be rude. I would have kept my distance from Edward. I most certainly would not have gone out to the willow tree to watch the fireworks with him and I would have never let him kiss me. And I would have never, ever, under any circumstances, allowed myself to fall in love with Edward Baker, Jr. I would have returned to D.C. with Sarah and Michael the day after the Harvest Ball and flown to California for answers. Why and how did he fake his death? What was I supposed to do now that I knew he was alive? Were we still legally married?

Would I have returned to Thomas Hall once I had my answers? My guess would be no. After all, I would have returned to the East Coast just around the time Senior was murdered. And since I normally do not attend funerals, I would have waited, if ever, to return.

In not staying, Senior would not have changed his will and I would not have been named head of the winery. Edward and I would not have become engaged and I would probably still be wandering aimlessly in search of someplace that felt like home.

In Edward's effort to protect me, he had given me the life I longed for. Career, family, love, friendship, home, everything. He may not have done the right thing by not telling me, but what he had done had changed my life for the better.

I knew Edward had not thought about the possible outcome when he chose not to tell me. He wore blinders where I was concerned. He only saw what he wanted to see. He may have been the detail-oriented CEO of a large corporation, but when it came to me, he was impulsive, passionate, and rarely thought through the consequences of his actions. As I sat in the darkness, I wondered if this was something I would be able to live with for the rest of my life.

It was not long before I had my answer, and when I did, I stood up and walked into the bedroom. I expected to see Edward sleeping, but the bed was untouched and still made from the day before. As I returned to the living room I caught a glimpse of the guest room door ajar. I walked over and quietly pushed it open. There he was, having banished himself to the guest room. He belonged in my bed, in our bed.

As I took the first step into the room, he sat up. "Cassandra, Sweetie, what's wrong?"

"You're in the wrong bed, that's what's wrong." I walked to the edge of the bed and took his hand. Silently, I led him to our bedroom and we crawled under the covers. I was asleep within moments, held tightly in his strong arms and at peace for the first time in over a week.

Chapter Twenty

"Did I wake you?" he asked as I stumbled into the kitchen and started the water for my tea.

"It's okay." The truth was I had only been asleep a few hours when I heard Edward rumbling around the kitchen and the smell of toasted English muffins floated through the air making it impossible to stay in bed. "I needed to get up anyway. I've got some reading I need to get done today."

"Winery?"

"Yes, I'm still trying to figure out why Thomas Hall isn't turning a profit."

"It was never designed to, Sweetie. It was Dad's pet project and he was no money manager."

"It should be making money with the number of bottles we're producing. There's a weak link somewhere and I'm certain I can find it."

"You sound more like a CEO than a geography professor."

"Speaking of CEOs, there's something I think we need to talk about."

"Hold that thought while I fix our plates."

Five minutes later, Edward and I sat across from each other at the table with breakfast in front of us. He knew I normally only ate toast at breakfast but he had gone all out and whipped up Eggs Benedict, adding some melon slices on the side. We ate quietly and each time I looked up, he was staring at me.

"What? Do I look that scary this morning?" I took a bite of my breakfast and the Hollandaise sauce was out of this world.

"No, you look that sexy."

I shook my head and wolfed down another bite, not realizing how hungry I was when I sat down at the table.

"Just wondering what you wanted to talk to me about."

"How stupid you are," I said as I looked down to soak up the sauce with part of the English muffin.

"Excuse me?"

"You heard me. Last night, among other things, I realized that when it comes to me, you're the dumbest smart guy I've ever met."

"Okay, you've insulted my intelligence more times in the last two minutes than anyone has, ever." His tone was that of sarcastic amusement. "You'd better explain."

"Edward, would you make a major decision about Chesapeake Biotech without consulting specialists within the company?" I asked.

"Of course not, that would be crazy."

"But you'd sneak out in the middle of the night and try to bribe Tony without consulting the person who knows him the best in this family. And would you go into a major merger and not disclose all relevant information?"

"No."

"So, why am I different?"

"Wait a minute, you're the one always accusing me of treating our relationship like a corporation."

"No, I said you try to run our relationship like the head of a corporation. It's different."

"How?"

"You can't be the boss here. We have to be in this together. You need to show me the same respect you show your company and I don't feel like you do."

Edward opened his mouth to speak but stopped before a single word left his mouth. During the silence, I picked up a slice of melon and ate a few bites. I didn't want to push him for an answer. I wanted him to think about it.

"I thought you were the one who knew nothing about relationships," he said. "I'm beginning to realize you know more than I do."

"How long was your longest relationship?" It was a question I had never thought to ask before.

"There was one, it my thirties, that lasted just less than a year, besides that, about three or four months."

"Mine was over seven years. I may be lousy at the dating thing, but I learned a lot about how relationships shouldn't be handled when I was involved with Tony."

"I guess so."

"Speaking of Tony, I need to ask you something. Who else knew that Tony was still alive before I arrived at Thomas Hall?"

"Besides the private investigators and myself, only one other person," he said. "Once Tony showed up I told you. And you told Mom."

"And Zoe, who I'm sure told Henry." I said. "My guess is Alex knows too."

"I would imagine so. You didn't tell Michael or Sarah?"

"No. And I'd like you not to tell anyone else," I said. "The fewer people who know, the better."

"Whatever you want."

"Who's the other person?" I asked as I sipped my tea.

"You might not want to know."

"Tell me."

"Dad knew."

I choked on my drink. "Senior knew?"

"I went to Dad when you showed up at Thomas Hall. He advised me to leave it alone. Looking back, I think he read you well enough to know you'd leave if you knew."

I had adored Senior. Hearing that he advised Edward not to tell me Tony was still alive was incomprehensible. I stood up and pushed my chair under the table.

I walked into our bedroom and lay across our unmade bed. I tried hard to mentally digest this additional detail but got nowhere fast. It seemed like only a few seconds before Edward lightly tapped on the door frame.

"Can I come in?" He whispered.

"Sure." He started to sit when I gestured to him to lay down. He followed my request and I rolled over and held him in my arms. His heart pounded as though it might burst from his chest.

"Sweetie, do you, do you want ...," he hesitated for a moment before continuing in a low, soft voice. "Should I call Dr. Rice to come back out to the house?" I knew what he was asking. He wanted to know if I was heading for another breakdown.

"No, I'm okay."

"I shouldn't have told you Dad knew. I'm sorry."

"No, I'm glad you did. It actually makes me feel better about the whole thing. It's nice to know you didn't make that stupid decision all by yourself." Edward smiled and I smiled back at him. "Do you have anything you need to do today?"

"No, it's Saturday. We can lie here all day if you want." There was a long, lingering silence before he continued. "Are you sure you're okay?"

"Yeah, just tired. I didn't sleep much last night." I closed my eyes, snuggled closer to him, and within moments was asleep.

I awoke to the sun beating in through the windows, alone in bed. The clock on the nightstand read two-ten. I was certain it was wrong. There was no way I'd slept for four hours. I sat up and picked up my phone, only to find the battery was dead.

I could smell orchids and roses. I looked around, but there were no flowers in the bedroom. However, the scent was so strong, it was overwhelming and I knew there were flowers somewhere in the house.

I heard voices in the living room. First Edward's, then Henry's, and after a few moments Zoe's voice joined them. I listened as I stripped off my nightgown and threw on some comfy clothes.

"I'd love to go with y'all tonight. God knows I could stand a night out. Sitting around, watching Cassandra like this is killing me," Edward said, causing me to frown. "But I can guarantee you she won't go. She doesn't even want to leave the house right now, let alone Thomas Hall."

"Maybe I could talk her into it," Zoe said. "It would do her a world of good."

"You think so?" Henry questioned. "I mean, if she's still feeling overwhelmed or doesn't feel safe, going out would only make things worse, don't you think?"

"Going out where?" I asked as I walked into the room. I could barely see over the mounds of flowers in vases. They were on every available table, shelf, and countertop. Edward had sent flowers. This is what he did when we had an argument or he had done something stupid. The first time, he had literally bought the florist out of everything and filled the house. While I appreciated the gesture, I reminded him that a house full of flowers wasn't necessary. He had scaled it back to a room full this time.

I tried to smile but quickly found the effort wasn't worth the results. Everyone was sitting in the living room, drinking wine, and examining my every move. As I plugged my phone into the charger on the desk, I noticed the small envelope that had come with the flowers. I opened it and read it to myself.

Cassandra, You were right. I shouldn't have kept it from you. I was afraid I'd lose you if you knew. I'm sorry. Forever Yours, Edward

I took a moment to ponder what he had written. It turns out he had thought about the consequences when he chose not to tell me about Tony. I was taken aback by the idea that he hadn't been impulsive and wondered if I understood my fiancé as well as I thought I did.

I walked over and sat on the armrest of Edward's chair. He slipped his arm around my waist, holding me firmly. I took the glass out of Edward's free hand, tasted it, and then returned it to its owner. It was one of our Merlots, but not my favorite. As he took the glass back from me, he buried his lips into my collar bone, kissing it softly.

"Zoe and I were going to try to talk you and Edward into going on a double date tonight," Henry said.

I thought about it for a long moment. I really didn't want to, but I knew Edward did. I also felt like I was in the dog house with

Henry. While he had never said a word, it was obvious he was disappointed with my behavior the day of my court date.

"Where to?" I asked, trying to sound upbeat.

"Dinner and bar hopping in D.C." Zoe said, with excitement radiating from her voice and eyes.

"No, not D.C., not right now. Too much press," I said, shaking my head in protest. "Maybe some other weekend."

"Maybe some place closer?" Edward suggested. It was becoming more and more apparent to me that we were going out somewhere. Whether I wanted to or not.

"But I can tell Zoe wants to go to D.C.," I said. "Why don't the three of you go without me?"

"That won't work," the two men said simultaneously, and then laughed at each another.

"Why not? I'll just get Victor to bring me dinner from the main house and I'll read. The new Charlaine Harris novel I've been waiting for came in the mail yesterday."

"Because you'll be alone," Henry said. "And that's not going to happen with Tony around."

"And because I wouldn't want to go without you." Edward slid me off the arm of the chair onto his lap then gave me a playful peck on the nose. I felt content for the first time in what seemed like a very long time.

"Okay," I said. "But does it have to be D.C?"

Zoe's response surprised me. I was sure she was going to say it must be D.C. or possibly suggest Fredericksburg or Richmond as an alternative. "Heck no. For all I care we can go to the new Italian place in town, and then go hang out at Lucky Shots. We can dance and play some pool. It'll be fun."

I looked down at my tank top and comfy sleep pants. "I guess I can't go in this, huh?"

"You could," Edward smiled, his straight white teeth showing, "but I don't think I have the energy to fight off that many men tonight."

Lucky Shots was the town's only bar and it was about half full when we arrived a little after nine. I was surprised to find how few cameramen and reporters were following us. There were only three and I wondered if it was possible the press had finally tired of us. I doubted it, but was grateful for a night off from the hassle they brought with them.

Alex was sitting at the bar and Brian came in a few minutes behind us. They both joined us at a small table we planted ourselves at in the darkest corner of the bar.

I had never spent any time at Lucky Shots but wasn't surprised by its interior. The dark paneled walls, dim lights, dart boards, and pool tables all screamed small town country-western bar. The music playing over the speakers confirmed the bar's look. Within five minutes of arriving, George Strait was blaring throughout the bar's sound system.

The waitresses were all in "uniform" so to speak. Cut-off jeans, cowboy boots, and tight yellow t-shirts with a shot glass on the front breast pocket and the Lucky Shots logo on the back. They were all attractive women, but one stood out from the rest. She was behind the bar, picking up a huge tray. Her fair skin and red hair made it undeniable who she was. I waited for her to return from her delivery, which took less than a minute, before speaking.

"Libby-Mae?"

"Hey, Miss Cassandra. What brings you in here?"

"Being forced to have fun," I said half-heartedly. "I didn't know you worked here, too."

"I don't, I mean, not on a regular basis. My uncle owns this place. I help him when he's short-staffed and two waitresses called out tonight, so here I am."

"Y'all talkin' 'bout me?" A burly man in his mid-to-late forties with a shaved head and tattooed arms walked up behind her, resting his large stubby fingers on her shoulders.

"Yes sir. Uncle Dave, this is Cassandra Martin, my boss over at Thomas Hall. Miss Cassandra, this is my uncle, David Jett."

He wiped his hand on his t-shirt, to insure it was semi-clean before reaching out to shake my hand. "Pleasure to meet you, Miss Cassandra. I hear you're takin' good care of Libby-Mae over there at Thomas Hall."

"Well, she's a great assistant."

A waitress walked up to Dave. "The Bud Light taps gone dry. You want me to try to change it?"

"Not after last time. I don't think we need a wet t-shirt contest in here tonight." He turned to me and said, "Nice meetin' you.

Come in at lunch sometime and we'll talk trash about Libby-Mae when I'm not so busy."

"Hey!" Libby-Mae protested with a smile.

"Thanks, I'd like that."

A man's voice from a large table across the bar called out, "Hey, Red. Another round."

"Guess I better get back at it." Without waiting for a reply, Libby-Mae turned on the heels of her boots and headed to work.

Alex bought the first round. Brian ordered Jim Beam on the rocks, Henry and Edward ordered a Sam Adams, Zoe went with a frozen margarita, and I had my usual Coke. When Alex told the bartender what the new head of Thomas Hall was drinking, I could hear the laughter across the room.

Alex brought the drinks back, as Libby-Mae was up to her ears in orders from a group of farm hands seated on the other side of the bar. When he handed me my drink, it occurred to me that Thomas Hall's resident ladies man was alone.

"Waiting for someone or just window shopping tonight?" I asked.

"Nope, just havin' a beer." This was out of character for him. I reached over and put my hand on his arm.

"Alex, what's going on?"

"Ever since the day your ex, well not ex, whatever you want to call him showed up at the winery, I've been thinkin' a lot about what I want in a relationship." He took a seat next to me.

"I've been referring to him as my 'not-so-dead husband," I said. "But what do you mean exactly?"

"Well, I've pretty much figured out how to get any girl into bed and that was fun for a while, but ..."

"But?"

"I want something more, something real. Like what you and Edward have. I just don't know where to start."

"You'll know her when you find her, trust me." As we spoke I watched Alex's eyes follow Libby-Mae as she worked her way across the bar.

"Yeah, that's the problem. I think I already have."

That's when all the pieces finally fell into place for me. Alex had fallen in love with Libby-Mae. I felt like the worst person on the planet. I had just assumed that Alex was looking to take her on as his latest conquest, but it was much, much deeper than that.

"Look, I'm sorry if I came down hard on you the other day about Libby-Mae. I was in a foul mood. I just need both of you at the winery too much. If the two of you got serious and things ended badly, it would be a miserable situation for everyone."

"I know. You're right. I can't handle her like the other girls I've had in my life, but I'm not sure exactly what I should do."

I was contemplating a second soda while Alex spoke. That's when Tony walked into the bar. The whole scene began to play out like a bad western movie. Bad cowboy walks into the bar, the whole place goes silent, and the barkeeper asks the bad guy to leave. The problem was that Tony didn't know why he was being asked to leave. He hadn't seen us sitting in the shadowy corner of the bar.

I was feeling fearless with so many people there to protect me from my soon-to-be ex-husband so I stood up with my empty glass in hand and walked straight over to the bar. The bartender looked over at me, then Tony. But Tony spoke before anyone else could.

"Baby girl, I didn't know you were here. I guess I'll go."

"No, you're good. Just leave us be, okay?"

"Look, I'm sorry about what went down at Edward's place. I was greedy and deserve what I got." He held up the cast on his arm a little. "I'll leave you alone, but let me buy you guys a round. I'll even deliver them."

Tony had never waited on me before and I was shocked by the offer. "Seriously?"

"Yeah. Why not."

About five minutes later Tony was at our table with a round that mimicked the first one. The only difference was Tony's drink, vodka and tonic, was on the tray as well. He kept true to his word and didn't linger, but thanked me for letting him stay at the bar instead of enforcing the restraining order I had on him. Everyone watched as he walked away from the table, and I'm sure most of them wondered if he had some sort of multiple personality disorder.

Once he was out of sight every head at the table turned toward me. All except Alex, who was far too fixated on watching Libby-Mae bounce around the bar waiting tables.

"He's not a total monster. He can be civil when he wants to be." The men at the table looked at me as if I had lost all good sense. Edward looked particularly annoyed by the fact that I would defend Tony and after I thought about it, I was a little annoyed at myself for having done so.

"Hmm," Edward responded after taking a swig of his beer. "Somehow I doubt for more than five minutes."

I took a long sip of my fresh drink before answering. "Does it matter?"

"No, because I got the girl." He reached over, and softly kissed me.

Zoe turned to Henry, "Let's dance!"

She grabbed him by the arm and within moments they were gliding across the dance floor. I had no idea that either of them knew how to two-step, but Henry led her around the floor as if it were the most natural thing in the world.

"Want to join them?" Edward asked. But I wasn't in the mood, so I gently shook my head. I was still feeling a little sleep-deprived and really just wanted to go home. Everyone else was having a good time though, so I sat and listened to the music.

Edward held my hand, brushing his thumb back and forth against the back of it. I wasn't in a talkative mood anymore, still aggravated with myself for defending Tony. The guys struck up a conversation about the Redskins and the Ravens and who was having a better season when suddenly, I felt nauseous and light-headed. There was no way I would allow myself to throw up in the bar. In a small town like Willow Creek, I'd never live it down, especially as the head of the winery. I let go of Edward's hand and stood up. The room started to spin and I could feel beads of sweat forming on the back of my neck.

"Sweetie, where are you going?"

"Just to the restroom. I'll be right back."

"Are you okay?" Edward asked. "You look a little flushed."

"I'm just a little too warm. I shouldn't have worn this sweater."

"Why don't we go then?"

"No," I said. "I'll be fine. I'm just going to go splash some water on my face."

Edward stood from his chair. "I'll walk with you."

"That's silly. Stay here. I'll be right back."

The bar was much more crowded than it was when we arrived and I had to weave my way through people before I reached the bathroom. I was almost to the door of the ladies room when I stumbled. I looked up from the floor to find Tony standing over me. I was feeling worse by the second. He reached out and helped me onto my feet.

"Baby girl, you okay?"

Then, as my knees gave out from under me, everything went dark.

Chapter Twenty-One

I VAGUELY REMEMBERED BRIAN'S arrival at the motel and the ambulance ride was only a blur. The whole event was more like a foggy dream or distant memory. However, one thing was certain, I had spent too much time at Community General since moving to Thomas Hall.

The emergency room was efficient enough, and being part of the Baker clan sped the process along even more, but I wanted to be home with Edward. I heard his and Fred's voices in the hall, but was rushed off to radiology for an x-ray before Edward was finished filling out my paperwork.

When I was brought back to the small room in the ER Edward still wasn't there but Brian and Fred were patiently waiting.

"I want to go home. The only thing wrong with me is that I'm tired and have a headache. I want out of here." I tried to stand but my legs felt like rubber. Brian and Fred caught me as my legs gave out and helped me back into bed.

"Cassandra," Brian said. "I think there's more to this than you realize. You need to stay put until the test results come back. While we wait why don't I finish my report so you don't have to come down to the station? I think I have all the facts in place but let's go over what happened, just so I'm sure I've got it right."

"Okay, Tony bought a round for us and delivered the drinks. About ten minutes later, I started feeling weird."

"How so?"

"I felt like I was so drunk I thought I was going to be sick. I wasn't about to let that happen in the middle of the bar. Could you imagine? I'd never hear the end of it. The head of the winery can't hold her liquor. Even though I wasn't drinking, I knew no one would believe me."

"You're right about that," Fred said, almost smiling. I had never seen him look that exhausted in my entire life.

"Anyway, I got up to go to the ladies' room. At least that's where I was headed. When I got to the restroom door, Tony was there and asked me if I was okay. The next thing I remembered was waking up, tied to the bed of the motel in nothing but my bra and panties."

"I bet that was quite a sight," Edward said, trying to sound light-hearted. He was standing in the doorway and the moment our eyes locked I saw it all. The torment that had plagued his unshaven face, the sleeplessness in the dark circles under his eyes, and the despair that left him empty until the moment he saw me.

If he had moved any quicker, his feet would not have touched the floor. His lips found me first. They were soft and wet and kissed every spot on my face. As he did, his arms wrapped around me lifting my body from the bed and cradling me. As terrified as I had been just an hour earlier, I now felt the complete opposite. I was loved, I was safe, and I was alive.

"Can we go home now?" I whispered to him.

"I just talked to the doctor Sweetie," Edward said, still holding me. "He needs to talk to you first."

I looked at the three men and wished I understood why they were so worried. Any other day I probably could have figured it out, but I was so sleepy I could not focus. Edward seemed to realize I was having trouble keeping my eyes open and gently laid me back onto the bed. He took a seat in the chair beside me and held my hand. It was strong, warm, and reassuring.

I saw Brian watching the two of us together. The expression on his face was one of acceptance. I'm pretty sure that was the moment he knew we would never be more than friends and that my heart truly belonged to someone else. "I think I'll head back and get this report filed. I'll be at the office if you need me."

I signaled Brian over with my finger and he bent over the bed in order to hear me better.

"Thanks for everything. I really mean it."

"I know you do." He kissed my cheek and then looked at Edward and said, "Take care of her. If you don't, I will."

Edward nodded his head. There was history to that comment, I was certain of it. But I didn't know what it was and wondered if I would ever understand the animosity between them.

After Brian left, Edward faced me with an expression I could only describe as perplexed.

"What?" I asked.

"He kissed you. I've never seen him do that before."

"Well, we are friends. Outside of you and our family, he's probably my best friend. And I was just kidnapped. When he showed up at the hotel he kinda had a job to do. I guess he wanted to give me a friend's goodbye and not a police officer's."

"You know, there are rumors in town," Fred said.

"You're not the first person to say that." I turned from Fred and looked deep into Edward's eyes. "You don't believe them, do you?"

He gazed back at me, lifted my hand to his lips, kissed it, and smiled. "Not for a second. I know you'd never do that to me. I like that you're making friends here. It's starting to feel like home to you, isn't it?"

"No, it *is* home. Speaking of home, I want to go back to Thomas Hall now."

"I know you do."

"Good, then help me get dressed."

"You can't leave yet," Fred said. "The doctor will be here soon. But now that I know you're okay, both physically and mentally, I'm going to head home. Molly's, well she's sick, and I need to get back."

He knew I would be fine but the worry that deepened the wrinkles around his eyes remained. The only times I'd ever seen him look this way were in the days following the death of my parents and brother. At first, I thought his concern had been solely for me, but it was obvious, at least to me, there was more. As he started to walk away, I grabbed his hand.

"What's wrong with Molly?"

"Nothing seri—"

"Don't you lie to me."

He sat back down and stared at the floor. "We don't know how bad it is yet, but she has cancer."

"Why are you even here?"

"Cassandra, I had to be. I had to do everything I could to keep you alive. Not being here was not an option."

"Go home, now," I said, sounding bossier toward my uncle than I ever had. "Be with her. Tell her I love her and I'll call her soon."

I didn't say the words "I love you" often. Okay, almost never. Not even to Fred, my only living relative. And it caused him to do a double-take at me as he stood.

"I will. But we'll be here for the wedding, I promise."

After the two men left, we sat in silence. As the quiet settled in, so did my ability to stay awake, just as it had in the ambulance ride to the hospital.

My eyes opened as I heard the divider curtain slide on its track. I saw what appeared to be a young doctor, but as we spoke his age showed in his voice and his eyes. He quickly shuffled through the niceties and got down to business.

"Ms. Martin, when you came in Detective Hayes had concerns that you might have been drugged. So we ran a full blood workup and drug screen and something suspicious came to light."

"Like what?"

"The guy who kidnapped you gave you at least two, possibly three very large doses of Rohypnol." Edward walked to the window, looking as though he might jump out of it.

"Rohypnol, what's that?" I asked. It wasn't until then I realized my speech was slightly slurred and I wondered if it had been all along.

"It's a date rape drug. I think the detective knew even before we ran the test. We've had a few cases reported recently and your symptoms matched the other victims. The thing is ... the amount that is still in your body right now should kill you."

"The test must be wrong because I'm not dead," I spoke slowly in hopes of sounding less drunk, but I was not sure if I succeeded.

"We ran it three times. Trust me, it's right. I'm afraid to let you leave until your tox screen levels come back closer to normal. Also, you're extremely dehydrated. I'd like to give you some IV fluids. My guess is you weren't given anything to eat or drink by your kidnapper."

"I don't remember."

"It is possible that you may never remember what happened. But, Ms. Martin, because of the nature and use of this drug, while you're here we'd like to run, well, some other tests." The doctor hesitated saying the words rape kit and chose the words "other tests" as he looked at Edward.

The thought of Tony raping me was sickening. I felt a knot in my stomach form as the list of repercussions of this violent behavior grew in my mind. STDs, HIV, pregnancy. As much as I wanted a child, there was no way I could live with that means of conception. I was certain Edward couldn't either.

"I understand." I looked at Edward who was still staring out the window. The thought of another man forcing himself on me, whether I remembered it happening or not, was torture for him and the evidence showed in his actions.

"How long do I have to stay here?"

"I'm not sure yet. Probably a day or two to get the Rohypnol out of your system. The tests will only take a few minutes."

"You have until nine o'clock tonight and then I'm going home," I said. "The only thing wrong with me is a splitting headache and sore muscles."

"Cassandra," Edward walked away from the window and stood next to me. "Just for today, promise you'll follow the doctor's orders. I couldn't bear the thought of something else happening to you. I think it'd kill me."

The doctor looked at Edward, then me, and shook his head. "Mr. Baker warned me you'd fight me on this. Why don't we see how things look at about eight o'clock tonight? You're likely to have more withdrawal symptoms before you're done and I want to make certain you come through this all right. We'll decide about going home later tonight."

"Fine." I figured I'd let the men in the room think whatever they wanted. I already knew where I was sleeping tonight and their overly precautionary state irritated me.

Edward made arrangements to get me out of the ER into a private room. The hospital was only half full and I think they were glad to let him spend the money, even if only for the day.

The relief of being wheeled away from the ER was indescribable. The noise level in that department, which was probably no louder than usual, increased the feeling of being stabbed in the head by tiny daggers. The relative quiet of the solitary room alleviated the pain to that of a slow pounding.

Much to Edward's dismay, I kicked him out of the room long enough for him to get some lunch and for the nurses to perform the rape kit tests. The nurses and I found it odd, that at some point, Tony had randomly drawn lines with a black marker on my body. One of the nurses documented it by taking photographs before helping me get a shower. Once I was scrubbed, dressed, and back in bed, one of the nurses hooked up an IV.

A short time later, the doctor came in to check on me. As he looked over my file, I felt compelled to ask a favor of him.

"Doctor, I need you to do something for me."

"What is it, Ms. Martin?"

"I don't want my fiancé, Mr. Baker, to know the results of the rape kit if it's positive. You can tell him if it's negative, but if it isn't I don't want him to know. Lie if you have to."

"Ms. Martin, I can't tell him anything you want to be kept private. It's the law."

I should have been relieved by this information but instead, my chest began to tighten, making it hard to breathe. The doctor noticed my distress.

"Are you feeling anxious?"

"Yes. No. I don't know. I'm not sure. What's going on? Why am I in a hospital?"

The doctor looked at the monitors and then at me. "Miss Martin, your blood pressure's spiking. I want you to take some deep breaths."

I did as the doctor advised but was unsure as to how much it helped.

"Don't panic. This is just a side effect of the Rohypnol. You're probably going to feel like this while you're withdrawing from it."

"Withdrawal from what?" I said, not remembering anything that happened over the last few days. A tsunami of panic tore through me. I needed to see someone I knew, someone I loved. "Where's Edward?"

The doctor calmly re-explained everything that was happening to me and that I sent Edward to get some lunch from the cafeteria. As he did, I took deep breaths and tried to relax. I asked him questions, probably the same ones I asked before, and he patiently answered each one.

As we spoke, my blood pressure returned to normal and I felt myself returning to a calmer state. Clarity found me once again and I remembered everything from the ER. It was not long before the nurse came in with the test results. The doctor read them and then silently handed them to me. Before I looked at the results from the rape kit, I braced myself mentally for the worst, and then carefully examined the paper where the doctor circled various facts. As I read, a sense of relief swept over me. I was fairly certain Tony had not raped me, but the power of suggestion caused me to second guess how well I knew him. He never wanted me, even when I was his, and the test results proved nothing had changed in that regard.

As I handed the paper back to the doctor, Edward returned.

"What's the paper?" he asked as he stood in the doorway, waiting for the doctor's permission to enter.

"The results of the tests," I said as I waved Edward into the room. The thought of this was a nightmare for him. Fortunately, I was going to tell him what he wanted to hear. "They were negative."

"Really?" he said, slowly and deliberately as though he was unsure of my honesty.

"Of course they were. Or did you forget that Tony is gay?"

Edward stared into my eyes for a moment as though he was trying to read my mind. Then he wrinkled his brow and turned to say something to the doctor, who had left the room before Edward could speak. He turned back to me. "Sweetie, you said *is.* You do understand that Tony's dead?"

Chapter Twenty-Two

After lunch, which consisted of some non-descript soup, a hard roll, Jell-O, and instant tea; I drifted off to sleep and was glad to do so. It felt like someone shoved my brain into a blender. Not only did I still have the worst headache ever, but I had several episodes of confusion with only brief moments of clarity in between.

Every hour someone would come in, wake me up, and draw blood. The doctor was afraid to let me sleep any longer than an hour at a time, fearing what could potentially happen. Every time I opened my eyes, someone new was in the room. It was a strange "Alice in Wonderland" kind of experience for me. Once they arrived, they refused to leave.

Edward had not left my side and Vivian showed up with Henry almost immediately after lunch. Zoe closed up the shop early and was there by mid-afternoon. Alex and Libby-Mae cut out of work early and rode into town together. Kelly drove down from D.C.

later in the day to bring Edward some papers and Brian returned when his shift was over. The most unexpected visitors, though, were Michael and Sarah. I was surprised Sarah had bothered and wondered if there was something worth salvaging between us after all.

Apparently, most of them felt guilty and thought the kidnapping was somehow their fault. Edward felt he failed to protect me, Henry and Zoe talked me into going out when I had wanted to stay home, and Alex watched me walk toward the bathroom, never realizing something was wrong. Brian was feeling guilty for not overriding my decision not to have Tony's restraining order enforced. Everyone felt that if they had acted differently, none of this would have happened.

As far as Edward was concerned, he was the most guilty of all. He thought he should have been more persistent about leaving when I first felt bad. He should not have let me drink anything Tony offered me. He should have stayed home with me in the first place.

Around six o'clock, the nurses changed shifts and my new one came in to check on me. She had fire engine red hair.

"Good Lord, what a party! Good thing I was invited." She walked in and gave Henry a kiss on the cheek and Vivian a hug. The nurse's name was Yolanda Harris. She had been Henry's mother-in-law until the recent death of Yolanda's daughter, Darla. The first few weeks after Darla's death were hard for her, but she never blamed the Baker Family. If anything it brought us all closer together.

"Cassandra, I must say, you can find more trouble than anyone I've ever met," Yolanda said.

"I know. It just seems to find me. Trust me, I don't go looking for it."

"Good. Now I'll be back in about ten minutes to take some blood. I'm supposed to call in the results to the doctor. I'm guessing you want to go home tonight?"

"I am going home tonight." There was no way I was spending the night in the hospital. I wanted to be at home in my own soft, warm bed.

"Sweetie, we talked about this," Edward said. "You're going to do what the doctor says. You promised."

"No, you asked me to promise. I never did."

"Damn it, Cassie!" He pounded the edge of the bed with both fists as he stood. "Why do you have to make this so hard?"

His voice echoed through the room and the others went silent. No one had ever heard Edward yell at me, let alone swear at me. I had heard him raise his voice to me one other time. But when I looked at him, I knew he was overly frustrated, stressed, and exhausted. He was feeling very passionate about the situation too, as he usually only called me Cassie during intensely passionate moments. Most were under very different circumstances requiring little or no clothing and absolutely no audience.

"Okay," I said quietly in hopes of calming Edward.

"Okay?" He repeated as he returned to his seat, already sounding more serene. He took my hand and pressed it between his.

"Okay, I promise, I'll do what the doctor tells me to do. But you don't get to talk him into keeping me either like you tried to do the day of your dad's funeral."

Edward let out a deep sigh, "Fine, I'll play fair if you do."

Vivian looked at me and smiled. "Unbelievable. Someone who can actually keep my son in line. You never cease to amaze me, my dear."

As she spoke, Yolanda came in to draw blood and a short, plump lady followed her in with my dinner. I looked at my audience. I guessed they were hungry too. Plus, I desperately needed a break from all of these people standing around, waiting for something to happen.

"Why don't all of you go over to the new Italian place and get some dinner?" I suggested. "It's just across the street."

"I'm not leaving you," Edward said. His hovering was driving me crazy, and as much as I loved him, I needed a break from it. I needed a plan but was in no shape to come up with anything elaborate. The only thing I could think of was food.

"But I want a cannoli or two from there, like the ones we had the other night. They were so good." I bit my bottom lip, raised an eyebrow, and then gave him the sexiest smile I could dream up in my condition. "Will you get some for me while you grab a bite? The doctor said I can eat anything I want."

He leaned over and whispered in my ear. "You're not playing fair, my love. The look on your face makes me want to make love to you right here, right now." Edward pressed his warm sweet mouth against mine and I wanted to be home, alone in bed with him. I wanted to be married to him. I wanted to have his babies. And I wanted it all in that instant.

Edward stood and announced, "Okay, looks like I'm buying everybody dinner and my wife dessert. Let's go."

Everyone said their goodbyes and headed out the door. Only Michael remained.

"Aren't you going to get some dinner with the others?"

"I'm not hungry," he said. "Do you mind if I stay?"

"As long as you don't mind that I'm going to eat."

Michael sat in the spot previously occupied by Edward while I ate. I gave him the remote to the television and he stole stale tortilla chips off my plate as he flipped through the channels, settling on ESPN's college football highlights with the sound muted until I was done eating.

"I hope they don't all come back from dinner. I know everyone is worried, but I'm feeling a little smothered."

Michael glared at me as if I were being an ungrateful toddler. "Cassandra, do you have a clue what we've been through the last couple of nights?"

I thought about it for a long minute. Everyone must have been panicked, mortified. They must have been searching everywhere. I, however, had been unconscious and completely unaware of what was going on. I was being inconsiderate and immediately felt guilty. "I hadn't really thought about it until just now. Will you tell me?"

He turned off the television. "Once it was realized you were missing, the police sent out an A.P.B. Then Edward made a call and within an hour there was a breaking-news report about your disappearance and the connection Tony had. That's when Sarah called me and we rode down together. By sunrise, search parties were out patrolling the woods and fields when Edward got the call from Tony."

"What call?" I asked.

His expression turned from that of focused news reporter to that of utter disbelief. "You really don't remember anything, do you?"

"I barely remember calling 911 this morning. Why would I know about this call?"

Michael sat, staring at me with his mouth open in amazement. "Tony called Edward. Told him he wanted fifty million dollars or you'd be dead within a day. Edward was worried you were already dead, so Tony made you talk to him."

"What did I say?"

"Edward wouldn't tell us, but whatever it was nearly killed him." I wondered what I could have said that upset Edward so much. I would never say anything to purposely hurt him. I knew I would have to find out what I said to Edward as soon as we were alone and apologize for whatever it was that upset him.

"Then what?"

"When Edward was a little calmer, he called some people, went to the bank. And before you ask, yeah, they opened for him on a Sunday. He then returned to Thomas Hall and did a sweep of the vineyard, even though the rain was coming down in buckets. He wouldn't let anyone go with him though. He said he had to do it alone."

"And everyone else?"

"They were following every lead that came in. When your clothes were found in the woods off of Northumberland Highway, Edward went out there himself, just to make sure they were yours."

"And they were." I said, half asking, half stating a fact.

"Yep, then it was dark. No one had slept in over thirty-six hours. We were all exhausted and the rain was turning to sleet and fog. So we met back at Thomas Hall to eat, shower, and sleep. When we woke up a few hours later, Brian, Fred, and Edward were gone and you were here."

"Wow."

"Yeah," he said.

We sat in silence while I tried to digest everything. But in the back of my mind, one question kept popping up. Strangely though, it wasn't from the kidnapping. It was from the first day Tony showed up at Thomas Hall.

"Michael, how did you find out I was in prison?"

"I was wondering if you'd ever ask. Remember my friend from college, Andrew Forlin, the linguist?" I nodded and he continued. "He works at the Chinese Embassy in D.C. About a week after your arrest, he called me and said we needed to have lunch together, as soon as possible. The next day, we sat outside at that great bistro Sarah took you to in September, and he told me an American had been arrested in the Tibetan region of China and he thought it was someone I knew. When he pulled out your picture, I thought I was seeing things. I mean, you were the last person I expected to see on that piece of paper."

I smiled. "I guess so."

"I never understood exactly why you were arrested."

"Visa mix up. I got my visa at the embassy in Moscow and the lady who wrote out my papers must have misunderstood me. My Russian really isn't what it should be. Anyway, I told her I wanted a business visa so I could stay in the country for more than a month, but she issued me a thirty-day visa instead. Since I can't read Chinese, I didn't notice the error. It wasn't until a guard asked for my papers after they had expired that I realized there was a problem and I was arrested. What happened next at your end?"

"Andrew put me in touch with an attorney who specializes in U.S. citizen arrests in China. I paid him his retainer and he told me that we could go through the country's judicial system or I could just pay off the judge and buy your way out. I chose the latter."

"Speaking of money, did you get the check?"

"Yeah, but I didn't expect you to pay me back. The money wasn't important, you were. You still are." I didn't know what to say. Ever since I learned about Michael's feelings for me, I found myself second-guessing everything I said to him. "I wish you'd talk to me."

"I just want things to be the way they were after Crush Weekend, before Tony came back. But I don't know if that's possible."

"Can we try? I wasted too many years pretendin' to be mad at you. I don't want to waste any more time."

"You're right, we should try, but you know, I think things might be beyond repair between Sarah and me."

"Actually, I don't know what terms you two are on," he said. "She was in the process of moving out the night you called."

"I'm so sorry. But you haven't talked to her at all? That must be awkward. How are you two going to work together?"

"She quit her job at my dad's accounting firm the same day."

"And this is the reason why." Sarah stood in the doorway with her arms crossed in front of her, eyes narrowed and focused on me. "The thought of you being in love with her while you were married to me is just more than I can handle, from either of you."

"Wait a minute! I didn't even know. How can you blame me for this?" I could hear the heart monitor attached to me beep faster and louder. I took a deep breath in hopes of calming myself, but it didn't work.

"It doesn't matter. She's leaving," Edward said as he walked past her and stood next to Michael, and glared at Sarah. "I don't want you upsetting her."

"Is this what you want?" she said, looking at me. "I hope so because it's what you're getting. Goodbye C.C." And she turned around and walked out of the room. I knew it would be the last time I would see her for a long time, possibly ever.

I was not discharged from the hospital until Tuesday afternoon. I promised Edward I would follow the doctor's orders and I did. He stayed with me Monday night, although I asked him to go home and get some rest. First thing Tuesday morning Henry and Zoe came by with breakfast for Edward and clothes for me. Before we headed home I asked Edward to stop at the police station. There were two problems I needed to address, neither of which Edward had any knowledge.

When we walked in Brian smiled. "Missing something?"

"Something I hope you found in the motel room."

Brian opened his desk drawer, pulled out an evidence envelope, and handed it to me. When I opened it, I breathed a sigh of relief. I pulled my engagement ring from it and slid it back onto my finger.

"Does it have to stay here as evidence?" I asked, not wanting to part from Edward's token of love for me.

"No," Brian replied. "I talked to the police chief and we both agreed that there is no reason we need to hold on to it."

Edward picked up my left hand and held it. "You should have told me it was missing. I just assumed you didn't have it on when we went to Lucky Shots."

"I always wear it. Why wouldn't I?"

Brian knew Edward didn't want to talk about the things that had transpired between us, so he changed the subject. "I haven't got the autopsy report for Tony yet, but I'll call you when I do."

"Why would you call me?" I asked.

"Technically, you were his next-of-kin at the time of his death."

I stared at the ceiling panels and swallowed hard contemplating the thought that was plastered to my brain all morning.

"What is it, Cassandra?" Brian asked.

"Is it possible, I mean is there any way I could have killed Tony?"

I dropped my head to look at the two men whom both adored me. They both looked confounded that I thought I was capable of doing such a thing.

"I don't see how you could have," Brian said confidently. "First, when I arrived, he was dead and you were tied to the bed."

"You said first. Is there a second?" I asked.

Edward answered for him and Brian nodded in agreement as he spoke. "I just don't think you have it in you to kill someone, even Tony."

"But Brian, you said it yourself, everyone has their limits. What if I hit mine?"

"I don't think so, but I am trying to get a list of suspects together. Anyone you know who might want to see him dead?"

"Yeah, everybody. You want a list?" I was joking about the list but Brian pulled out a pen and waited for me to begin.

"Well, the obvious, me and Edward. My Uncle Fred, Sarah, Michael—"

"Why would any of them want him dead?" Brian asked.

"Tony spilled a big secret of Sarah's," Edward said. "Fred and Michael's reasons are a bit different."

"How so?"

It was less than a second before I realized I was going to have to tell Brian everything. "Apparently Michael has had a thing for me for years."

"I'm sure several men have," Brian said, smiling. Edward just glared at Brian. "But Michael found out how Tony treated me when we were married, so did Fred." I knew what the next question would be and really did not want to tell Brian this piece of my past. When I looked up, Brian's eyes were brimming with anger. He had already figured out the answer to the question he was about to ask anyway.

"Exactly, what did he do to you while you were married?" He spoke slowly, trying to reign in his emotions.

I looked back at the linoleum-tiled floor, counting the black specks that were randomly mixed into the cream-colored squares. I took a moment and disconnected myself emotionally from what I needed to say. It was a hard thing to do, but I could manage it for brief moments of time, as long as I stayed focused. "He broke my nose once, I had the occasional black eye, and a rib got cracked every now and then. But the worst was probably the dislocated—"

"Enough." I looked at Brian. His face was ashen. His voice was still soft, but breaking up as he spoke. "It's a good thing he was dead before I found out, or I'd be on the suspect list, too. But Cassandra, what in the world …? How in the world did you let that happen to you? You're smarter than that."

"That's what everybody keeps telling me."

Chapter Twenty-Three

As I stepped into the bedroom from the steamy shower I caught Edward watching me from bed. A contented smile sat easily on his face as he watched me dress in a burgundy wrap dress, stockings, and black heels. Most women would have chosen to wear tights over stockings considering the cold windy weather, but I had grown comfortable wearing silk stockings and did regularly. I was even considering getting rid of any pantyhose or tights I owned as I rarely bothered wearing them anymore. As I tied the dress and began brushing out my hair, Edward cleared his throat.

"That's a beautiful dress, but isn't it a bit much for the production rooms. Big meeting today?"

"No, I want to be at the courthouse around nine." I pulled my still damp hair up with a single clip as we spoke, thinking I might let it down later. "You want to come?"

"Sweetie, you don't have to go. Tony's dead, remember? A divorce is not necessary now."

"I know, but I need to pick up a copy of his real death certificate. If you come with me we could get a valid marriage license while we're there. Edward, if we're going to get married next weekend, I want it to be legal."

"You still want to marry me?" He sounded surprised at the idea. "Even after I didn't tell you about Tony?"

It was only then I realized I never told him about the conclusions I arrived at the night before my kidnapping. I decided not to tell him. I figured when the dust had settled from all the craziness, I'd explain everything to him. The only thing he needed to know was that he was out of the doghouse.

I sat next to him on the bed and put the back of my hand on his unshaven cheek. "Honey, did I ever give you the impression I wasn't going to marry you?"

"Well, you did kick me out of bed and you seemed determined to postpone things."

"I'm sorry if that's what you thought. I was just trying to be realistic with the wedding. I know I probably shouldn't have kicked you out of bed last week, but I didn't intend for it to be forever. I guess with everything that's happened over the last few days, it all stretched out longer than it should have. I'm sorry if you got the idea I wasn't—"

He sat up, leaned in and kissed me. It was intoxicating and I felt as though my insides were doing somersaults. The thought of crawling back into bed became very tempting. I wanted to be naked, wrapped around him like a bow on a Christmas present.

He pulled his lips away from mine and I tugged on his bottom lip, holding it gingerly with my teeth before letting go.

"Why don't we go to City Hall, get all this paperwork straight, and then see where that kiss goes." he said, smiling.

I walked to the dresser to retrieve the necklace I planned to wear. As I did, I decided to ask Edward one last time about a topic of constant conversation already knowing the answer I would get. "I guess there's no chance of you signing the prenup so we can get it filed at the same time."

"Why is that so insanely important to you?" His annoyance of the whole idea was in his voice.

"I told you, I'm just trying to protect—"

"No, Sweetie, the real reason. There's something you're not telling me. I know you're holding back, I just don't know why."

I felt like a kid who just got caught cheating on a test. My face was hot and my stomach churned. I looked away from him before answering. "This is going to sound stupid, I know it is. But I don't want people to think I'm marrying you for your money. I don't like being called a gold digger, even behind my back."

He went into the living room, quickly returning with the papers. He opened his nightstand drawer, retrieved a pen, and signed them. When he handed them to me, he gently rested his hand on my cheek just under the spot where a faint bruise had risen to the surface. I did not know how I had gotten it, but could only imagine it had been caused by Tony.

"Why didn't you just say so in the first place?" His voice was soft and calm.

"Because I know it shouldn't matter what other people think. But it does to me, at least where you're concerned."

Less than two hours later Edward and I walked out of the courthouse into the blinding sunlight and cold breeze. We hurried down the steps of the courthouse toward the limo when my cell phone rang.

"Cassandra Martin," I said.

"Hey, it's Brian. How ya doin'?"

"Better today, what's up?"

"I just read Tony's coroner's report and I think you're gonna want to see this. You want me to bring it out to Thomas Hall?"

"You could, but I'm standing in front of the courthouse." I looked over and watched as he lifted the blinds in his office and waved to us. I waved back. "I could just come get it."

"Sounds like a plan. I'll go make a copy of it right now."

We walked across the street and the officer at the front desk waved us through while listening to an elderly lady complain about the high school kids cutting through her back yard after the football games. We walked down the hall into Brian's empty office. I had just taken a seat when Brian walked in behind us.

"Happy Thanksgiving. Sorry it took me so long. The copy machine ran out of toner." I stood up and hugged him. He held me for just a moment longer than he had in the past. I wasn't certain if it was because of his feelings for me, his new knowledge about my past, or some combination of the two. Edward made a faint grunting sound, disapproving of Brian's behavior, and stepped into his office.

"Happy Thanksgiving. Did the girls and your mom get back okay?" I asked.

"They're still in Pennsylvania. In what godforsaken place does it snow eleven inches in late November?" Brian laughed. "Look, I won't keep you. But I thought you might want to know what the coroner's report said. It came early this morning. I would have called you sooner, but I wanted to follow up on a couple of things."

He handed me a manila envelope. I opened it and slid the enclosed report out and scanned over the pages quickly.

"Poison?"

"Yep. Something he ingested. But not chemical."

"So, am I reading this right?" I asked. "Someone was slowly slipping a natural toxin in his food in order to kill him?"

"No. It was a one-time ingestion. That's what I was following up on. I tried to track down where Tony had been eating. It was something he would have eaten within seventy-two hours of his death." Brian took a seat on the corner of his desk before continuing. "He ate nearly every meal at either the Blue Star Diner or had something delivered from Main Street Pizza."

"The man did love his pizza," I said. "But it kind of wipes out your suspect list."

"Yeah, I've got all but about two meals accounted for. I was hoping you might know where else he ate or who he ate with."

"I was trying to steer clear of him, so I had no clue what he was doing for meals. The only place I can think of is Lucky Shots. Did he eat there?"

"I didn't even think about that. I'm not sure the timing's right but I'll call David Jett and ask if he ate anything that night, just to be sure."

"Besides that, I'm afraid I can't be of much help."

"There is one more person," Edward said. "Tony's grandfather, Poppy Scarpelli, saw him Saturday."

"As in the—"

"Yes, as in *that* Poppy Scarpelli," I said, having repeated that line one too many times recently. "But he didn't do it."

"Why would you say that?" Brian asked, looking at me like I was delusional.

"Because he would have told me if he had. It's the kind of man he is."

"Okay then," Brian said sarcastically.

"Actually, now that I think about it, she's right. After meeting him I could definitely see him being that way."

Brian swallowed hard. "You've met him?"

"He spent the night at Thomas Hall," Edward said. "Nice guy. You'd be surprised."

"Well, I'm not going down that road unless I have Scarpelli's fingerprints on the murder weapon and since that's not possible, I guess I'll take your advice and let it go."

We talked a few minutes longer and Brian thanked us for stopping by. As Edward and I left, I turned back one last time toward Brian.

"Hey," I said. "Why don't you join us for dinner tomorrow? No one should eat alone at Thanksgiving."

"Cassandra's right." Edward reluctantly agreed and I knew it was strictly for my benefit.

"Thanks, but I picked up a shift. When you're a cop, holidays equal double time and Christmas is coming."

"Well, at least stop by and we'll whip you up a plate to go." I said.

"Now that I can handle," he said with a smile.

We were making out in the back of the limo within seconds of beginning the fifteen-minute trip home from Willow Creek. Neither of us could keep our hands off each other and I was glad there was a divider between the driver and the backseat. Edward's hands were wedged between the seat and the back of my legs and he had managed to pull up my dress past the lower edge of my favorite lace panties. His lips were desperately searching for more bare skin at my breasts, a common occurrence when we were alone together. I could feel the intensity of Edward's rising passion as he ripped off my black silk undies.

"Edward! That was my favorite pair," I teased.

"Fine, I'll buy you the company." He was untying my dress as I slid his sports coat off and undid his tie. He pulled my dress back away from my body and immediately buried his head into my cleavage. As he did, I began to feel self-conscious of my surroundings.

"Edward, are we really going to do this here? Now?"

He stopped to growl his reply without looking up. "Problem?"

"It's just I've never done this anywhere quite like this."

He looked at me with a mischievous grin on his face, having made his way to my inner thigh with this mouth at lightning speed. "Sweetie, we have got to broaden your horizons." And without removing a single article of his own clothing, that's exactly what he did all the way home.

And he did not stop there. The moment the front door to our house was closed, I found myself naked and Edward undressing faster than I'd ever seen him move. By the time he stripped all our clothing off, he guided me into our bathroom, where he gently picked me up and sat me on the counter. "Before too long I will have made love to you in every room of this house."

"Every room?" As I asked, Edward put his strong hands on my waist, coaxing my hips to the edge of the counter. "That's a little, um, unconventional, isn't it?"

"Not in my world." His lips were forming a path of kisses up the side of my neck.

I started to respond, but he pressed his lips to mine, wiping away any comment I could have made. As I felt his warm hand slide up to my breasts I knew one thing was certain; he meant everything he had just said.

After a late dinner, I found myself in a bath full of bubbles, drinking Champagne with Edward. We had a lot to celebrate. Tony was dead, we were getting married, and I had the perfect wedding dress. Things were starting to fall into place.

As Edward refilled my champagne glass for the third or fourth time, I decided I needed to ask him about the phone call. I was originally going to wait until we were in bed before asking, but I was already feeling tipsy and worried I might not be coherent enough to ask later.

"Honey, Michael told me when Tony was holding me hostage that we talked on the phone." As I spoke, I watched the color drain from his face. "What did I say to you? I don't have any memory of it but I was given the impression it was quite upsetting."

"I won't tell you, Sweetie." Tears began to fill his eyes. I had never seen him cry before and wasn't sure I was prepared for it. His voice continued to drop in volume until it was barely above a whisper. "You don't want to know."

"I think I do."

"No, Cassie, you don't." He hopped off the counter where he had been seated and stepped into the tub, without bothering to take off the sleep pants he had on. He lowered himself to his knees, wrapped his arms around my bubble-coated body, and cradled the back of my head with one hand. He pulled me up to him kissing me as though it could be the most important moment of our lives.

"Not telling you what you said is my gift to you. I need you to trust me on this, okay?"

"Okay," I said quietly as though we were having a private conversation in a room full of people. For all the pain my words had caused him, he knew what I said would hurt me more.

I brushed my wet fingertips along his lips before wondering how I had ever been so lucky as to find a man who loved me so much.

"What?" Edward asked, knowing I was deep in thought.

"I love you."

Edward's lips were back on mine in less than a second. In the process of kissing, we began to splash bubbles over the edge of the tub and it made me laugh uncontrollably. Edward smiled as he watched me and when I had finally worked all the giggles out of my system he said, "Now this, here, now, ... this is something to be thankful for."

Chapter Twenty-Four

The main house overflowed with love and happiness. If this was Thanksgiving, I couldn't wait until Christmas. Vivian was in full holiday-event mode and her sisters were following her orders and fluttering about the house. Phoebe had come up the night before with the kids and Henry and Zoe were there as well. The only ones missing were Alex, Fred, and Molly. Alex was having dinner with his mother and her family. I missed his presence, along with Fred and Molly. They stayed in Florida, as Molly was due to have surgery first thing the next morning.

When we sat down at the table, I took a long look at the setting. It looked like a photo spread for Southern Living Magazine. Beautiful fall flowers were arranged in low circular vases along the length of the table and the linen tablecloth and matching napkins were the color of golden fall foliage. The silver was freshly polished at each place setting and I was glad my parents had taught me at an early age which fork to use for which course.

The meal was everything Thanksgiving should be and more. All the traditional favorites were there; turkey, stuffing, gravy, sweet potato casserole, and cranberry sauce. In addition, there were regional specialties as well; salt-cured ham, fried oysters, greens and stewed tomatoes. We all ate until we were so stuffed we could barely move. Then, after dinner, everyone retired to the sunroom for coffee and dessert.

Henry looked around with a sad smile as we silently ate. "You know, this would be about the time Dad would start telling us stories about Thanksgiving when he was a kid. Anybody want to tell one?"

"What about you, Aunt Cassie?" Noah asked, snuggling up next to me on the sofa. "What was Thanksgiving like when you were a kid?"

Noah was the younger of Phoebe's two children and he and I got along well. He was a miniature version of Edward. Whenever I knew the kids were going to be at the house, I tried to make sure there was something fun for them to do. Thomas Hall wasn't exactly kid-friendly, but I was doing my best to change that fact.

Edward's video game collection had grown in ways he would have never expected. Noah and I spent one rainy Saturday afternoon playing Super Mario Brothers and Pokémon while Edward caught up on some paperwork. My fiancé was a gamer and had been since he was a child. However, his tastes ran more towards games like Resident Evil and Call of Duty.

Edward was sitting on the opposite side of me and leaned over to get a better look at his nephew, peering at him from underneath his broad brow. "I don't think she likes to talk about her past too much. And who gave you permission to call her Cassie?"

"Aunt Cassie did. Right?"

"Yes, I did." I wrapped one arm around Noah as I spoke. "Let me think about what story to tell you while someone else goes first. How about that?"

"Viv, why don't you tell the poison mushroom story?" Virginia commented.

"Oh, no, not that one again," Phoebe said.

Norah looked up from the floor where she was sprawled out reading. "I like that one. Who wouldn't want to be an only child?"

"Now you've got to tell me the story," I said. "I'm curious what mushrooms have to do with being an only child."

Vivian smiled and shook her head from side to side and the twins began to giggle. "Now you have to understand," Vivian said. "I was an only child for six years before the twins were born. So I wasn't crazy about having two toddlers following me around. Anyway, when I was little my dad used to take me on long nature hikes. He loved the outdoors and everything about it. The weather, terrain, animals, everything. He had a special love of plants. He knew the scientific name and common name of every plant in Virginia. When we went on our walks, he pointed out all the edible plants as well as the poisonous ones."

"Yeah, and you obviously paid so much attention," Violet said sarcastically.

Vivian ignored her and continued. "Anyway, the Thanksgiving the twins were two, I decided I wanted to be an only child again.

So when we were playing in the fields, I convinced the twins we needed to have a snack. I had them pick mushrooms from the forest's edge and we rinsed them under the garden pump. Then I got a blanket and spread it out so the three of us could have a picnic. I made three piles of mushrooms for us and pretended to eat mine while the twins gobbled up theirs."

"How did you get two year-olds to eat wild mushrooms?" I asked.

"Oh, I told them they were magic, chocolate flowers. The girls were just finishing their 'flowers' when my mom came out to see why I had gotten a blanket from the house. Well, she was mortified to see the girls finishing off the end of the mushrooms. Like me, she knew the forest on our property was covered with poisonous mushrooms."

"Oh Viv, you didn't?"

Henry laughed. "Oh yes, she did. Now you know why we don't let her cook."

Everyone joined Henry in his laughter, except Violet. "Sure, you can laugh. Your first childhood memory of Thanksgiving isn't having your stomach pumped only to have the doctor discover the mushrooms you ate *weren't* poisonous."

"Yep," Vivian said. "I fed them the wrong mushrooms. I was so upset with myself for failing that I immediately began reading every botany book in the house."

"Until Mom and Dad sent you off to boarding school when you were ten," Virginia said.

"Ah, but it got me away from the two terrible toddlers. Who I am very glad were not poisoned at age two." She reached over and patted Virginia's arm.

"You were lucky Vivian," I said, shaking my head.

"Yes I was, but now I know the difference between every poisonous and non-poisonous plant in Virginia."

"Grandma," Norah said. "Will you teach me? I think I might like to be an only child."

Norah was joking. At least I thought she was. She had a dark, brooding sense of humor that matched her personality. Phoebe worried about her daughter. During her recent divorce from the children's father, Norah had taken to wearing all black and referring to everything as stupid, including me, but only behind my back. Still, Phoebe forced her to apologize to my face every time she said it. I continued to try to get on her good side with very limited success. We both liked to read, so that was the common thread I tried to build from. I don't think the problem was me though, at least not directly. Edward and Norah were very close and she seemed threatened by my presence. Until I came along, Edward never brought a date to family events. He always claimed Norah as his date for the evening, but my arrival into her world changed all of that so I tried not to take it personally.

"No," Phoebe said with an authoritative tone. "She will not teach you a thing about botany young lady and you will not be an only child."

"Aunt Cassie's lucky," Norah continued, unknowing. "She doesn't have a younger brother. Brothers are so stupid."

Edward, who was mortified, looked to me for a reaction. But, I did something for the second time in a month that I hadn't been able to do in a decade. "You're right, brothers can be stupid. I had an older brother and you wouldn't believe some of the stupid stuff he did."

"Had?" Henry asked, unaware I had any siblings. This was a fact Edward had chosen to keep to himself.

"Lewis died when I was fifteen." Norah sat up, looked at me, then her brother. "But talking about stupid brothers, I just figured out what story to tell you, Noah."

"Is it a 'brothers are stupid' story?" Noah asked. "'Cause I don't wanna hear one of those."

"No, not exactly. More like a 'brothers are weird' story." Norah laughed out loud, which was something I'd never heard her do.

Edward leaned into me and whispered, "You don't have to do this."

"I'm fine," I said. Then I told them the story of the concussion Lewis got during a football game the day before Thanksgiving, and how he was convinced in his delusional state that I was the Tooth Fairy. I'm not the best story teller, but everyone in the room seemed to enjoy it and even laughed when I told them the part about Lewis insisting I was hiding wings under my dress. I had never told anyone that story, and the memories of my brother and I as children, for the first time in my adult life, brought me joy. By the time I was finished, Norah was leaned against the sofa with her arms wrapped around her brother's legs.

That night, I sat in bed next to Edward and read Tony's coroner's report again. Poison. Someone had intentionally poisoned his food with an organic substance. All but two of his meals were at the same places. They were public restaurants. If it had been something unknown in the food, dozens of people would have died, not just him. Where else would Tony have eaten?

Oh my God! I thought to myself, but managed not to say out loud. Meals. Poison. Organics. I knew who killed Antonio Martin.

I looked at Edward, wondering if I should say anything to him. At first I was certain I should. But the more I thought about it, the more I decided I would talk to this person first. I must have been in really deep thought because I snapped back to where I was as I heard Edward say something his brother said to me frequently, "Earth to Cassandra. Come in, Cassandra."

"Sorry, I was just thinking." He looked down at what I was reading.

"Trying to figure out who killed Tony?"

"I guess."

"I'm surprised you even care," he said, with genuine curiosity.

"Edward, we were together a long time. I even loved him more than life itself at one point. When you love someone like that, no matter how vile they turn out to be, you always care, at least a little. Whether you want to or not."

Chapter Twenty-Five

Sometimes the simplest mistake, like picking up the wrong piece of paper, can have unimaginable consequences. Edward left earlier in the day to go Christmas shopping with his brothers and I was preparing to head to Evergreen Funeral Home. Poppy called me that morning and asked if I could pick up Tony's cremated remains and bring them to Thomas Hall. There was someone en route to get them, but a snow delay at Chicago's O'Hare Airport would have his courier arriving after the funeral home closed for the night.

At the last second, I decided to grab Tony's death certificate in case I needed it and glanced at it as I made my way to the door. As I reached the threshold, I noticed the date and realized I grabbed the wrong one. I walked back and picked up the other death certificate, laying it on top of the one already in my hand. I examined the new certificate and then the old one once more.

"No way," I muttered to myself. I picked up my phone and dialed Brian. His phone went straight to voicemail.

"Brian, call me when you get this message. Something weird is going on. Tony's death certificate was signed by the same coroner both times. And that's how he faked his death the last time. He paid off the coroner. Something's not right. Anyway, I've got to run into town and pick up Tony's remains from the funeral home for his grandfather. Call me." As I hung up the phone, I wondered if I was making a mountain out of a molehill.

When I opened the funeral home door, the brass bell, which hung over the entrance, rang. I walked to the counter and set my purse and keys on top of it. A petite man with feminine features came out of a back door labeled employees only and stepped onto a stool behind the counter in order to meet me.

The moment I made visual contact with him, I felt as though someone had tied my stomach into a square knot. This was the same man who handled Tony's remains the first time around. This was no coincidence. First the death certificate and now this. I was feeling better about my decision to call Brian before leaving Thomas Hall with each passing second. Now I just had to get out of this place with the hope he did not recognize me.

"You must be Ms. Martin. I'm Mr. Kerber."

"Yes sir, I got a call that Tony Martin's remains were ready to be picked up."

When I began to speak, Mr. Kerber's eyes widened and I knew he had made the connection. I kept telling myself to stay calm even though I was feeling far from it. I began to retrieve my checkbook from my purse as he began to speak.

"Of course, Mrs. Martin." He pulled out a clipboard and looked it over. "It appears the bill has already been settled by a Mr. P. Scarpelli."

"Oh, very well then," I said, returning my checkbook to my purse. I wasn't aware that Poppy had settled the bill, but it was the least of my concerns.

"Well," he said. "Why don't you follow me to the back to get his urn, and I'll put it in your car for you."

I found it odd that he asked me to follow him but I was in no position to argue. The sooner I had the urn in my possession, the sooner I could get out of the building and go to the police station.

We made our way down a wide corridor with doors on both sides. Each door had an electronic key pad designed to keep out intruders without the proper code. I had never been behind the scenes of a funeral home before, but the security for the doors seemed extreme. At the end of the hall was a cinderblock wall with an emergency exit and circuit breaker box.

At the last door on the left, Mr. Kerber stopped, punched in a four digit code, and opened the door. He held it open for me and as I walked into the darkened room, I felt a chill as I heard the door slam shut behind me.

I tried the handle. The door was locked from the outside. I looked through the port-hole-sized window and Mr. Kerber was looking up at me from the hallway side of the door.

"Hey, let me out of here!"

"I don't think so lady. You know too much."

"What are you talking about?" I asked, pretending to be clueless. "I just came to pick up the urn."

"Don't play dumb with me. I know you recognize me. I never thought we'd run into anyone in this ass-backward hick town that we'd scammed before. You'll be staying in there for a while until I figure out what to do with you." He walked away, leaving me in the cold and dark, with only the light from the door's window to guide me.

I could not see anything but an empty hallway through the window, so I pressed my ear to the metal door. I could faintly hear the funeral home director on the phone. I couldn't make out what he was saying, but he was yelling.

I was getting colder by the minute and when I turned around to check out my surroundings I knew why. I was standing in a walk-in cooler. Why Mr. Kerber had put me in the cooler room, I had no idea. One thing was certain though, I needed to find some way to keep warm, and I needed to do it fast as I left my coat, along with my cell phone, lying in the front seat of my car.

I looked around only to find gurneys of body bags. Full body bags. There were at least two dozen bodies in the room with me. Willow Oak was a small town. It was a busy week for the funeral home if more than two obituaries were in the Herald on any given Thursday. Where had all these corpses come from?

As morbid as it was, I prayed one of the bodies was dressed. I was shivering and the slacks and cotton blouse I was wearing wouldn't be enough to keep me from developing hypothermia. I unzipped the first bag in hopes of finding a body still dressed. However, inside was a male teenager, maybe seventeen, naked with surgical incisions. There was something about the incisions that bothered me, but I couldn't put my finger on what it was so I zipped the bag back up and moved on to the next body.

Next was a woman, also naked and in her mid-thirties. I remembered hearing about her. She had been driving drunk and wrapped her car around a pole. Someone told me she was the vice-president of the PTA. A mom with three kids. I wondered how someone with so much to lose could do something so foolish.

When I opened the next bag, the arm of a teenage girl fell out. When I saw her face I knew who it was. It was one of the teenagers that had recently gone missing; Juliet of the Romeo and Juliet teenagers. Luckily, she was small enough that I was able to drag her body bag over toward the door to get a better view. Light from the window showed she was naked and her body had been sliced up like a Thanksgiving turkey. The incisions were in the same place as the male teenager and I could see where organs had been removed from her body. I lowered myself to the icy floor as I felt a wave of nausea come over me. It was all falling into place. The surgical equipment and cooler in the motel room, the weird marker lines on my body. Tony had intended on using me as an organ farm. I had always assumed that black market organs were an urban myth, like alligators living in the New York sewers, but there was obviously some truth to it. Tony just hadn't lived long enough to execute his plan.

I could faintly hear sounds outside the door but knew what they were and after I stood and peered out the window my suspicions were confirmed. It was the gulping of liquid leaving a gas container and splattering across the floor. Mr. Kerber was about to torch the place. I watched as he poured gasoline down the hall and propped open the back door. He then began splashing the flammable liquid along the back wall of the building as he moved out of view.

No sooner had I watched Mr. Kerber leave did Edward's face appear across from me in the glass.

"Cassandra? Thank God. Are you okay?"

"Be careful, the floor's covered in gasoline. The director's getting ready to torch the place. You've got to get out of here now."

Edward pulled on the door but the electronic locks held tight. "I'm not leaving here without you!"

"The only way out is to disable the locks. If you kill the electricity it might unlock the doors."

He looked around frantically. As he did, smoke began to pour through the door and down the hallway. "How?"

"The circuit box." As soon as I said it, I remembered seeing it as Mr. Kerber and I walked down the hall. "It's on the back wall."

The flames grew higher and Edward began to choke on the smoke-filled air as he moved toward the wall. Less than a minute later, he was back in front of the door.

"I can't get to it."

"Then get out of the building. I'm safe in here. I'm trapped but the smoke and fire can't get in." For that moment, the statement was true, but for how long I wasn't sure.

"I'm not leaving you again."

"Edward, don't be foolish. You could die and I couldn't live with that kind of guilt...." I stopped mid-sentence as I watched the flames turn the corner and come into view.

When the fire hit the circuit box it created a pyrotechnic display. The room went black and I heard every electronic sound cease. I looked through the window at Edward and simultaneously, we both reached for the handle and the door opened. Along with an escape route, the open door created a wall of smoke that filled the room.

I spun in a circle, disoriented by the smoke, and then felt the panic freeze my legs into place. The smoke-filled my lungs and the sensation of drowning overwhelmed me. The room seemed brighter and I felt certain the flames were edging closer, but I stood, unable to move. I tried to inhale once more, but there was no air. Then a pair of hands reached around my waist and my feet left the floor. I knew whose hands were holding me. Edward scooped me up from the refrigerated room and out the front door so quickly I was barely aware we had moved. It wasn't until I sat on the curb across the street and fresh air filled my lungs, that I looked around and realized what was going on.

The fire trucks had already unloaded their hoses and were spraying the back of the building. The outside was in flames and the inside was rapidly following suit. A firefighter raced passed me and I touched his ankle. He bent down and I was surprised to see myself face to face with Libby-Mae's uncle, David Jett. I had a flash of déjà vu before I spoke.

"Dave?" I paused to cough before continuing. "Bodies in the frig. Shouldn't be there. Missing people." I knew he did not understand everything I said, but he understood the significance of my words. He stood and turned to another firefighter.

"There's a bunch of bodies in there. We gotta get 'em out." Then he disappeared into a pack of others wearing the same yellow gear.

As David walked away, Brian bent down so he was eye level with both Edward and me.

"You two okay?" We both nodded our heads and he turned to Edward. "I picked up Kerber just as he was backing out of here. We've already picked up his wife at the hospital and taken her to the station. She's talking like there's no tomorrow. You'll explain it all to Cassandra?"

"Yeah." His voice was as harsh as sandpaper from the smoke he inhaled. "I'll tell her."

Brian reached out and put his hand under my chin. "Will you do me a favor? Try to go at least a week before you get yourself killed again. I haven't finished the paperwork from the last time yet."

I tried to laugh but found myself coughing instead. The paramedic walked over with a large box in hand. I watched as she wrapped a blood pressure cuff around my arm, but when I looked back at Brian, he was gone.

Edward put his arms around me and held me to his chest. He held me as if I were his only possession. I turned my head to him and when my eyes found his, I knew with absolute certainty, he would be the man I would spend the rest of my life with.

Against all common sense, Edward refused to go to the hospital to be checked out. The paramedics and I spent a good twenty minutes arguing with him before we realized it was pointless. He continued his stubborn streak by insisting on driving my car home.

"I wish you'd let me hire a driver for you," he said. This was not the first time he had brought up the subject.

"I don't need a driver."

"But the driver could double as a bodyguard. I don't think you should be alone, not just because of all this, but because of me."

He did not need to elaborate because I knew what he meant. Being married to Edward meant living in a world where the wrong type of people would see me as a great kidnapping victim, especially since they knew he would pay or do anything to keep me safe.

"You're probably right, but I'd rather not. At least for now." I paused for a moment and watched the scenery as we made our way toward Thomas Hall. "Honey, how did you know where I was and that I was in danger?"

"You can thank Brian for that. After he got your message about the death certificates, he made some calls and found out the coroner had done time for forging death certificates."

"So how does she have a license?"

"She bribed someone in Ohio to expunge her record so that she could get a license to practice in Virginia."

"Okay, so what's the coroner's connection to the funeral home?"

"That one's pretty much common knowledge if you've lived here for more than a year. After what seemed like a lightning-quick courtship, the coroner and the funeral home director got married. Mr. Kerber is her husband."

"Oh," I replied. The downside of being the new person in a small town is that you tend to be unaware of its history and scandals.

"Anyway, Brian decided to pick up the coroner for questioning and was worried about you being alone with Mr. Kerber. He didn't want Kerber to panic either though, so he asked me to stop by and make sure you got in and out okay. Brian was afraid sending another officer would raise too many questions and I could pretend to be the guy who was trying to hunt down his fiancée because she wasn't answering her cell phone."

"Yeah, sorry about that. I'd left the phone in the car."

"It's okay, we knew where you were heading. When I arrived, I saw the smoke coming out of the building and your car parked out front, and I knew—" Edward's phone rang and I answered it for him, putting it on speakerphone so he could hear while driving.

"Hey, it's Brian. How are you doing?"

"All right. I'm a little hoarse, but I'll live. Cassie's on speakerphone with me, too. We're on our way back to Thomas Hall in her little clown car."

"Hey!" I said and listened to the men laugh until Edward began to cough. I gave him one of my "See, you should've listened to me" glares as I rubbed his back with my left hand. "I like having something to drive that doesn't cost more than the value of my life insurance policy."

"That's another thing we need to talk about," Edward noted.

"Later," I said with a tinge of aggravation, already knowing how that conversation would play out.

"Are you two fighting again?" Brian asked.

"You wish." The words flew out of my mouth before I could stop them. I pressed my lips together and looked at Edward, who looked at me with an expression that could only be described as somewhere between curious and terrified. "We're just trying to get all our ducks in a row before the big day."

I leaned over and kissed Edward behind his ear. I knew the effect it would have on him and his expression changed to something a little more R-rated as his Cheshire Cat grin spread across his face. As I watched him, I directed my question to Brian. "What's up?"

"I went by the hospital to get your statements only to discover you'd never shown up."

"Please tell me we don't have to turn around and come back," I said. I was exhausted and wanted to get Edward home to rest as well.

"No, I'll swing out tomorrow and I'll take your statements at the house. It'll cost you a glass of iced tea, though." Brian was a southern man through and through. And his two favorite drinks proved it: Jim Beam on the rocks and sweet tea.

"You said the coroner was confessing down at the station when we saw you earlier," Edward said, watching the road as he spoke. "What did she say?"

"You know I'm not supposed to tell you that, but it looks like Cassandra stumbled on something bigger than we could have suspected. She's confessing to everything to avoid jail time. I'm pretty sure Kerber won't get off as easy though."

"What do you mean?" I asked.

"Apparently forging death certificates isn't the only thing Kerber and his wife were up to in Ohio and here."

"Wait a minute, I thought they just got married," Edward said.

"That's what they wanted everyone in Willow Creek to think too. They've been married to each other for over eight years. The whole running off to Vegas and getting married thing was a cover so they could start living under the same roof without any questions."

"You said they were doing other things?" I asked.

"Yeah," Brian paused. "I don't really want to tell you this, though. This is going to freak out at least one of you. It makes me sick just thinkin' about it."

"It has something to do with selling black market organs," I said.

"Now how in the hell did you know that?" Brian asked.

"When I woke up in that motel after Tony kidnapped me, all the evidence was there. And trust me, Tony wasn't smart enough to know how to sell the organs once he had harvested them from me."

"What!" Edward screamed and slammed on the breaks. Luckily, no other cars were on the rural route that led us home. "Why didn't either of you tell me about this? What was in that room?"

"Calm down," I said in a soft, calming voice. "I thought you had read the police report." I knew Brian hadn't finished the paperwork yet, therefore making it impossible for Edward to read.

"Sorry, I thought Cassandra told you." Brian wasn't about to sell me out to save himself.

"I'm still a little confused," I said, rapidly changing the subject. "Besides a forged death certificate, how was Tony connected to these two lunatics?"

"It's a small town. It didn't take long for Tony to run into the Kerbers. According to the coroner, Tony threatened to expose their operation if he didn't get a cut. He even offered to help find donors."

"Of course, it all makes sense," I said. "They'd harvest the organs, and then cremate the bodies so that when they forged a death certificate, there would be remains to go with it."

I paused for a moment to think about what I'd just said. The remains I had buried when I thought Tony was dead the first time belonged to someone else. I would never know if they were someone's mother, brother, sister, or father. The only comfort I would ever be able to find was the fact I had given them a Catholic funeral service.

"Exactly," Brian replied. "From what the coroner is saying, Tony told her he went into Lucky Shots that night with the intention of finding a 'donor'. When he saw you there, he figured he could kill two birds with one stone. He would blackmail some money out of Edward, and then Kerber would harvest your organs. When they found out who you were and how much Rohypnol was in your system, they told him there was no way they would use you. You were too high profile in this town and they knew Edward would never stop hunting down his fiancée's killer."

"So the idiot decided to try it himself," I said.

Edward inhaled so hard I was worried there would be no oxygen left in the car for me. When I looked at him, it was obvious the thought of what Tony could have, *would* have done if he'd had the chance, made Edward feel physically ill. I opened the passenger's side window just a crack, in order to let the cold, fresh air pour into the car.

"Yep, there was no way he could have known he wouldn't live long enough to actually do it," Brian said.

"Man, it's been a hell of a day," Edward said, provoking Brian to agree.

"Welcome to my world guys." And that's when I think they began to understand exactly what my life was like.

Chapter Twenty-Six

I NEVER FELL ASLEEP that night. I snuggled next to Edward in our warm, soft bed, watched him sleep, listened to his racing heart, and thought about men. The one lying next to me would be my husband in a week. The thought of marriage still terrified me. The only thing keeping me from running as fast as I could was my love for him. I had never known anyone who could capture someone's heart so quickly and completely. He scooped mine up the day after I arrived at Thomas Hall. Maybe even sooner, but I would never admit it.

Then there was the man who had my friendship but wanted more. The kiss we shared replayed in my mind. While I was madly in love with Edward, a little piece of me wished I was attracted to Brian the same way I was to Edward. It would have made my life so much simpler.

Finally, there was the man who had made me so afraid of marriage, love, and men. Tony was absolutely dead this time. While there was no part of me that was sad he was gone from my life; a little piece of me still mourned his passing, again.

I was fairly certain I knew who killed him, but I needed to know for sure. So when the first rays of light hit the vines, I got ready for the day, and wrote Edward a note telling him where to find me when he rolled out of bed.

Vivian did not seem surprised when Victor announced my arrival as I strolled into the sunroom. I sat across from her and within seconds, Victor returned to the room with a breakfast tray for me.

"How did you know I was coming up for breakfast this morning, Vivian?" I asked as I took the first sip of my hot tea.

"I didn't. My guess is someone saw you walking up the path and called the kitchen. But you know you're always welcome here."

"I do. And it means a lot to me." I looked up to find Vivian's eyes peacefully examining my reaction. "It feels like home."

She smiled and we sat in silence as she drank her coffee and I nibbled on my breakfast. I finished drinking the last of my tea and settled into the task at hand. "Vivian, I need to ask you something, and I might be completely off base, but I'll go crazy if I don't know the truth."

"What is it, my dear?"

I hesitated for a moment, thinking about how foolish I'd feel if I was wrong. I felt a few beads of sweat form on the back of my neck as I looked at her. "Exactly how did you kill Tony?"

She smiled as she looked up from her coffee cup.

"I wondered when you'd figure it out. You're too smart not to. When did it come to you, dear?"

"Thanksgiving Day. When you were talking about your dad and the poison mushroom story, I started putting the pieces together but it didn't fall completely into place until later that evening. What did you put in Tony's lunch the day you cooked for him?"

"Eupatorium rugosum, White Snakeroot. It's an herb that grows wild all over the East Coast. I didn't have to roam far to find it either. I scrubbed it well, chopped it up, and added it to his salad. I wanted to make sure Tony could never destroy your world again. Especially since your world is Edward's now."

"God help me, but I'm glad he's dead."

"And I'm glad you're not," Vivian said. "I was so worried Tony would kill you before he'd die from the poison. I wondered if I'd made a mistake bailing him out so I could kill him."

"So he wasn't lying when he said you'd bailed him out." I took a minute to digest that fact before continuing. "That must have been terrible for you. Knowing he was going to die, and possibly for no reason at all."

Vivian leaned across the table, frowning. "Don't you ever say that again young lady. If he had killed you, he would have definitely deserved to die. I can't think of a single scenario where that scum deserved to live. You are far too special for anything to ever be done in vain where you're concerned. Do you understand?"

"Yes, Ma'am."

"But you don't believe me, do you?" she said, leaning back into her chair.

I shrugged and smiled. She was right, of course, I didn't believe her. But I wasn't going to argue with her either.

I never said it out loud and she never questioned me about it, but Vivian understood that her decision, her actions, her secret, would forever be safe with me. From the moment I arrived at Thomas Hall, Vivian had watched over me as if she were my own mother and this was the ultimate proof she always would.

I woke up to find Edward gone. It was Monday morning, after all. I knew I'd never be satisfied with this arrangement, but was thankful to have him at Thomas Hall as often as I did. I got up and headed to the bathroom. After showering, I opened the drawer to my dresser to retrieve a bra and underwear. In the top of the drawer was a plain white box with a blue ribbon. I laid the box on the bed and finished getting dressed.

Once I was dressed, my hair pulled up into a loose bun, and ready to go for the day, I sat by the box, staring at it before opening it. Inside were two large manila envelopes and a single sheet of paper, with Edward's perfect penmanship.

Sweetie, Enjoy your wedding gifts. These were my idea.
Love, Edward

I carefully opened the first envelope and a pair of panties, similar to the pair he destroyed, fell out. I smiled. As I began to lay the envelope on the bed, I noticed it wasn't empty. I reached in and pulled out a certificate, a stock certificate. One thousand shares of stock in a high-end lingerie manufacturing corporation. After all, he had promised me the company.

"Only Edward," I muttered to myself.

As wonderful of a gift as the first envelope was, the second meant more to me. It was fat and contained a large file. The front of the folder had a sticky note posted to it.

Cassie, Now you know what I know. Forever Yours, Edward

When I flipped through the file, I pieced together what it was. It was my life. Everything the private detectives discovered while investigating me. The guys he'd hired had done a pretty good job, but a few important things were missing. Edward didn't quite know everything about me and it made me smile. It was nice to know he still had a few surprises left to discover where I was concerned.

I called the main house and asked Victor to have my VW brought to the production building. I needed to look at a couple of things and talk with Alex and Henry before I headed into Willow Creek. I walked out into the sun, but it was so cold that my face was numb by the time I got into Henry's office.

"You look frozen. You want something hot to drink?" Henry asked.

"No, I just popped over for a few minutes before I headed into town. I still need to get your brother a wedding gift."

"You know he told you not to get him anything."

"I know, but I'd like to get him a little something. Just to mark the occasion. Any ideas?"

Henry smiled at me, knowing I had made up my mind to find Edward a gift. "Well, he does seem to constantly lose cufflinks. I think Mom's bought him a hundred pair over the years."

"Well, that's simple enough." It wasn't the most creative wedding gift on the planet, but it would suffice. When I got to town, I would go to the jeweler's and get him the nicest set of cufflinks they had in stock. As I stood to leave, Henry walked up and hugged me.

"Sis, try not to get yourself killed today."

"Trust me, I never try."

I listened to the radio on the way into Willow Creek. The radio reception of the D.C. stations was iffy at best, but it was unusually good that day. The morning talk show hosts had started their countdown to the Baker wedding in their gossip segments. Luckily, today had nothing to do with me directly. It was all about how the town was losing their most eligible bachelor and who was expected to be at the big event.

I listened to their babble and sang along to the songs. The car was the only place I ever sang, and even then only when I was alone. Needless to say, I was in a pretty good mood, until I heard the weather report.

"... The weather will continue to be unseasonably cold with temperatures fifteen degrees cooler than normal for this time of the year in Northern Virginia. The highs will continue to drop throughout the week, with a chance of flurries on Friday and Saturday..."

I continued to listen to the forecast and my mood soured. As soon as I parked on Main Street I dialed Edward's number.

"Hey, Beautiful."

"Did you know they're calling for flurries this weekend?" I asked, not even bothering to say hello.

He laughed for a moment, knowing my hatred of cold weather. "I heard that too. But we never get snow in early December, so don't worry. It never happens."

"I hope you're right," I said. "Oh, and I found my wedding gifts. Now those I really liked."

"Anything for you, Sweetie."

As Edward and I said our goodbyes, I noticed Brian sitting at his desk through the open blinds of his office window at the police station. I went into the coffee shop and ordered a chai latte for me and a large mocha latte with an extra shot of espresso for him. I had no clue if he would like it or not but I thought it might be a nice surprise.

I walked past the front desk, not waiting to be waved through, and tapped on the door frame of his open office door. "Thought you could use an energy boost."

"Cassandra." He smiled and I walked into his office and handed him the cup. "For me?"

He took a sip and smiled. "Hey, this is good. Thanks. Any special reason for your visit or just fueling the rumor mill?"

"I was in town and thought I'd say hi." I took a seat in one of the wooden chairs across from his desk. I had stopped by his office a half dozen times over the last couple of months and he never asked for my reason before. But in light of all the craziness, I wasn't shocked by his question. "I am still allowed to do that, aren't I?"

"Of course, I'm glad you did. I didn't know if you'd feel comfortable dropping by like this anymore after that kiss."

"Kiss? What kiss?" I asked with a smile. "I don't remember any kiss."

He smiled with a thankful, but slightly sad expression about him. We sat in silence, enjoying our morning caffeine, before continuing our conversation.

"I guess the wedding is still a go then?" While I knew Brian would be at the wedding, I think part of him was still wishing for a last-minute change of heart on my part.

"The only thing ever stopping us was Tony, so yeah, Saturday at four." Every time I thought about a whole day of people staring at me, I felt my stomach turn somersaults and this discussion was no different. Brian could see the change in my demeanor and moved the topic of discussion in another direction.

"Has it warmed up any out there?" he asked.

"No. The sun is deceiving. It's colder than Chicago in February."

"Speaking of Chicago, I wish I had some news for you about who poisoned Tony."

"I don't think anyone cares at this point," I said.

"While I agree, you know it's still my job to investigate."

"Brian, as your friend, I'm going to tell you not to waste your resources. It seems like a dead-end case.

"Why do I have the feeling you know more than you're telling me."

"I'm just saying, if it looks like a dead-end case, it probably is." I looked up at him and tilted my head and raised my chin just a little bit.

"You know who killed him," he said. "But you're not going to tell me, are you?"

He was right. I wasn't ever going to tell him, or anyone else for that matter, what I knew about Tony's death. Vivian did what she felt was necessary to resolve the situation. And while I could never have done it myself, I was glad someone did.

So the only thing left for me to do was focus on my wedding day.

And the weather.

Chapter Twenty-Seven

I STARED OUT THE window in utter disbelief as I held the phone to my ear. Nothing had improved since I first opened my eyes. In fact, things had gotten worse. "Tell me again why eloping in Vegas was a bad idea?"

"Cassie, Sweetie, it's just a little snow. It's really not that bad." Edward was trying his best to keep me calm from the other end of the phone. However, nothing he could say or do was going to fix the weather.

"Not that bad? Twelve hours ago there wasn't a flake of snow in sight and now, now there's fourteen inches! And it hasn't stopped yet!" I couldn't bear to look out the window any longer. I walked away and stretched out across the bed. It had been a lonely night, but if Edward was going to insist on having a proper wedding, I was going to make him do it all, including not seeing his bride before the ceremony. When I slept in his childhood room I thought the chill in the air was from sleeping alone, not from what was silently happening outside. When the weatherman mentioned "a chance of flurries", no one could have anticipated this was what Edward and I would wake up to on our wedding day.

"It will make for a memorable day." I could tell by the tone of his voice that he was smiling. He was happy the day had arrived, regardless of the weather, and no blizzard was going to alter his happiness.

"You think this is funny, don't you? Your poor mom is running around like a chicken with her head cut off and Zoe is having trouble getting her hair and makeup people here."

"What about you, Sweetie? How are you? I mean really, not what you think I want to hear, but the truth."

"The truth? I wish it wasn't snowing, I wish Fred was here, I wish I didn't feel like I was going to vomit, I wish ..." I didn't want to say the last thing out loud because I feared it might bring me to tears.

"You wish what? I'll make it happen."

I sat in silence for a moment, knowing he would never be able to deliver on that statement. "I wish my parents were here."

"I know. I wish Dad was here too. I can only imagine how hard it is for you some days."

"Most days aren't too bad. It's the big events you never get past without thinking about them." I looked out the window as I tried to push back my vision of what the day would be like if my family were still alive. However, the deteriorating weather conditions shifted my focus quickly. "It's never going to stop snowing, is it?"

"Well Sweetie, I can't fix the snow, but the second an airport within a hundred-mile radius opens, Fred will be aboard the jet on his way here. My pilot flew down last night before the weather turned and he and your uncle have already flown as far as Raleigh this morning, so it won't take him long to get here."

"I know, but the whole thing is turning into a disaster." I sat up on the bed and stared at the floor.

"It'll be fine. I talked to Mom before I called you. She's taking care of everything. Try to stay calm."

"Calm? That's funny. I wouldn't be calm even if this blizzard hadn't hit and you know it." I heard the sound of muffled voices on the other end of the phone. As I tried to decipher what was being said, Vivian tapped on the door and then quietly let herself in. She walked to the window, looked out, and then snapped the curtains shut.

"Sweetie, Henry and Alex are here," Edward said. "They're going to have some coffee with me and then we'll work our way up to the house. Don't worry, we've been ordered to stay downstairs."

"By your mom, no doubt."

He laughed and we said our goodbyes. As soon as I pressed the end button on the phone, Vivian sat down on the bed and put her arm around my shoulders.

"My son?"

"I think he wanted to make sure I wasn't having a seizure," I said, smiling. "What's the latest news?"

Vivian smiled as she inhaled sharply. I knew this wasn't going to be good. "We had to move the ceremony to the house."

"No church?"

"I know you wanted a church wedding if you were going to do this, but there's no way the church can clear the parking lot out or if the roads to the church are even going to be plowed."

"But who will officiate? How will the guests get here?" I began to feel light-headed. "Maybe we should just postpone—"

"Don't even think about finishing that sentence, young lady. The guests you've invited from overseas are already in town and the kitchen's been going full steam since before dawn. As for Father Baxter, we sent a driver for him in the Hummer."

"We own a Hummer?"

"We do now." We sat for a brief moment in silence as I reflected on all she said.

"Vivian, I don't feel so good. I feel dizzy and I think I'm going to be sick."

"I felt that way on my wedding day too. Of course, I was four months pregnant with Edward."

"Really?" I had not known exactly when Vivian and Senior had married and never knew that Edward was not a honeymoon baby, but a pre-engagement one. "I didn't know that."

"I probably would have married Senior eventually, but Edward sped the process up a bit," she said. "You don't think you're pregnant, do you?"

"No." At least I was pretty sure I wasn't. I had not been feeling like myself lately, but after the month I just lived through, it was amazing I didn't feel more out of sorts.

"Well, maybe you'll make me a grandmother while you're on your honeymoon." She smiled and pulled out a small phone and called down to the kitchen. Within moments Victor appeared at the door with a tray of hot tea, toast, and fruit.

I sat and ate my breakfast as Vivian headed out to meet the florist downstairs. Zoe, her team of stylists, Phoebe, and Libby-Mae strolled in not too long after. Libby-Mae wasn't originally part of my bridesmaids' party, but she fit into Sarah's dress and I had grown fond enough of her to want her in my wedding.

"Good morning, Miss Cassandra. Happy wedding day!" I loved Libby-Mae's optimistic approach to life, especially since so much of hers had been difficult.

Zoe had already been working on the three of them. Their fingernails and toenails had a fresh coat of enamel and their hair had been freshly washed and blow-dried.

"You're just now eating breakfast?" Libby-Mae asked. "It's almost noon."

"Which means we only have four hours to get ready," Zoe said. "Hurry up and finish eating. You need to get in the shower."

"Why hurry? How long can it take?" I asked. "Besides, no one will show up, not in this weather."

Phoebe sat down next to me. "Everyone will be here. Mom hired a private snowplow company. They've plowed the winery road and parking lot and now they're plowing the road into town. She found a limo company with stretch SUVs and is picking up everyone in the area who doesn't want to drive."

"She's making sure this happens today, isn't she?"

"I think Mom's worried if you and my brother don't do this today, you never will. Or you'll elope."

That's what I had wanted to do all along, elope. But Vivian and Edward had other ideas and somehow, in a moment of weakness, I conceded. The more I thought about this day, the more nauseous I felt. I could feel breakfast working its way back up. I covered my mouth with my hand, stood up, and ran to the bathroom.

I thought I would feel better once I'd been sick, but as I closed my eyes and slid to the floor I realized I only felt worse. I heard someone else in the room with me and when I opened my eyes, Zoe was sitting next to me, holding a cold washcloth. She handed it to me as she spoke and I washed my face.

"Nervous?"

"Terrified." I felt the room spin but before my head could reach the tiles, Zoe turned my head so it was in her lap.

"You know, it's not too late to change your mind. My car is at Henry's house. We could be halfway to Savannah before the wedding's due to start." She was giving me an out if I wanted one. No one had done that for me since we had set the date. She was definitely my favorite bridesmaid. I thought about what she said before I responded.

"It's not the marriage I want out of, just all this wedding stuff. It makes me so nervous. All those people staring at me."

"It won't be that many people. You told Vivian no more than a hundred."

"Yeah, I meant one hundred people. She says she thought I meant one hundred invitations. So try two hundred and twenty people." My stomach upped the intensity of its somersaults. "Oh God, help me."

Zoe carefully lowered my head gently to the tiles and stood up. "Try to relax. I'll be right back."

She raced out of the room and I heard the women talking so quietly that I could not understand them. A moment later Phoebe returned in place of Zoe with a glass of water and a pill.

"Take this, you'll feel better."

"The last future sister-in-law who said that was trying to kill me." Phoebe burst into laughter even though it was true.

"No, I want you to live. It's just a Xanax. It will even out your nerves a little. My doctor gave them to me right after my ex and I split up. Trust me."

I took the pill and popped it into my mouth. I figured even if she was trying to kill me, at least it would get me out of walking down the aisle with everyone watching my every move.

"Good, now into the shower. Take a nice long, hot one. By the time you get out, you'll feel much better."

Phoebe was right. When I exited the bathroom thirty minutes later, I felt great. My hands, which shook when I was on the phone with Edward, were now steady and the tension in my neck and shoulders had subsided.

The women unwrapped me from the oversized towel and slipped me into the beautiful flannel-lined white silk robe Vivian and Phoebe gave me as a wedding shower gift. I tied the sash and was guided to the beautician's chair that had been brought in the day before.

When I looked at Zoe and Libby-Mae, their hair and makeup had been done since my trip to the bathroom and Phoebe's make-up was in place. The hairdresser was pulling her hair up into a fancy do as the makeup artist started her magic on me.

Zoe was putting the finishing touches on my hair when Victor entered the room with fruit, cheese, bread, chocolates, and cham-pagne. We thanked him and then shooed him out. It only took a minute before we all noticed a velvet, rectangular box, wrapped in a ribbon on the tray. The card tucked into the bow simply said, "Forever Yours, Edward."

I could feel nervousness creeping up on me, so I downed an entire glass of champagne before opening the box. When I saw the contents, I had to sit down in order to catch my breath.

"Well, nothing says forever quite like diamonds," Phoebe com-mented as she examined the spectacular necklace that lay in the silk-lined box, along with matching earrings.

"Then that necklace is screaming eternity," Libby-Mae said. "It's amazing." Amazing was an understatement. The circular necklace was a string of respectable-sized diamonds with smaller stones clustered in a circular fashion between each diamond.

"Here, help me put it on." I handed it to her, with my now shaky hands. But hers were shakier. I wondered why she was nervous until I realized that the necklace she was putting on me cost more than her mother's house.

Once Libby-Mae hooked the clasp, I took out the earrings I was wearing and replaced them with the ones that came with the necklace. When I looked in the mirror, the sight of myself with my hair and makeup done, wearing nothing but a white silk robe and a necklace that looked like it should be in a museum, I hoped I wouldn't hyperventilate. However, Zoe handed me a paper bag to breathe in. She knew me well and had come prepared. When my cell phone rang, Libby-Mae answered it.

"Yes. Yes, sir, she got the gift. No, I'm sorry you can't talk to her right now. Why? Because she's busy hyperventilating. Oh, okay." She stuck the phone out in my direction. "He wants to talk to you."

I stopped breathing into the bag, took the phone from her, and tried to calm myself. A moment later, Phoebe brought me another Xanax. While I probably should have asked about the dosage, I opted to just take it and hope it helped as much as it did the first time.

"Hi."

"Hey, Beautiful. Are you all right?"

"I think so. I don't feel sick anymore. I guess that's good." I could hear Edward laughing through the phone as well as the echo of him in the hall. "Are you outside the bedroom?"

"Yes. Do you want me to come in?"

"No! It's bad luck."

"You and my mother are taking this whole luck thing way too seriously," he said. "If you change your mind, I'm right here in the house."

"I know. Honey, the necklace is, well, it's ... I can't even describe it." The second pill Phoebe gave me was starting to kick in fast and I could feel my body relaxing. I felt no worries at all.

"As soon as I saw the necklace I knew it would be perfect for you. You probably think it's too much though, don't you?"

"The money probably could feed the entire continent of Africa for a day, but I do like it. I don't know how many occasions I'll have to wear it, though."

"Then we'll just have to make occasions." I smiled as I thought about what he'd said. I must have thought longer than I was aware because I heard him say, "Sweetie? Are you still there?"

"Yep."

"The only time I've ever heard you say yep is when you're drunk. Have you and the girls been drinking?"

"Just one glass. But Phoebe gave me a couple of Xanax. They seemed to help calm my nerves."

"Good, then while you're calm I'll tell you why I called. Sweetie, Fred's not going to make it."

"Oh." I had already resigned myself to the fact that my uncle probably wouldn't be able to complete his journey due to the weather, but it still stung a little knowing my only living relative wouldn't be in attendance. I'm not exactly sure why, but I handed the phone to Phoebe.

I sat on the edge of the bed, silent. I'm not sure for how long, but it was long enough to cause concern. Zoe sat down next to me and placed her hand gently on my back. "What is it?"

"No Fred. The airports are still closed." I stood up and walked toward the window and Zoe followed me. Then, I made my biggest mistake of the day. I drew back the curtains.

The snow was no longer gently falling to the ground. It was a complete white-out. You couldn't see more than twenty feet away. I turned to Zoe, took her champagne glass from her hand, and downed the entire thing in one large gulp. I heard the door open and turned around to find Vivian, looking amazing as always. Today she was wearing a deep purple, full-length, silk dress with an intricate lace overlay. She was the classic example of what the mother of the groom should look like.

"Dear, it's time to get you into your dress," she said.

I stared through her for a long moment before I spoke. "I can't, I can't do this. I can't walk down the aisle by myself."

"Oh dear, your uncle's not going to make it?" I couldn't find the right words. I noticed Zoe was no longer in the room. "I was afraid that was going to happen. I'm sure Poppy would walk you down the aisle if you'd like."

"No," I said. "I think that would be a bad idea. I love Poppy but I don't want the winery connected with his line of work."

"Probably a smart idea," Vivian said. "Don't worry, we'll figure something out."

I was beginning to feel a little zombie-like. It was as if I was going through the motions, but not feeling anything. I walked to where my dress was hanging and stopped. I needed to put on underwear, stockings, and crinolines. Phoebe helped with the under-skirting and Libby-Mae put my shoes on my feet. I could only compare the experience to being dressed up like a doll. As Vivian brought the dress to me, Zoe walked back into the room.

"Cassandra, once your dress is on, there's someone outside who'd like to talk to you."

"I told Edward he can't see me until I walk down the aisle."

"It's not Edward," she said and helped Vivian get me into the dress.

Once I was in the dress, Vivian walked around to the back to zip it up, but the dress didn't get tighter. "Zoe, come help me, dear."

Zoe fiddled with the zipper and then said to Vivian, "Go get your sisters. And tell them to bring some thread and a needle."

"I'll go," Phoebe said as she slipped her shoes off and scurried out the door. As she did, I could feel my chest tighten and I turned to Zoe.

"What's wrong?" I asked.

"Nothing, nothing's wrong." Libby-Mae snapped out, already sounding panicked. "Right Zoe? Everything's fine."

Zoe knew Libby-Mae was trying to keep me calm. However, before she could respond, Vivian chimed in. "It's nothing serious. The zipper isn't working quite right. It keeps pulling apart. Don't worry though, Violet and Virginia will fix it."

As if on cue, the two sisters walked in and turned me around. One inhaled deeply while the other threaded a needle. "They just don't make zippers like they used to."

"Can you fix it?" Libby-Mae asked.

"Yes and no. We'll replace the zipper after the wedding, but for today we're just going to have to sew Cassandra into the dress." I wasn't even aware they were already doing just that. Within a few short minutes, they were done and the veil was pinned to my head.

As I looked in the mirror, I saw the reflection of Zoe opening the door to let Henry in the room.

"This is who wanted to talk to you," Zoe said. "Is that okay?"

I nodded my head and then Zoe did something I had not expected. She asked everyone to clear the room. Within seconds, the room was void of people, with the exception of me and Henry.

"Wow!" Henry said. "You look amazing."

I smiled and opened my mouth, thinking I would say something. Like how great he looked in his tux or how glad I was to see him, but no words came out. After a moment, Henry gave me a hug.

"You look like you're in a daze. Are you okay?" I could only shrug and smile in response. He smiled, understanding my state of being both in shock from the way the day was unfolding and also being moderately medicated. "Look, I know I'm not your dad or your uncle, but if you'd like, I'd be honored to walk you down the aisle."

I knew that tears would flow at some point that day, but I had no idea that Henry would be the facilitator of them. As they began to fall, Henry handed me his handkerchief and I dabbed the tears from my face. I nodded my head, hugged him again, squeezing him as tightly as I could, and then loosened my grip. Henry smiled at me.

"Well, now that we've gotten that straight, I need to go tell Edward about the change in plans. I'll be back in a few minutes for our trip down the aisle." I tried to give Henry's handkerchief back to him, but he took my hand and folded my fingers around it. "You keep it, just in case."

I would love to say in all honesty that I remember every detail of the ceremony, but I don't. I remember being terrified of descending the staircase. We hadn't practiced that sort of entrance and the bulk of the dress lent itself to disaster on any set of stairs. But Henry and I took our time and found our way to the bottom with no major incidents.

I know I repeated the vows the Anglican priest said to us, but I have no idea what they were. For all I know, I vowed to hand over the winery to the church. I do not remember the music either, but I am certain it was beautiful as everything Vivian arranged was perfect.

The one thing I remember from the ceremony was Edward. The look of awe on his face as I walked down the aisle, the touch of his hands cradling mine when Henry gave me away to him, and his kiss, soft, wet, and warm on my lips the moment we were pronounced man and wife.

Immediately after the ceremony, Edward and I had a brief moment alone in the library. He took a seat on the leather sofa when we walked in and I sat as close to him as I could in the expansive yards of silk I was wearing. He brushed the back of his hand softly against my cheek.

"You are really drugged, aren't you?" He asked.

"I don't know. I feel pretty good though. Is it that obvious?"

"Not really, I just know you well enough that this day, with all of these people, should completely freak you out and you look as cool as a cucumber."

I giggled quietly and Edward leaned in for a kiss. Suddenly I had the unyielding desire to make love to my husband. It was the first time I had thought of him as my husband and it provoked feelings in me I had not quite anticipated. The next thing I knew we were lying on the sofa and I was running my fingers through his wonderfully thick hair until I reached the nape of his neck. I could hardly contain myself and I pulled Edward closer. When I finally let his hungry lips leave mine, he moved his mouth down my neck to my breasts.

"By the way Sweetie, amazing dress," he said between his traveling kisses. As he continued to kiss and nibble at my skin, I tried to think of how I was going to get out of the dress I was sewn into. But before I could come up with a plan, Edward found this special spot at the top edge of my cleavage and it left me breathless.

And then I heard Phoebe's voice. "Good God! Can't you two at least wait until after the reception?"

Edward turned his head to her and I buried my face in his chest.

"I think the answer's obvious," Edward answered. He and I sat up and I could feel my face ablaze and knew it had to be beet red. When I looked toward the door, not only was Phoebe standing there, but Vivian and the entire wedding party, desperately holding back their own amusement, along with the photographer as well. I had forgotten the reason we went into the library – wedding pictures.

Zoe walked over, looked at the two of us, shook her head, and smiled. "Edward you might want to remove your wife's lipstick from your face and neck before we start taking pictures. And you, young lady, need a touch-up."

She reached over and grabbed a makeup bag from a side table, which I assumed she'd placed there earlier for pre-picture touch-ups. As she worked her magic, I continued to breathe heavily, thinking about the wonderful things that surely would have happened had we not been interrupted. Within moments Edward was sitting next to me again, having slipped into the powder room to wash the makeup off his face.

And just as the photographer began snapping pictures, Edward leaned in and softly said to me, "Don't worry, Mrs. Baker, we have the rest of our lives for that."

Somehow, the photographer managed to see the moment and capture the perfect photo of Edward whispering in my ear as I smiled at the words "Mrs. Baker".

It continues to be my favorite picture of the two of us. Every person who has seen it asks what Edward said to me, but we kept that our secret, our own Baker family secret.

Acknowledgments

There is no friend like a childhood friend, and one with over a dozen years of law enforcement experience has been invaluable. A special thanks to Melissa Flora for finding the answers to all of my bizarre police and legal questions.

Next, I'd like to thank my amazing team of readers. I will forever be indebted to these brilliant women and the feedback they provide. Ashley Knight, Betty Bryant, Katy Hines, Kim Bryda, Lynn Whitt, Tracy Voyles, and Stefanie Lewis; I am a better writer because of each of you.

And finally, a big thank you to my wonderful family. Michael, Zach, Sarah, and Phoebe, your love and support makes me the best wife, mother, and writer I can be.

Also By Beth Sorensen

The Thomas Hall Series
Crush at Thomas Hall – Book One
Divorcing a Dead Man – Book Two
Waiting for Time to Tell – Book Three

www.ingramcontent.com/pod-product-compliance
Lightning Source LLC
Chambersburg PA
CBHW071236300726
48975CB00002B/445